A Flash of Red

By Sarah K. Stephens

pandamoon
publishing

www.pandamoonpublishing.com

Jacket design and illustrations © Pandamoon Publishing
Art Direction by Don Kramer: Pandamoon Publishing
Editing by Zara Kramer, Rachel Schoenbauer, Jessica Reino, and Kathy Davidson: Pandamoon Publishing

Pandamoon Publishing and the portrayal of a panda and a moon are registered trademarks of Pandamoon Publishing.

Library of Congress Cataloging-in-Publication Data is on file at the Library of Congress, Washington, DC

Edition: 1

ISBN-10: 1-945502-14-2
ISBN-13: 978-1-945502-14-9

And she, remembering other things, to me trifles but torturing to her, showed me how life withers when there are things we cannot share.
—Virginia Woolf, *The Waves*

Dedication

To my parents, Norma and Stephen Holowach

A Flash of Red

Part I
Friday – Saturday
March 17 – March 18

Anna

Anna's heart skipped a beat in a wave of involuntary fear. There were only two eggs in the refrigerator.

Anna had descended the stairs five minutes before, perfumed and fully dressed, ready to begin her day. With each step, Anna had recited to herself the tasks for her morning: she would make pancakes for her husband who was still asleep in their bedroom, she would wash fresh raspberries to put on top, she would lay the table with care, all to set a pattern of comfortable predictability for herself, to ensure the day would unfold in a way she could control. But now, everything was skewed by yet another ordinary situation somehow turned inexplicable in Anna's life. Or at least she preferred to see these blips in her daily routine as having no reasonable explanation, because the most reasonable explanation of all was unacceptable.

She'd checked last night before going to bed—everything she needed had been there. A full carton of eggs, their twelve white orbs nestled neatly in the divots on the side of the refrigerator door. Anna always took them out of their cardboard container after returning from the grocery store and moved them lovingly to their designated place. So where had they gone?

And that's when it rushed over her. Standing in front of the pristine refrigerator, its cool air pouring over her chest and thighs through the thin satin and crepe of her dress, Anna thought again about the dark spot inside her head, the one we all share, the one where our brain oversteps the rules of generosity and creates a reality for us. She had learned this small biological fact with indifference in college. Now, when it shoved its way into her conscious thought, as it had just now, the sheer density of it warped her mind like a black hole, devouring everything around it. *How else do our minds betray us? How will mine?* Anna knew only part of the answer.

Anna blinked rapidly in an attempt to clear the blur in front of her. She could fix this. Everything could be put back in order. Ignoring the skittering thoughts inside her head, Anna amended her plans. She had two eggs. She would make them sunny-side up for Sean with two slices of her homemade bread and the strawberry jam she had canned herself last summer. The fresh raspberries she would put on the side for him in a bowl.

Anna took a deep breath. And another one. Then she shut the door to the refrigerator and placed the eggs on the counter by the stove, careful not to crack their fragile shells. Putting her favorite cast iron pan onto the heat with a bit of Portuguese olive oil drizzled inside, Anna wrapped her slim fingers around the first egg, feeling the tensile strength of the shell shift slightly under the pressure. In one swift and practiced movement, Anna split the shell against the edge of the skillet and poured the viscous contents out, the yolk centered perfectly within the white that emerged in the sizzling heat. Yes, that was better.

* * *

"I'm off. Have a good day!" Sean stood in the hallway, draping his black coat over his broad back before putting his left arm inside and buttoning up the double-breasted flaps. He didn't look over at her.

"Okay, honey." Anna could feel the clip in her tone and urged herself to stop. Throwing out another spindle for him to grab, she called out from her seat at the kitchen table, "Hope you enjoyed breakfast."

She could see Sean's movement pause for a second. A blip of joy fluttered up inside her throat when he turned around and settled his gaze on her face. She smiled, anticipating his compliment.

"Sure," Sean's voice was thin, stretching itself down the hallway, "but I thought you were making pancakes."

2

What could Anna say to that? She scrambled for an explanation that didn't suggest a failure on her part. "When I woke up this morning, I just thought you might like something a little lighter." She added with a soft laugh, "And don't worry, I'll clean up the dishes."

Sean's face was unreadable. Spontaneously, he covered the expanse of the front hallway in three broad steps, bent down to kiss Anna on the cheek, and then was just as quickly out the door without another word. The smell of his shaving cream lingered on Anna's cheek for a few seconds before diffusing into the kitchen's sunlit air.

The first task of Anna's day was done.

After clearing up the dishes and wiping the table of crumbs, Anna settled down to her second task. The notecards were embossed at the top with her initials, ALK, in silver lettering. She took seven, one for each day of the upcoming week, from the stack in the kitchen drawer she'd designated for writing utensils and other note materials. Choosing a blue pen first, she began to write in her flowing script,

Hope your day is wonderful. I love you!
XOXO

Anna

Anna placed the card upside down on the table, picked up the next card, and began to write. She was traveling to visit her parents tomorrow and only had a few more minutes to prepare for the week ahead before leaving for her office at Ambrose University. A busy day awaited her: morning meetings with colleagues, class at 1:00 p.m., and office hours later in the afternoon. No one, Anna thought with satisfaction, could call her inefficient.

* * *

A Flash of Red

Sprays of slush from the footfalls of passing undergraduates slapped Anna in the face, capturing her attention. Although she had always loathed winter as a child, constantly searching for the hint of loamy earth on the breeze that would preface warmer days, Anna had come to love the colder seasons. It seemed as if her bones and sinew had grown tougher over the years and now icy sleet and chilling wind fortified her tolerance for the injuries of daily life: the dead monotony of grading, her husband's halo of ambient blue light, the gritty underbelly of potential.

As Anna traveled across the quad, she chose the diagonal pathway that had clearly been laid only recently, a result of repeated traipsing by undergraduates. Anna was always impressed, if a bit stunned, by not only the efficiency with which students could communicate their need for greater convenience, but also by the complete lack of creativity or ambition she often found in their supposed need to be educated.

Taking in her surroundings, Anna noted it was the point in winter where the peaceful snowfall that cocoons December in holiday-anticipation had long since given way to the post-celebratory regret of excess. Snow lay arrayed across the inlets of grass, path, and brown brick buildings in patches of hardened gray mounds, each adorned with the detritus of months of biting cold: cigarette butts, lone gloves, and the ubiquitous college accessory of empty Starbucks cups. It wasn't until graduate school, Anna reflected, that the educated masses found it necessary to budget by carrying in caffeine from home.

Anna felt her grip on the heavy briefcase filled with exams and lecture notes loosen as she made her way across campus and paused a moment to readjust herself. As she paused, she caught sight of one of the few visual consolations of winter: a cardinal, crested head of red resplendent against the bleak midwinter backdrop, perched atop one of the many ancient oaks lining the pathway. She had loved these crimson ambassadors of goodwill ever since her mother had taught her to identify them in childhood. As he called out his charming reverie over the desolate grounds, Anna's second thought was how one's beauty benefits from the decline of those around. But her first thought was the same as it always was when reminded of her mother.

Resuming her steady stride, Anna rolled the word "decline" around in her mind. She worried it like a not-yet-smooth piece of glass found at the beach, its jagged edges catching on the rough surfaces inside of her. Anna avoided self-pity, but the facts of her life remained, austere and foreboding in their precision.

Anna cast her view across the quad to Klingersmith Hall, where her well-appointed and organized office awaited her, along with a busy day of lectures, office hours, and meetings. A cold wind was now blowing across the lawn and the cardinal had flown away during Anna's brief pause, probably to find shelter in a nearby pine. As Anna headed towards her destination, she wished she shared the same sensibility.

* * *

Anna did not expect today's class to be challenging, even with its familiar undertones. She was a professional, after all. Her abnormal psychology course was always an easy one to teach, undoubtedly because the topics captured students' interests and the material was fairly standardized. Each class or, depending on the amount of material, set of classes was devoted to a specific disorder within the DSM, the all-encompassing manual for mental health diagnoses. The diagnosis she was introducing today, with its fantastical set of symptoms that seemed to embody the word *insanity*, never failed to pique student interest.

Her classes at Ambrose University were small, as at most private colleges. This classroom in Holland House, one of the many smaller tutorial buildings peppered across campus, provided thirty padded retractable seats aligned in three rows of ten. The chairs sat facing the large projector screen for professors' lecture slides and, hiding behind the screen, an outdated chalkboard.

A Flash of Red

With the lights dimmed to aid the clarity of the PowerPoint slides, the room assumed the air of a small documentary film house. Anna sometimes enjoyed the feeling of anonymity the classroom created for her as she presented the material through the gauze of the dimmed lights and luminescent screen. Although she often loved the spotlight lecturing inherently provided for her, on the rare days when her anxiety got the best of her, she'd pretend students could only hear her voice as the narrator of the moving slides.

"One diagnostic hallmark of the illness is the experience of delusions. Patients might encounter exaggerated feelings of paranoia; these are the classic delusions of persecution"—Anna moved to stand at the opposite side of the screen, sweeping her eyes across the room as she did so. Sitting smack in the middle of the clustered desks was her one male student, Bard Avis, his eyes following Anna intently as she moved—"where the patient feels they are under attack by some fantasized perpetrator, like the 'Government' with a capital 'G'." Anna held his gaze for a moment, but soon shifted it to Julie, the nervous girl who always sat towards the front.

Moving towards the back of the classroom, Anna continued. "Other patients might experience delusions of grandeur, where they believe they're someone famous—or infamous—or that they have superhuman powers." Anna was at the back now, free from everyone's line of sight. "I'm sure you've seen the clichés on TV. The homeless man who thinks he's Jesus Christ or the teenager who jumps to her death because she thought she could fly. Just remember, in the case of this disorder, these clichés are often quite accurate."

In this 400-level course, her class comprised only ten students. Almost all of them were young women, dutifully noting her lecture material down in notebooks or laptops as they gathered the knowledge necessary for graduate school exams, licensure, and a career as active listeners. At this point in their training, Anna knew most of them by name and, if not by name, at least by sight. However, Anna had never taught Bard prior to this semester and was surprised to only have encountered him within this upper division course at Ambrose. Typically, she saw students in her lower level general education courses first, and had a sense of who they were prior to meeting them again in advanced coursework. Bard, though, was anything but typical.

Stockily built, with the broad shoulders and plumpish waist of a man who had been a defensive lineman on his high school football team, his shock of copper hair sat in soft curls around his face and highlighted his sea-glass green eyes. His face was full of freckles that undoubtedly had lightened from childhood into adulthood, as they were only a faded sienna now. Today, as on all other days Anna had seen him, Bard was immaculately dressed: ironed corduroy trousers, a button-down sky blue shirt with an argyle sweater vest partially covering it, and polished brogues.

Anna clicked the remote mouse to reveal the next bulleted point on her PowerPoint slide. "De Clerambault's Syndrome" flashed up on the screen. *Shit shit shit.* She'd forgotten to remove this from her presentation when she was prepping earlier this week. Two mistakes already today.

Bard had adopted his typical listening posture of feet flat on the floor, his back rigid against the chair, with his eyes fixed on Anna or, when she was behind the group of students, on the illuminated screen. Anna stayed at the back of the room.

Clearing her throat, she trudged onward, preferring to get through the material quickly rather than admit her error and skip to the next bulleted point. "De Clerambault's Syndrome gets its name from the psychiatrist who first described the condition. It refers to a delusion where the patient believes a person of higher social status, such as a politician or a celebrity, shares a secret affection for the patient. Often, the patient sees secret signals in the ordinary behavior of the object of their obsession." Almost finished, Anna took a breath. She had spoken quickly, and tried to slow down with this last bit of information to ensure she wouldn't have to repeat herself.

"For example, one of the original cases De Clerambault encountered"—Anna looked up to see that Bard had departed from his typical posture and had swiveled to face her at the back of the room, his sturdy body squeezed horizontally into the gap between desk and chair—"was that of a

7

woman who believed King George of England was showing his love for her by moving the curtains in Buckingham Palace."

Anna immediately clicked the remote mouse again, advancing to her next category of *Hallucinations*.

This was by no means the first student Anna had encountered who fixated on their professor during lecture, although generally students tended to avoid eye contact. In the rare instances when she would catch a student's eye while presenting, he or she would almost involuntarily look away, as if with embarrassment at having initiated such intimacy. Bard, though, appeared to share none of this concern. If Anna looked at him during lecture, the severity of his gaze continued or intensified. His mouth remained neutral while his forehead furrowed, giving his face a cast of disdainful concentration. And then there was his gaze, his eyes boring into her with a confidence she found unfamiliar in an undergraduate. At the beginning of the semester, she had been so surprised by Bard's composure that the first few classes saw her stumbling over her words and losing her focus on the material, a mistake that she chastised herself for afterwards as amateurish.

She emphasized to her class that hallucinations manifested themselves as experiences occurring external from the patient, whereas delusions embodied themselves within the patient's belief structures. After moving smoothly through the common hallucinations of the disorder, Anna addressed the topic of etiology. The heritability of this diagnosis was well-established, she informed her students. Out of all the diagnoses housed within the DSM, this illness had one of the strongest genetic foundations, she explained, her voice catching on the last part of the sentence despite her efforts to the contrary.

She spotted movement out of the corner of her eye. Bard's hand was raised.

"Yes?" Anna let her impatience show. With only a few minutes left of class, she just wanted it finished.

"Is it likely…I mean, *can* a parent pass this onto her child?" His voice was sonorous and amber in tone, with a soft hint of a southern dialect.

Anna felt sick, but managed to push back the bile that had risen into her throat from her empty stomach. She hadn't had time for breakfast. Anna reminded herself that this was a legitimate question, and that any student could have asked it out of his or her own general interest. But as Bard quietly stared at her in wait, she thought she saw his face transform for just one moment as the corners of his mouth sagged downwards. A glimpse of distaste or sympathy, Anna was unsure. For the first of many times to come, she wondered what Bard might know about her life.

"Compared to almost all other mental illnesses, this disorder has one of the strongest likelihoods of occurring in both parent and child."

And with that, class was over.

* * *

After class, Anna headed back to her office. She had an article to review for one of the professional journals she volunteered her time to. *Service* was what they called it in the academic sphere. The three-legged stool of tenure-track faculty: teaching, research, and service. Anna was well on track for making tenure early and, in all honesty, she'd never doubted for a moment that this would be the case.

Anna knew how to work hard, and she knew how to set a goal and reach it. Unlike many others, including Sean, she had navigated the serpentine path of graduate school with ease after only a few minor hindrances at the beginning. Her first advisor, a supposedly brilliant psychologist who had just acquired a government grant for over two million dollars to examine the links between domestic abuse and child abuse (a topic Anna felt was rather obvious and overdone), had returned Anna's first draft of her master's thesis proposal as a bloody carcass of corrections and derisive feedback. Anna had worked for weeks on the proposal, leaving Sean at home by himself until the early hours of the morning while she pored over academic articles only available in hard copy at the university library, in order to gather the proper background information for her hypotheses. She knew she had worked harder than the other members of her cohort in the clinical graduate program, dismissing their overtures for dinner and drinks after the end of their three-hour statistics class in lieu of a quick call home to Sean for reassurance followed by more hours at the library. Looking back, her long work hours may have been a way to avoid dealing with the issues that had recently emerged in her life. Illness in any form always casts a shadow of grief. Even still, she knew her work was quality.

Anna recalled Prof. Dernham's face when they had met to review Anna's proposal. The woman clearly enjoyed the opportunity of showing Anna her supposed missteps in logic, the misinterpretation of previous studies, even her grammatical errors. Prof. Dernham had spent over an hour with Anna, deliberately examining each and every problem in the manuscript. In one section, the distinguished professor noted that Anna's interpretation of her summarized research findings was totally dissociated from the reality of what the experiment actually proved. Anna struggled at that point not to be visibly appalled.

"These problems are egregious, but if you follow my advice it might be salvageable," Prof. Dernham said in her high-pitched voice that seemed to originate from her nose rather than her mouth. She had spent the entire hour in her chair behind her desk, her old veiny hands arched into a steeple over Anna's proposal, staring at a spot on the bare wall just over Anna's left shoulder, as if she were too proud to offer Anna even the courtesy of eye contact. Her office had been spotless, with real cherry bookshelves and a desk clear of clutter except for an old-fashioned immaculate cream blotter. Apparently, Prof. Dernham was one of those archaic academics who preferred to keep their computers to the side of their workspace, as if they weren't essential.

Anna had sat through the meeting doing her best impression of respectful and active listening. After she was dismissed with a gesture towards the door and a perfunctory "Keep at it," Anna promptly headed to her program's main administrative office and demanded to meet with the head of the department.

Within a few days, Anna was happily partnered with the most grandfatherly and close-to-retirement faculty member in the department. He had no grants and hadn't published any research in years, but when Anna had met with him during recruitment weekend in the spring, he had made a point to comment on her talent as a writer and how much he had enjoyed her personal essay. After their first official meeting as mentor and mentee, Anna was sent away with a draft of her proposal that was marked only with gentle suggestions and an assurance that she would be able to defend within the year. When the prediction came true the next spring, during Anna's second year of graduate studies, Anna and Sean celebrated at the best restaurant they could afford. Over a glass of the cheapest red wine on the menu, Anna and Sean toasted her success along with the pending departure of Prof. Dernham for some obscure position in northeastern Canada. Sean had told Anna his opinion of Prof. Dernham when he first heard Anna recount their meeting, and Anna was happy to have him remind her once more that Prof. Dernham was just an old jealous bitch as he celebrated his wife's achievement. Back then, Sean had been her biggest supporter.

Anna scanned her own professorial office as she entered it. It was well-appointed and organized, much like Prof. Dernham's, she thought with some bemusement, although her computer took center stage at her desk. She kept her workspace free of clutter, organizing any pending paperwork in the labeled trays stacked in the left-hand corner of her university-issued faux-cherry desk. Her decorations and personal touches to the small space were simple, but also communicated a rich life. Her three degrees were professionally framed and hung strategically so that visitors could view them easily from their seats. Her framed photographs included a picture of her parents smiling together at her wedding, a picture that would now be a stark impossibility. There were also pictures of her and Sean throughout their relationship: smiling in cap and gown at their undergraduate graduation, beaming at their wedding, drenched in sun as they wrapped their arms around each other on their last vacation, which had been almost three years ago. Impossibilities-in-waiting.

A Flash of Red

Catching herself, Anna redirected her attention. She settled into her desk and clicked on her mouse to illuminate her monitor. Opening her e-mail, Anna saw she had twenty unread messages and several drafts she had yet to send. There was much to be done.

Sean

It was difficult to focus. Sean sat at his desk, observing the last bits of what was meant to be a working lunch. Anna always packed his lunches, and he noted once more her attention to making sure he had everything he might need or want. Today, she had prepared a turkey and ham sandwich with a container of mayonnaise on the side. She knew he hated when the bread of his sandwich became soggy from overly-applied condiments. With a similar intention, she also packed his tomato and lettuce separately, wrapped in a fresh paper towel to absorb excess moisture. A can of sugar-free iced tea, a round and juicy pear, and one of Anna's homemade oatmeal cookies completed the package.

Sean had eaten his sandwich with care, if not with enjoyment, and now only a few stray crumbs and one slice of tomato were left. The pear and cookie, though, would wait for later. The proposal he was working on sat to the left of his desk, so that he could read it while eating without getting any food on it. At this stage, the proposal was lacking in form. The client was building a retirement home and found the ready-made plans of the other architectural firms available to be below his standards. The client wanted an original, something you couldn't just "pick off the truck." *Well, Baker and Bigwell may not be the company for him then*, Sean thought. The firm Sean worked for specialized in pre-fab designs that carried a reassuring whiff of the generic, with a few touches of the inspired thrown in. Under-cabinet lighting and Jacuzzi suites were the most exciting additions Sean's firm offered. If he were honest with himself, Sean would say he'd never had a sincere interest in his job. That he'd settled for it because Anna had been offered a job at Ambrose University and at the time, they had found themselves happy in the flow of their relationship. Just before Sean had accepted the offer, Anna had suggested they try to start a family.

He decided today was a day to work from home. He packed up the remaining components of his lunch, eliminated any garbage from his desk, slid the uneaten food into his lunch bag to return home, and took a fleeting glance at the note nestled inside the bag.

Hope you have a great day. I love you!
XOXO

Anna

Sean smiled and, walking out of the office with his coat, carefully flung the note into the recycling bin.

* * *

As Sean stepped in the door, he breathed in the smell of their house. Anna enjoyed cooking and upon entering, Sean could always smell the hints of past dinners and baked goods. Today, the air carried the faint smell of cinnamon and roasted garlic.

Hanging his coat in the closet, he removed his shoes and wiped the salt from their leather uppers. Placing them on the shoe rack in their entryway, he moved into the main portion of their house. Sean liked their home, but he didn't love it. He would've preferred to have designed a house for himself and Anna, one that was distinct from the McMansions of today's suburbia. When they were first settling into their professional lives after Anna finished graduate school, funds were adequate and supplied reasonable comforts, but they couldn't manage the luxury of a self-designed home on their starter incomes. With his father unable to provide any financial backing, and Anna's parents already stripped of their nest egg, they had settled on 349 Bristol Avenue.

Built in 1935 in that decade's rigid style, their home consisted of four bedrooms and two and a half baths. "Plenty of room to grow into!" Anna kept saying throughout the purchasing process. Children had always been part of their family plan. The house had two stories plus a basement. All four bedrooms were located on the top story, branching off a wooden stairway and landing. The kitchen was placed at the end of the first floor hallway; a living room and den, which Sean used as an office, branched off in opposite directions from the entranceway. The den was situated ideally for working from home. With its windows facing out onto the front lawn and sidewalk, Sean had positioned their desk such that he could both view his computer screen and look out the window to see Anna walking up the path to the front door. He was often able to catch her eye as she walked up and could quickly close various windows open on his computer before moving to open the door for her. Sean didn't want to give Anna any further evidence of his inadequacies.

Sean changed from his work button-down into one of his baggy college sweatshirts, and then headed back downstairs to his office in the den. It was in these moments of anticipation that the bittersweet element of what he was about to do was most firmly in place. How he wanted it so, so much. How the small steps he had created around this pleasure extended his longing, molding it into a desperate need. And he would delay the finale, to the point that he ached inside.

Sitting down in his comfortable black mesh office chair, Sean adjusted the blinds on the window. They needed to be perfectly straight and opened just a quarter-inch between the slats, to let light in and create an atmosphere of sensual tenderness while also allowing him a full view of the front walk. Next, he used a special lint-free cloth to wipe the monitor of fingerprints and smudges. The keyboard was askew for some reason, so he set it perfectly parallel to the edge of the desk. As if going through a checklist in his mind, Sean ticked off the tasks until everything was ready. Finally, seated in his chair, he pulled his sweatshirt over his lap and, concealed by the shirt's tented fabric, unzipped his pants. He didn't touch himself yet, though. He liked to show himself that he could wait—that he was in control in this room, in this small facet of his life. Today, he waited for a very long time, longer than was usual, his eyes peering through the slats of the blinds at the sun-dappled pine trees outside and the black-headed chickadees playing on their branches. His hands began to shake. It was then, when he hit the cliff where he could no longer force himself to resist, that he let himself plunge in with a hunger he now reserved only for this. Only for them.

Working himself with one hand and the mouse with the other, Sean navigated through his favorites in a never-ending loop of satisfaction. www.hotbox.com/ginger. www.hotbox.com/marlene. www.evesapple.com/claudia. He sought them out with the eagerness of boyhood indulgence. Their naked bodies, their glistening mounds, their heart-shaped asses. *Take me to the women who give and give and give and expect nothing in return. Where they are always happy to do what I want.*

Sean rotated through the images, the videos, bringing himself to the edge and then stopping at the brink again and again. Minutes turned to hours, and hours turned to eternities of self-affirming love. They wanted him, unconditionally. He was always good enough for them, he always did enough, said enough, loved enough. Their faces, their pussies, their asses. They always wanted him. "More, give me more" they seemed to say from their pursed mouths and gaping holes. You are perfect. A perfect man. And today, like every other day, Sean tried to believe them.

The end would often be brought about by two things: exhaustion or interference. For Sean, the first ending was, of course, preferable. Hitting the point in his enjoyment where he achieved his climax and ended spent and satisfied was the best. But having Anna come home early or unexpectedly, with her confident stride—he had to admit that he hated her in that moment, when he knew he would need to leave this world of unconditional acceptance to enter one where his performance was always under scrutiny.

Sean had not always relied on this form of self-love, nor found so much comfort in it. Like most guys his age, he had been introduced to online pornography soon after his first uncontrolled erection. A high-speed internet

connection paired with an absent mother and an inconsolable father had left
Sean with a great deal of freedom during his teenage years. But back then it
had only been recreational, a way to ease boredom or achieve a quick burst of
enjoyment. With Anna, at least in the beginning, it had still been just a quick
outlet for him when he knew Anna was unable to fit another round into her
schedule. Now, though, it was his medicine for a difficult life. Just like a
prescription, he felt the side effects if he didn't get the proper dose.

In the early times, Sean had relished their sexual experimentation.
Being so young and in love left him feeling drunk. His and Anna's love knew
no physical limits. Often, behind closed dorm room doors, Anna and Sean
would explore the boundaries of pleasure. Prior to his relationship with Anna,
Sean had slept with a few women and had enjoyed it, but it wasn't until his
commitment to Anna that Sean had realized the world of possibility in his
sexual life and how much he wanted to explore it together with her. Anna had
been a virgin when they first came together, and Sean took it upon himself to
introduce her to the sexual world. In return, Anna gave him, for a period of
time, her complete devotion and trust. Whatever he asked of her, she tried to
do. Difficult positions, insertions of toys and other objects, playing out of his
dirtiest fantasies; Anna accepted them all in exchange for Sean's constant
attention and his acquiescence to her needs in daily life.

With her mother's absence, though, Anna had fallen into a deep hole
of depression. In the privacy of her relationship with Sean she had unleashed
all of her sadness, while with everyone else she was still the capable, strong
Anna. Her desire to attend to his needs became nonexistent as she coped with
her loss. Sean knew she was grieving, and he tried to be the understanding
husband she deserved, but Sean had never been very good at selflessness.

Sean had liked Anna's self-confidence at first. It was their own private
joke. She was the demanding partner in their outside world, but in the privacy
of the bedroom, or kitchen, or park bench, it was Anna who bent to his whims
without question. When he had been a teenager, Sean thought changing
yourself for the women you loved made you a pussy, but that logic was horribly

flawed. Sean had learned that the hard way. He knew how special his wife was and that she needed to feel that every day, and he was happy to oblige as long as his own private requests were met.

Caught in his reverie, Sean noticed his train of thought wasn't doing much for his one-handed efforts. Indeed, looking down he saw the perfect metaphor for how he felt inside. Zipping up and pausing the frantic video on the screen, he walked to the kitchen and poured himself a glass of water from the sink. Leaning his long body against the edge of the steel basin, the memories came tumbling in and he let them fall haphazardly in his mind. Best to get them all out, Sean decided—those memories tinged with the dark ink of rejection—and then maybe he could go back and make himself feel better. And so Sean conjured one of the first in the bitter stream of his marriage's memories.

It was an evening in the deep of Indiana's winter, where the days are short and dark and most residents stay inside after the sun sets. It had been already six months since Anna had, for all intents and purposes, lost her mother and also five months into their first year of graduate school. In typical Anna fashion, Sean reflected, she had refused to defer her enrollment for even a semester.

They had eaten a dinner of reheated lasagna and salad, and afterwards Sean had taken care of the dishes while Anna had lain down upstairs. Earlier that day, Sean had decided that tonight would be the night for them to reignite the passion in their relationship. Sean felt it was time to get back to normal.

Sean saw Anna laying on her side of the bed, the lights off and the drapes open to let in the dim light of the moon hanging in the dull February sky. He could just make out her figure, the soft inward curve of her waist and her small perky breasts flattened in her prone position. He knew from her breathing that she wasn't asleep. Sean approached cautiously, but with confidence. This would be the night that everything broken got fixed, he'd thought.

Stretching himself next to Anna, his chest and thighs pressed against her left side, Sean murmured in her ear, "You're so beautiful." That was how they usually began, and Anna would take his compliment as a cue for what was being asked of her. That night, Anna didn't reach her hand down to touch Sean or flip over to press her ass into the cave of his pelvis. Instead, she quietly and neutrally removed her blouse, pulling it over her head in one efficient movement, followed by her bra, slacks, and panties. Anna did all of this without moving her eyes from the crease in the wall where it met the ceiling, her face blank and passionless. Sean didn't know what to do with her.

He reached up and cupped her chin in his left hand, turning her face towards his own. Anna was pliable to his touch, and she smiled at him when their eyes finally met, but Sean didn't feel the familiar warmth of her naked and exposed body. Instead, he felt reluctance, hesitation, remorse even. *What was wrong? Why didn't she want him?* And just when his mind screamed out these agonized questions, Anna whispered up at him, "I like it when you kiss me first." And so Sean had done that. He had followed her orders and kissed her. And then she said, "Touch me here," pointing with her pale fingers at the soft rise of her abdomen. Sean did that too, tracing his fingers from her navel to her small thatch of blonde-brown hair. Just as he placed his hand on the back of Anna's head to push it towards his crotch, hoping for a return to their familiar roles, Anna whispered again. "I don't want to tonight. Is that okay?" she said. *No, it was not okay,* Sean thought. Definitely not okay, but what could Sean do with his exposed wife basically telling him that their old bargain was off? The night proceeded with lots of instruction, much more foreplay, and a small burst of relief at the end, not because he had enjoyed it, but because his fucking performance, literally, was finally over.

Now in hindsight, that evening served as a marker for Sean of when the decline in his marriage had truly begun. Gradual, and in fits and starts, but there all the same.

In the months and years to follow, his orgasms began to decline in intensity and functionality. While inside his wife, he found himself no longer able to let go of consciousness at the point of climax. Instead, he clung to his self-conscious state of being, aware that behind Anna's looks of adoration there was a scorecard being checked off for performance measures: kisses, 5; loving eye gaze, absent; foreplay, minimal.

Sean's proposals in the bedroom eroded until they became mere suggestions open to interpretation. Instead, I-language reigned, as in "I feel dirty afterwards." "I want you to try this." "I didn't cum." Sean may not be as brilliant as his wife, he thought, but he could still read between the lines. She may as well have said them out loud, every last one of them. "You are a freak." "You don't satisfy me." "You are pathetic." Sometimes, being around his wife made Sean feel as though he had no skin.

More recently, newer and even crueler accusations had been added to the hidden conversations of their sex life. After Anna had revealed the doctor's findings that Sean couldn't give Anna the baby they both wanted, bringing their intimate life to a standstill, Sean had become crueler than he thought possible. Lately his actions had reminded him of how he had behaved in the last few months of his own mother's life, but he found he couldn't stop himself from punishing Anna. She had abandoned her unspoken promises made almost ten years earlier, in the bed of his dorm room, the most important being that she would love him for who he was.

There. He had scoured his memory and come back with the same message he always heard: *your wife hates you*. Sean set his glass down and brought his body and mind back to his sanctuary. Online, every type of woman was there for his viewing pleasure and each clearly approved of what he was offering. Their eyes signaled openly that they wanted him, their mouths wrapped around and slavered those enticing, milky words: *You are good enough*.

Still, Sean reflected, as he settled back into his chair and un-paused the clip, in his times of greatest sadness, he could only achieve that final peak of release and self-love if he pictured Anna as one of them, too.

Bard

Bard left Dr. Kline's afternoon lecture unsure of where to go. He was a young man who typically knew his next step at any given point in his day, but Dr. Kline's class had proven overwhelming. The implications of what he had learned swirling in his head, he finally decided to walk across campus to the library.

Bard turned into the wind and began his commute past the naked oaks that littered Ambrose's campus. The cool air rippled across the wool of his jacket and pinked the apples of his cheeks, giving him the look of an overgrown moppet in a book of fairytales. One of the great benefits and disadvantages of his complexion was that he always looked younger than he was. Although twenty-two, Bard could easily pass for sixteen or seventeen if wearing the proper attire.

Passing into the library through the revolving glass door, Bard noticed once again the book drop to his left, its gleaming metal mouth shaped to give the illusion of pompous security that an ATM deposit box might. In today's age of electronic print media, Bard enjoyed this remnant of the past. The idea that students would be so desperate to return a printed book that they would rush by after-hours to do so seemed ridiculous to him. Still, he was on his way between classes to see what the library had to offer on the subject matter currently causing his mental panic. Walking into the quiet hush that all libraries across time and space seemed to share, Bard wasn't sure what he hoped to find.

Admittedly, Bard had wondered for a long time if he would follow in his mother's warped footsteps. He'd always thought the indentations she had left in his life were like imprints in the sand of an ocean's shoreline, deep impressions at first and then diminishing as the force of time swept over them again and again—but he'd been wrong. However faint his mother's voice— however delicate her imprints on his interests, his mannerisms, his memories—her influence had begun surfacing like violently colored mushrooms on his consciousness soon after he entered Ambrose. Bard had at first thought it strange that while his childhood home and all of the landmarks of his developing years had served to dull his memories of his mother, of Claire the woman rather than Claire the patient, now the form of his mother was fully realized for him in a place distinct from his past.

But Bard had come to understand what initially appeared so unexpected, so contrary. His family had worked for years to create a "new normal" for themselves (that was what his therapist had called it; his father had insisted he go to therapy after the visits with his mother were ended). One that essentially erased their mother from their daily lives.

Eating, sleeping, schooling, praying, working, gardening, loving—all of the tasks of daily life became distinct from what they had previously been. Food came from a catering service and was delivered daily to be reheated by their newly hired housekeeper, Mrs. Delamont. Gone were his mother's signature vases filled with fruit in the bottom and bursting arrangements of wildflowers, and sometimes weeds, at the top, instead replaced with vases of fresh hydrangeas in the spring and summer and dried hydrangeas in the fall and winter. Admittedly, Bard preferred the sterility of Mrs. Delamont's arrangements. They were, if anything, at least choices that pointed to a pattern of sane predictability, a predictability Bard lost when he began his new life at Ambrose.

And now Bard was in the library seeking the same assurance of predictability. The library was almost empty, which surprised Bard. The large vaulted ceiling of the main entrance was flanked by a checkout desk housing a dour-looking student employee reading Faulkner, her oversized black-rimmed glasses sliding down her ridged nose. *Pretentious.* Bard had first read Faulkner in high school when he was fifteen. And he hadn't needed to show off that he was reading it, either. Passing the young woman on his right as he headed to the computer kiosks that now served as card catalogues, he restrained himself from walking over and whispering "Kill your darlings" in her ear. More than likely, she wouldn't have got the reference anyway.

The kiosks were all deserted and Bard was able to secure one that was more privately situated towards the back of the broad room. He wasn't terribly self-conscious, but he'd prefer to keep his errand more private than not, at least for now. Faced with the flashing cursor in the empty white search field, Bard needed to decide on the search terms. He was at a loss. His courage was failing him—all of his options seemed so bleak. Eight years ago, no one would have predicted Bard would be here, staring at an empty screen trying to decode the best words to unlock what had happened to his mother.

After she had left, school had become a rote task of achievement for Bard, who had little difficulty excelling in his academic work but still preferred to be the student who set the curve for comparison, so he learned to work hard and push his efforts past adequacy into the realm of perfect outlier. If it hadn't been for his sister's extracurricular exploits, the Avis household would have become a family vault of well-preserved manners and clearly defined roles. Bard, as the middle child but first son, was destined to assume the family business once he finished his undergraduate degree.

Bard was happy to take on the role. He had no real career interests in mind and was ambivalent about the other options for someone of his stature and intellect: doctor, lawyer, politician. Egomaniacs, misers, and cretins. No, Bard preferred to option his life to a path without any hidden agendas: he would work to earn money and to then earn more money for his family. There would be no guise of helping others, helping society, or helping the common man.

At least then he would never be a hypocrite, a posture he had come to loathe as he watched all of the well-heeled professionals in their family's social circle (the people-loving doctors and the fighting-for-good lawyers and the local saving-the-community politico) dwindle from their family's existence even as they called across the chasm of social rejection, "If you need anything, just…"

A Flash of Red

Well, assholes, you could help me right now. How would you *describe my mother?* Immediately, though, Bard chastised himself for being so childish. No one knew better than him, except maybe his father, what his mother had gone through. He had been her little darling, her big boy. But this made it that much harder to dilute her down to a label. The empty white box still stared at him. *Come on Bard, stop being such a coward and admit to yourself what you're really looking for.* His bag felt incredibly heavy on his shoulder, its strap cutting in despite his heavy wool coat and reminding him of the extra weight inside. Why was he carrying around that book today, of all days?

Away at Ambrose University and separated from the rituals of the Avis lifestyle, Bard's severed connection to his mother began to repair itself with its own sense of agency. As he had packed for his first semester, Bard had brought his confirmation present from his mother, the *Lives of the Saints*, without any real intention. He had simply cleared off his bedside bookshelf and shoved all the books into the packing box to be shipped up north into the Midwest. When the shipment arrived a few days after he had already settled into his apartment, Bard surprised himself by pulling the book out and leafing through the pages that evening after completing the backlog of assigned readings for his classes. As a freshman, he'd unknowingly gone to class without having prepared the readings for the first day. It was a mistake he wouldn't allow himself to make again.

Having lost any religious fervor well before his mother even left—a side effect of his mother's zealous insistence on church attendance, on kneeling prayers before each meal, and on fasting from Saturday vespers until after Sunday's communion—Bard had not examined the religious figures of the Catholic faith since his catechism classes in middle school. Away at college though, the stories of the saints, especially those of women who had suffered for their love of God, intrigued him. His freshman year found Bard examining the book each night before bed. In that exercise, his exhausted mind was allowed to release what he had learned in the day, the basic foundations of economics along with the content of his general education courses, and his thoughts could float over to the elaborate stories of the saints, filled with sacrifice, despair, visions, and miracles, but all ultimately ending in death's triumphal surrender and the supposed glory of their reunion with Christ in Heaven.

At first, it was like reading a genre novel, maybe a romance or a mystery, where the stories offered singularities but the arcs of the plots followed the same familiar and comforting contours.

Over time, Bard noticed that he began to approach these stories with a bit more reverence, a bit more intensity. He wouldn't have called it devotion, but he certainly began to admire the women he read about: St. Bernadette's bravery in the face of excruciating pain as she battled her cancer, St. Teresa with her pious disregard for misogynists and royals. Although it may have been difficult for some to reconcile capitalism with spiritualism, Bard saw no difficulty in the matter. As long as his business ventures were honest and, most importantly, respectful of the men and, perhaps more so, the women he encountered, he felt reconciled with the values he was taking away from his readings: honesty, fidelity, and loyalty. Throughout the stories, it was those three tenets that seemed to demarcate the saints from the sinners. And Bard felt he possessed each of the three in abundance. Of course, he, much like the saints, was discerning about where his devotion was deserved, and also where there were those unworthy of it.

And so semesters passed and the camouflaged traces his mother had left on him revealed themselves to Bard more and more, like wild deer in the forest who remain invisible until they flip their white tails running towards salvation. He saw his deepening fixation as a harbinger of his future, and he began to question whether he was really inspired or simply traveling the path his own mother had taken, to end up screeching religious fanaticism. And yet his mother had been so beautiful, so poised, so loving.

Now, just when Bard felt he had resolved these fears by driving a clear divider between his mother's life and his own, Dr. Kline had given him reason to doubt his solution.

Students were trickling into the library, using it to cut across campus and shorten their commute between classes. Bard saw the same categories of students he always saw at Ambrose: pajama/slipper wearers with morning breath still at 3:00 p.m., freshly-pressed kids trying to convince people they weren't from Kentucky and therefore not white trash (personally, Bard had never felt embarrassed by his origins, but he knew many other natives of his home state felt the need to apologize for their presence in Indiana), and the largest category of generic co-ed, slightly overweight with the pudge hidden by jeans and a baggy Ambrose sweatshirt, t-shirt, or hoodie. Bard could feel the room getting warmer with the influx of bodies. He had delayed long enough.

Breathing deeply, but not so deep that he could smell the students who hadn't bathed yet today, Bard typed in the word that he knew he needed to type all along, admitting to himself how serious this so-called errand was to him. The results came back immediately, with a variety of options buried deep in the library's stacks.

Bard left to locate the proper floor and shelf. The third floor of the stacks occupied the compressed portion of the library where the ceilings seemed to be only two-thirds the height of a normal floor. Bard thought it was an odd way for an institution of education to house what was once the primary support of its existence.

The close room was arrayed with stacks, six shelves high, spanning floor to truncated ceiling, in parallel rows. A few desks were littered throughout the jumbled space, with a poorly groomed boy in pajama pants sleeping at one. The area was otherwise empty of people.

Bard found his sought-after section in the middle of the fifth row of shelves. Pulling three books out, each dusty from lack of use and ranging in date of publication from the late eighties to only a few years prior, Bard surveyed the titles. Opening the newest book first, *The Neurobiology of Mental Illness*, he scanned the index for the most relevant pages, turned to them, and began to read.

Twin studies indicate a strong heritability for psychotic disorders. Some estimates suggest that the likelihood of an individual experiencing a psychotic break or other dissociative symptomatology increases by 1000% if they have at least one first-order biological relative, such as a parent or sibling, with a diagnosed psychotic disorder.

Bard's breathing sped up and his stomach filled with the dead weight of confirmation. Fact after fact answered the questions in his mind. Feeling dizzy, Bard sat down with the books at the closest desk, which was mercifully at the opposite end of the room from the sleeping boy who appeared to remain blissfully unaware of Bard's crisis. Blinking his eyes to focus and chastising himself for losing his composure, Bard concentrated on his breathing until it had regained its normal cadence.

Feeling more stable seated in a chair, Bard forced himself to review again what he had just read. He needed to be sure he wasn't misinterpreting the meaning of the bland scientific prose.

No, it was as he had first thought. Bard closed the book and considered his options.

He needed to speak with Dr. Kline.

Anna

Office hours are an unknown for professors. Often, her door remained ajar and the entire hour would pass without a single student crossing the threshold into Anna's office. Other times, a line of students would wait outside her door, clamoring to get ten minutes with her to discuss a grade. Over the semesters, Anna had begun to recognize the patterns of increased student need around exam time and paper due dates. Today though was a week with no upcoming deadlines or pending projects and Anna anticipated having the hour to herself.

Engrossed in replying to requests for letters of recommendation and filtering announcements of upcoming colloquia, Anna didn't hear the knock on the glass pane of her office door at first.

"Ahmm," the visitor cleared his throat.

As she turned around in her chair to face the doorway, the periphery of her gaze at first caught a glimpse of what she perceived to be a shapeless face engulfed in flames. The disconnect between perception and reality startled Anna—she was unsure how her brain could so significantly misrepresent the world. As was her habit when faced with evidence that she was her mother's heir apparent, Anna's mind sought confirmation of her lucidity. A memory from her undergraduate perception class, where she had learned about how our mind creates notorious illusions in response to stimuli, reassured her. Calmer, she turned fully around and focused on the person in front of her: Bard.

"Can I help you?"

"Hi, Dr. Kline." Bard nodded as he took a seat at Anna's table in the center of her office. "I wanted to talk about today's class." His soft twang told

Anna he had not grown up in Indiana, and she wondered for a brief moment where home was for him.

"Certainly." Anna sat down opposite him, her hands folded into themselves on the table and her feet primly hooked at the ankles. She'd met with many students before, ones who made her uncomfortable on a variety of levels. Bard was no different. Anna had discovered her best defense was to remain constrained and impregnable in body posture. Neutral voice. Formal language. Calm demeanor, even if provoked.

"In class today you said it—schizophrenia—was really likely to go from parent to child." Bard stared down at the fake wood grains of her table. "I guess I was hoping you could tell me *how* likely."

Anna felt it coming, but managed to relax her face before her cheek muscle contracted. Despite her best attempts at composure, there were two topics that triggered a reflexive, angry shame. One was her husband's rejection of her. The other was, of course, her mother.

* * *

Looking back now, Anna could see her mother's health had begun to deteriorate in the months leading up to her marriage to Sean. In her ungenerous moments of reflection, Anna sometimes wondered whether Sean would have married her if her mother's mental health had been questionable at the time. Anna could be, and was, the perfect wife for him in so many ways even now, but none of that seemed to matter to him. In hindsight, Anna could see the seeds of displeasure growing deeper and deeper roots in her husband, like a tsunami quietly drawing up the shore, with the point of origin being her mother's illness.

Prior to that night of gnashing and gleaming things where everything changed for Anna, the signs had been subtle and easily disregarded. As Anna set up appointments for the caterers, dress fittings, and florists, she had assumed her mother would go with her to all of them, this being one of the benefits of attending college close to home. She loved both her parents, Lena and David Lichner, deeply but it was her mother who embodied the ideal combination of adoration and unconditional encouragement that characterized, in Anna's mind, the most loving of parents. As a bride-to-be, Anna couldn't imagine approaching marriage without her mother's unflinching confidence in her.

With the wedding in June, only a few weeks after graduation, many of the details needed to be finalized in February and March. Anna and her mother traipsed through the slush of winter's tail end from appointment to appointment, weekend after weekend. Anna preferred that Sean's interest in the plans remain minimal—she said all he really needed to worry about was showing up, and that she would take care of the rest. Sean had seemed relieved by the removal of responsibility from his shoulders.

It was before one florist appointment that thin cracks had begun to appear, much like the lines on river ice shiver out in webs before finally shattering. She was meeting her mother at a little coffee shop near campus prior to the appointment and had looked forward to having time to chat about their day-to-day affairs before meeting the florist. Her mother had arrived immaculately dressed, as always. That day, Anna remembered her mother had worn a deep purple cashmere sweater with a long silver pendant. Her chestnut hair was combed sleekly back into a bun at the nape of her neck, with her signature streak of gray nestled across her temple and tucked behind her ear.

When her mother walked in the door Anna rose from her seat to wave her to the section of the café, but hesitated for a second. Lena stood on the edge of the entrance, peered around the corner of the doorway furtively towards the parking lot, and then slowly inched herself inside. Her hands were shaking.

"Mom, I'm here. What's wrong—are you hurt?"

Anna had walked across the room and had stood next to her mother with her arm on Lena's shoulder. She had thought, with admittedly some irritation at her mother's bad timing, that she was having a stroke.

A Flash of Red

Her mother stared at her for a moment as if looking at a stranger. *She doesn't know who I am.* The thought darted through Anna's mind, ricocheting off the edges of her rational self. But just as real fear started to seep into her stomach and the acid of her cup of coffee surged into her throat, all returned to normal. Recognition finally brightened her mother's face, and she spoke in the crisp authoritative voice of a lifelong educator.

"I'm fine, just fine. I was out in the parking lot and I ran into a man I've been having a…a disagreement with—but I took care of it. Everything's all right." Her mother turned towards the counter and picked up a menu. "So what's good here? Shall we have a bite before we go?"

And just like that, Anna had let her mother brush the episode away. She could have asked more questions. *Who was he? Someone from work?* She could have looked for the man and checked to make sure he had left. She could have called the police.

But Anna had done nothing and admittedly, with all of her mind occupied with her own plans, she hadn't worried much beyond that day either. In the cloud that is memory, Anna could only vaguely recall a few episodes over those next few months where her mother's symptoms emerged.

Once, during a meeting with the caterer, Lena had stopped mid-sentence in her castigation of pasta with red sauce. "It is atrociously common and instead we should…" Anna and the caterer, an earnest man who had diligently taken notes during the entire meeting, had stopped in anticipation of Lena completing her thought. They had waited in vain for an uncomfortable period of time while Lena stared off into the center of the round table where they were seated. The caterer had started to fidget. Anna had taken her mother's hand, which had seemed to rouse Lena back into the present. "What's next on the list?" Lena had inquired, with only the slightest hint of annoyance.

Another time, when they were sitting in the car waiting for the light as they headed to a dress-fitting, her mother had described her day at work. As a middle school assistant principal, Lena shared stories with Anna about the students' awkward forays into romance and delinquency that came across her desk, or about the teachers' equally awkward attempts at adulthood.

"The poor girl honestly believed that the applicator was supposed to be inserted as well. She could barely stand up by the end of the day—weaving this way and that. Mr. Herbert finally sent her to my office, under the assumption that she was drunk," Anna recalled her mother sharing. The light had turned green and Lena had eased her foot off the brake expertly as she continued, "Well, I got to the bottom of the entire incident and told her that men were poorly schooled in this topic and didn't really understand women in the slightest. I clued her in on the secret of womanhood: that my thoughts and her thoughts were more powerful than any man's. Too powerful, sometimes."

It was finally after Anna had gone by her parents' house to pick her mother up for an appointment to taste wedding cakes one afternoon that she had decided to talk to her father about it. When Anna used her key to open the front door, she had expected to call out to her mother in the kitchen; she instead had found Lena sitting on the couch abutting the front wall. All of the curtains were drawn and Lena sat staring ahead, oblivious to Anna's entrance.

"Mom, what're you doing?" Anna didn't bother to hide the annoyance in her voice. They were running late as it was.

Lena turned her blank stare towards Anna, the same stare Anna had seen in the café a few months earlier. "He's out there, isn't he?" Lena's voice was scratchy and weak, as if she had been sitting for hours waiting to say the words, practicing forming them with her mouth and tongue. "Did you see him? My thoughts can't seem to push him back this time."

"Who...what?" Her annoyance gone, Anna's voice wavered on the edge of desperation at the sudden insight that her mother might need, rather than provide, care.

A moment later, Lena turned her gaze towards Anna and again, her eyes were lucid and her voice was steady.

"Are we late for our appointment? Let me just freshen up and we'll head out." She was always skilled at communicating normalcy. Like she'd observed in so many other mothers, Anna recognized in Lena a sense of responsibility to keep calm when really most afraid. After that afternoon, Anna had decided it was time to speak with her father.

David Lichner was one of those affable men who took on their familial roles of husband and father with joviality. All was well. All was *always* well. Anna had completed a series of abnormal psychology courses in her undergraduate work and was familiar with the broad spectrum of mental illness. When Anna laid out her concerns to her father, he listened patiently from across the kitchen table in the house he had shared with Lena for the last twenty-five years. Anna documented the patterns she'd recognized: the paranoia, the lapses in rationality, the communication dysfunctions. Finally, Anna found the courage to bring up the question she dreaded, the one that would confirm it for her.

David blinked and wiped his hand over his face, as if someone had just splashed him with their drink and he was flicking the imaginary wetness away with a shake of his hand.

"It's ridiculous. Your mother's family has always had the better health, you know that."

Anna did. Her father's side was wrought with drinkers, adulterers, and individuals with personality disorders. Her mother's family had always seemed bucolic in comparison.

"Okay, but don't you think Mom should go for a check-up? Haven't you noticed anything strange?"

"No, I honestly haven't, honey. But tell you what—I'll make an appointment for Mom with Dr. Glinchesky just to make sure she's still fit as a fiddle. She's been under a lot of stress at work, anyway, ever since that one poor boy, well...you know."

Anna did know. Six months earlier, seventh grader Bobby Haines had hanged himself by his belt from one of the shower bars in the boys' locker room. The gym teacher had found him during one of his routine checks of the facilities. Bobby had been rushed to the hospital and was still in a coma in the

ICU. No one seemed certain of the extent of the brain damage he had suffered. Anna's mother had seemingly taken it all in stride. After all, as she put it, she wasn't the school counselor; she only encountered children when they were in trouble and Bobby had never gotten into any trouble. But Anna knew the scrutiny from the local papers and the parent backlash had spawned sanctions from upper administration, and all of this had taken its toll on Lena. And Anna also knew her mother wished Bobby had gotten into some trouble earlier.

Anna pressed her father to make the appointment as soon as possible. Her wedding was only a few weeks away.

Her father promised to make the appointment at the earliest time available, and he had. He and Lena went to see Dr. Glinchesky, had a "lovely chat" as David later put it, talked all about Lena's stress at work and her emotional and physical responses to it, and left with a prescription for a weekend getaway and more regular aerobic exercise. Afterwards, in true Dad fashion, they had gone out for ice cream. Over the phone, he assured Anna that her mother was fine, that the doctor had told them all her symptoms were natural reactions to the higher levels of stress Lena was experiencing, and that they should all focus on positive aspects of life, like Anna's wedding, if they wanted to help Mom. Relieved and unburdened, that is exactly what Anna had done.

The day of the wedding had come and gone, with much joy and fanfare and with little concern for any undercurrents of mental disruption. Anna and Sean's wedding was a large affair, with over five hundred guests by the time her family had finished contributing to the guest list. Anna wore a bias-cut silk dress with a plunging back; Sean wore the suit Anna had painstakingly picked to match the modern styling of her dress and the flowers worn in her hair, and Lena and David mingled, danced, and enjoyed the entire affair. After the months and months of planning, it was a relief for everyone to finally be living in the moment.

Anna and Sean flew off directly for a two-week honeymoon in Italy, a gift from David and Lena, and then returned home to settle themselves in their new "married" apartment and prepare for graduate school that fall. David and

A Flash of Red

Lena met the couple at the airport and drove them home. At the gate, Anna was relieved to see that all appeared in order. Her mother was just as relaxed, lucid, and happy as when she had left her two weeks earlier. Even though she'd learned about remission in her undergraduate coursework, Anna couldn't have predicted how convincing a spontaneous respite from symptoms could be.

As the summer continued, Anna focused on her new married life. It was intoxicating to be able to spend the night with Sean without any lingering guilt or the need to hide reality when her parents called early in the morning or stopped by unannounced. Although Sean and Anna's sexual relationship had begun with intensity well before their marriage, Anna knew her parents preferred to deny that sexual intimacy a few weeks after beginning a relationship was now the societal norm, and they welcomed any opportunity to continue believing in their daughter's virginity. Now officially married, Anna no longer needed to pretend that she and Sean didn't share the same bed. Other intimate details, though, she still found necessary to obscure from everyone in her life.

Anna and Sean frequented yard sales, forever the venue for furnishing the apartments of graduate students, and slowly pieced together a home that reflected what Anna considered her impeccable taste and eye for quality. The couch was a real find for fifty dollars: deep brown leather with only a few scuffs and one snag along its upper right arm. Their kitchen table reminded Anna of something she had seen in her grandmother's *Better Homes and Gardens* magazine from three decades ago; it seated twelve around its heavy walnut leaves, and at seventy-five dollars she couldn't pass it up. When it came to their desk, Anna was almost smugly satisfied with it. It resembled a Biedermeier with its sleek lines and pale ash wood, and the two pedestals curving up to the unblemished desk face with its hidden drawers imitated the curve of a woman's waist. Anna thought it was beautiful, and imagined the compelling ideas she would produce while sitting at it over her graduate school years. At the time, Anna had felt it was the perfect symbol of their domestic bliss: a harmony of the intellectual and the sensual.

It was towards the end of this nesting phase that Anna's earlier fears were realized, and the blow they struck was both surreal and revealing. At home one evening attempting once again to competently make chicken à la king, a favorite dish of Sean's from childhood she had yet to master, Anna decided to check in with her Dad, whom she hadn't heard from in a few days. As she sautéed the pale pink meat in the pan waiting for its juices to flow, she knew she'd have a few minutes.

"Hi, Dad. How's it going?" And for the rest of her life, Anna would remember the answer he gave.

With his voice sounding as if it was coming from the center of an echoing cavernous place, David said, "She's gone." And then he began to cry, his voice racked with heaves and gasps over the line.

"Who's gone?" Anna's voice broke on the last word.

The pause that followed seemed to last for weeks, for months, as Anna hoped and wished that his answer would be something different. When it finally came, it was its synchronicity with what she already knew that leveled her.

"Your mother."

"I'm coming over. Now." And Anna hung up.

She rushed to the room in the apartment designated as their office and, without knocking, burst in upon Sean, who had retreated there earlier that day to catch up on some paperwork for the teaching assistantship position he had been wait-listed for. Anna had had no time to wonder about Sean's flushed face or embarrassed expression.

"Mom's in trouble—I have to go." And with that, she rushed out of the room, grabbed her coat and keys, and slipped on her shoes as she headed out the door. Before leaving, she paused briefly to see if Sean would get up from the desk and try to catch up with her, but no movement came from the hallway. And then she was gone.

The night was typical of late August in the Midwest, hazy with the ebbing balminess of the day. Through the misty humidity of the air, Anna could easily see the pulsing lights well before she pulled onto the block where

37

her parents lived. A police car was there, lights revolving in blue and red on the top of the car, but no sound was emitting from it. Anna parked haphazardly at the side of the road and rushed onto the front lawn of the Tudor-style two-story house she had known since childhood. As she went up the front path, she heard a rustling in the boxwoods that lined the front of the house. Looking over, she saw in the darkness three pools of light reflected, the smaller two set closely together and another lower, horizontal and parallel to the ground. The lights moved together, and she could just discern a figure uniting them. Then the figure moved a bit further into the light, and she could see the streak of gray hair within the red. And the knife.

* * *

Bard gazed back at Anna, waiting for her reply. Anna noticed his hands, clasped together so tightly that his knuckles were white from the exertion. His foot tapped below the table, rocking it gently with each percussive stroke. *He's really scared.* And her heart opened a little for him.

"Schizophrenia is around 65% concordant between identical twins, which we talked about in class. If a child has a first degree relative with schizophrenia, like their mother or father, there's about a 10% likelihood that child will develop it too at some point."

Anna saw Bard's face relax a little. She continued, "That's higher than the 1% probability you get in the general population, but it's also not a guarantee that children of schizophrenics will become ill too."

Even as she provided these factual statements calmly, Anna chastised herself for how sterile she was being. Likelihoods, predictions. The poor boy just wanted to know whether he was destined to go crazy, but the perfectionist in her wouldn't allow Anna to give that blanket reassurance. She had wrestled with this same question herself consistently since her mother had been institutionalized, and had yet to assuage her fears with what the numbers told her.

"I see," was all Bard said.

His grip did not loosen and his leg continued its rhythm. Anna could imagine the stream of words flowing through his head at that moment. *When will it happen, when will I stop being me, when will I become a menace, a burden?* She wanted to tell him that he was not alone, but also feared revealing the most vulnerable part of herself to a student.

"Why do you ask?" Even as she said it, Anna regretted the question's invitation for further intimacy.

Bard hesitated and then, with an exhale of breath, loosened his hands and shifted his gaze from the table up to Anna's face.

"After lecture today, I went to the library. The books I looked at said exactly what you just told me. I guess I was hoping you might tell me something different. See, my mom had a nervous breakdown when I was fourteen." Bard drew in a ragged breath and smiled weakly, "At least that's what Dad called it. It was really…hard, on all of us. I used to get letters from her, but then I'd have trouble sleeping so—"

Bard looked at Anna, as if waiting for encouragement to go on. Anna tried to remain neutral, but still found herself raising her eyebrows involuntarily at the pause in conversation.

"So Dad put a stop to them. The letters *and* the visits."

How long had it been since he saw his mother? Anna wondered.

Bard continued, "You see—she would say such terrible things, about evil and about sin. It was awful. And then, in class today, it was like all these things that I'd let myself forget just came back." His voice was terribly small now. Small and embarrassed. "It's scary."

Anna knew how this type of recognition could play with a person's reality. How you start to question the reality of what you see, hear, and feel. She had wrestled with the same uncertainties so many times in her own mind that she almost felt relieved to encounter another person in her life who had the same experiences. How many times had she forgotten about a dinner date with Sean, only to have him call her from the restaurant to say he'd been waiting for almost an hour? Or gone into the fridge to make dinner with the ingredients she remembered purchasing the day before only to find half of them weren't there? Or she'd misplace something, only to have Sean to locate her keys or phone exactly where she remembered leaving them, despite her repeated checks in that very spot. Each time something like that happened, she'd tried to ground herself in what she knew about memory and thought. *There is a rational explanation for this,* she tried to assure herself. But of course, one of the rational explanations that needed to be acknowledged was that she was losing herself, and that scared Anna more than anything.

Sharing her worries with Sean was unsatisfying. His reassurances that he would know when she was crazy, and that she wasn't there yet, were far from the universal affirmation she craved: that it would all be okay, that he would love her no matter what, that he wouldn't let her go crazy. She wanted him to say that he would love her out of it.

Anna could remember a time when this level of sincere support was instinctive to Sean, but even though their marriage persevered, Sean's efforts to soothe and comfort her slowly but surely decreased. After a few discussions where Anna tried to articulate what she needed and Sean repeated phrases like a recorded message, her willingness to open up to him about this slipped away. She eventually learned to push the worry from her mind when she was with him, but this only forced the thoughts to rush back during times of solitude or when she should have been engaged in work. Too ashamed to reveal her vulnerability to even her closest friends, and with a husband who refused to acknowledge it, Anna had nowhere to lay down her burdens, and she sensed Bard felt the same.

She wanted to help this young man, and the temptation to let him help her was palpable. Anna leaned forward in expectation of what she might say, letting her posture slip for the briefest moment. But, she reminded herself, she should be cautious. He's a student, not a friend. From the standpoint of Ambrose University, the rules of engagement were clear.

"I'm so sorry, Bard. That must have been really difficult for you and your family." Standing up from the table and moving towards her desk, Anna grabbed a green Post-it and a pen. "I'm writing down the number for counseling services. It might be helpful to talk to someone about this."

Bard seemed surprised at first, and then his shoulders drooped as he mumbled a brief thanks and took the proffered Post-it Note with the number on it. Anna could see it in his face—she had disappointed him. Trying to make amends without compromising herself, Anna continued, "And remember, our genes are not our destiny." The prefabricated phrase rolled off her tongue, as was to be expected. She'd told herself the same thing often enough.

After Bard left, Anna moved to the window to watch his departure. She was glad to have maintained the integrity of her emotional armor, despite the tempting release Bard had offered to her, but she also felt her response had been inhumane, robotic, a conditioned response instilled by the closed system of bureaucratic higher education. Trained mice and dogs respond in the same way.

As she looked out the window, Anna saw many students filing past on their way to their next classes. The sun was out now, and some of the slush from past snowstorms was melting into puddles on the sidewalks. She must have missed Bard, because as she watched for the next few minutes she didn't see him walk by. As she was turning away, though, she noticed the cardinal she had seen earlier in the day had come out and was splashing in one of the puddles.

Bard

Leaning back in the sculpted plastic chairs of his Econ 301 class, Bard tried to focus on his professor's explanation of a chi-square calculation. Looking around at his classmates, Bard saw yawns and grimaces in equal abundance. One girl with curly black hair was asleep on her desk, pencil still poised over her notebook. Bard appreciated his educational opportunities—his transcript clear evidence of this—but admittedly his hard work didn't arise purely from a general love of learning. As a teen, Bard started equating his ability to focus on even the dullest lessons as confirmation that his mind was running smoothly. Not surprisingly, Bard had been a very good student for a very long time.

Still, there were times when Bard found his mind wandering. Today, despite his best efforts, his mind retreated again and again from the present, where Dr. Turnbild's chalk squeaked across the outmoded blackboard at the front of the indifferent classroom, to a reenactment of his meeting earlier with Dr. Kline.

Leaning over his desk, pen in hand, Bard mimicked the familiar posture of an absorbed student but surrendered his train of thought to something more pressing. He let himself think about Dr. Kline.

During the meeting and immediately afterwards, Bard had felt disappointed in Dr. Kline's packaged replies. Initially, he saw her responses only as those typical of all professors dealing with distressed self-disclosing students. But as he continued to mentally separate his own health from the umbilical tether to his mother's, Bard's memories of that discussion took on a different hue.

A Flash of Red

Bard recognized objectively that Dr. Kline, as a woman, was a unique variant of attractive female. Slight in build, with a rigid posture, long lithe legs, and a nipped-in waist regularly accentuated by the cropped jackets she wore over trouser jeans and a camisole, Dr. Kline was more fit and stylish than the traditional academic. He'd noticed, in his observations of her over the duration of the time spent in her class, that her face had an oddness that could be pleasing. She had a high forehead and pale blue eyes; her dark brows contrasted with her straw-colored hair. Her lips, like a misshapen archer's bow, were fuller on the top than the bottom, and broke up the contiguity of her slightly prominent nose and dimpled chin. Not traditionally pretty, Dr. Kline's physicality offered an artful combination of components that beckoned the onlooker to examine her further. And this Bard had done without remorse. He prided himself on appreciating beautiful things.

It was this scrutiny that, upon contemplation, showed Bard what he'd missed at first in his meeting with her. Composed and perfect in decorum, Dr. Kline did not stray from her professional presentation in her academic role. Over the course of the semester, he had quietly looked on before and after class as Dr. Kline subdued students' complaints over grades, received confessions of serious illness, and discussed one young woman's revelation of rape with the same distanced but empathic demeanor. And yet he replayed his own meeting with her in his mind only to notice a softness in her that had been absent in all of these other interactions he'd seen.

The way her shoulders had melted towards him, especially after he'd disclosed his fears to her. And her face—it was an open invitation to tell her everything. Yes, Bard saw her tenderness as clearly as if she had spoken it aloud. Coming to that realization, Bard found himself surprisingly pleased that she offered up her humanness to his circumstances more readily than to other students. Why she found his story warranted the offer of greater vulnerability on her part, he could only guess. Regardless, the release she had offered to him with her words and gestures had been profound.

Looking up again, he saw that his professor, Dr. Turnbild, was coming to the end of his lecture. With his note page almost entirely blank, Bard realized he had wasted the majority of the class thinking about Dr. Kline. He would have to make up for it by working harder at home to master what he had missed.

* * *

After class, Bard walked across the campus quad, breathing in the biting air and clearing his head and lungs. He preferred to walk at a fast pace, which necessitated passing by other students who preferred a more leisurely stroll as they crossed campus from one destination to the next. Bard enjoyed eavesdropping on the snapshots of conversation that flowed around him: "...she woke up with him the next morning..." "I can't believe he puked all over her..." "...and the doctor said it wasn't infectious, but that I needed to..."

Bard had observed over time that the topics covered in personal conversations at Ambrose University inevitably revolved around three topics: alcohol, sex, and the interaction of the two. Bard himself was not as easily seduced as his fellow co-eds. Ever since his mother's removal from daily family life, his father had sought nightly solace in Jameson's amber-hued comfort. Over time, John Avis' ritual had extended earlier and earlier into the evening, until Bard began to associate a glass with chinking ice with his father's entrance into any room at any time of day. It was perhaps a blessing that his family was wealthy, on both his father's and mother's sides, and that real daily work was not necessary for the survival of this wealth.

After his mother had been institutionalized, his father set about securing the family fortune in solid investments and trusts, then descended into sodden grief. Hailing from Kentucky, the Avis family had staked an early claim in the coal mining operations of the state. Before Bard was even born, the Avis family had turned the day-to-day operations of the company over to others, allowing the family to reap the benefits of their majority share in the company without having to trouble with running the operation. Ensconced in the Avis family mansion at a prominent crest on Old Richmond Road, Bard's childhood with his siblings, Rosalind and Henry, had been one filled with financial and interpersonal security, the latter only beginning to disintegrate after his mother was diagnosed.

Turning right onto Willow Avenue, the street running adjacent to campus that marked the threshold where the university ended and the town began, Bard continued his transit, brushing shoulders with other pedestrians and jostling a few that proved unaccommodating to his faster pace. With a quick turn left onto Butler St., Bard reached his apartment in under five minutes. Bard surveyed his apartment building, which was really just an old family home that a profiteering local had bought and refashioned into four apartments, and felt once again satisfied in his choice to rent the attic apartment rather than the more expensive second or first floor accommodations. Although more inconvenient to access and slightly smaller, Bard felt the privacy and quiet it afforded were worth the sacrifice of other amenities. He climbed the outer wooden staircase, rickety with old age, and entered his studio apartment.

As was his habit, Bard immediately turned on his computer and monitor. MacBooks and iPads were for upper-middle-class college kids who didn't really know anything about computers. He preferred a double monitor set-up with a customized tower built to his own specifications, his computer skills having been honed in his high school programming classes. He had read in *Forbes* as a teenager that programming skills would be the keystone of successful businesses in the near future, and Bard had followed the advice with his typical acumen. After making a cup of espresso in his Italian-made machine, the only other artifact in his apartment besides his computer indicative of his family's wealth, Bard sat down to his afternoon tasks.

He had taken a job to help gain independence from his family's money and to move himself away from the problems that came with financial entitlement, like laziness and general douche-baggery. Prior to taking his current position, which had been ambiguously advertised in the university paper as "Programmers Needed for Exciting New Opportunities in Online Business," Bard had never had much to do with pornography. Like most young men, he had stumbled upon it a few times online and had had a few links shared with him from male classmates during the early semesters of his undergraduate life. He imagined the flow tapered off with time as his cohort realized that graduation would not happen of its own accord. Still, he'd never really seen the appeal in it. Certainly, being gay limited him to a more select group of sites than the variety available to heterosexual men. Even still, Bard's sexual impulses had always seemed subtler and less urgent than those of his peers. He rarely thought about sex and certainly didn't crave it regularly. He would have welcomed an emotional love and sometimes dreamed of lying in bed with a partner, caressing each other as much with words as with their bodies. But without the mutual adoration of the heart, Bard recognized in himself how intense his own need was to keep his physical boundaries intact. Generic college sex was really of no interest to him, and public sex performed for money was seen by Bard as the basest form of human connection.

Strewn over his desk were various books cleared from his bookbag, including his confirmation gift with the simple black cover. It was uncommon to be Catholic in Lexington, but Bard's family was adamant that he be raised in the faith and complete the necessary rites of passage for Catholic youth. Although his family's devotion deteriorated after his mother's illness, and his sexual identity technically put him at odds with the church's doctrine, Bard's devotion had apparently lain dormant, not dead, only to bloom again when he was on the precipice of adulthood.

Logging onto his computer, Bard checked for any new work orders on the Gmail account his employer had requested he create. No new messages. Currently, his employer had ads placed on one hundred different high-traffic porn sites. The ads moved through three rotating offers: reducing belly fat, erectile-dysfunction treatment, and IQ enhancement. Each ad offered an all-natural herbal supplement that had been "proven" to effectively produce the indicated outcome. The customer would click on the ad, link to another website that would request shipping and credit card information, and then one to two weeks later a box of sugar pills with the appropriate label would arrive. Bard had nothing to do with this, though, and had only gathered these facts from fragments of information in e-mails from his employers. His work began once the credit card information was entered. Bard was assigned one site at a time, from which he compiled all of the credit card numbers and identifying information for each customer, encoded them into an encrypted document, and then sent this document off to a specified Hotmail account. Apparently the sites used for ordering these products were changed regularly, as Bard worked on three to four different sites each month. The work was easy and paid well, in cash. Every two weeks, Bard would receive an envelope with his earnings in the PO Box he was required to lease at the local post office.

Bard realized his job carried with it some ethical complications. He had guessed early on that the credit card numbers were being sold for a high profit, although his employers were careful to keep him segregated in his position and uninformed about the other components of the business. He had read in an article in the *New York Times* a while ago that this compartmentalized approach to identity theft was common and effective. Crises of conscience were rare in Bard, and he had decided early on that people who were willing to devote part of their life to the consumption of porn, in contrast to so many examples of people living lives of chaste devotion, didn't deserve his compassion.

Bard worked tirelessly through the remainder of the afternoon, completing the assignment for his econ class and reviewing the material he had missed earlier. He usually felt annoyance that so many professors posted their lecture notes online, making class attendance unnecessary, but today he was thankful for the redundancy. After a light dinner of cucumber salad with tomatoes and feta, he settled into his next installment of paid work. Opening his Gmail account, he read the new assignment that appeared in his in-box. Apparently, much success had been had with the IQ Enhancer lately. The last several sites assigned to him used similar titular codes embedded within their

html: "Brain Fitness = Clit Wetness. Oozing IQ will make her Ooze too."
Bard had long since grown accustomed to the desperation of weak men.

Picking through the code, he extracted the name, address, and credit
card information of each customer, cataloguing it into the soon-to-be-
encrypted text file. The names varied in their ethnicity, although it was clear
that the customers were primarily men. In all the lists over the months since
his employment had begun in September, Bard had come across only a few
names and addresses he recognized: a neighboring businessman from
Lexington, a former classmate from his freshman year. Once, he had
recognized the name of a professor in the biology department. Bard had
unceremoniously entered each of them into his database.

Today, he came across a name that made him stop. "Kline, Sean, 349
Bristol Ave., Winnetka, IN." The time stamp read "Wednesday, 3.1, 13:00."
Bard knew that Kline wasn't an entirely unique name, but the likelihood of
another Kline living in the small town that housed Ambrose University seemed
unlikely to Bard.

*Dr. Kline's husband perused sex acts at 1:00 p.m. on a weekday while she was
teaching her abnormal psychology course?* Bard copied the information diligently into
his text file, but then also created a separate document on his desktop where
he copied it once more. After compiling the remaining names and data points
into the original text file, he encrypted it and sent it off. Unsure of what to do
next, he reached for the black-covered book on his desk, thinking of Dr. Kline
as he felt the soft cover under his fingertips.

Anna

It was time to go home. Anna stood and shut down her computer, clicking the small button on the monitor as she leaned over her desk and collected the papers she needed to review at home before Monday's classes. She buttoned up her red caban-style coat, piercing the buttons through the holes with practiced ease. Sean had made the mistake one year of buying her a winter jacket for Christmas, choosing a black double-breasted pea coat. She had laughed when she opened it at how absurdly generic it looked. She had thanked Sean for his initiative, but promptly returned the coat the next day. Luckily, since then Sean had stuck to the gift lists she made for him.

With her outerwear secured, Anna locked her office behind her and strolled down the hallway to the outside doors. She always loved the university at this time of day. Early evening settled on campus like a down comforter, encasing the ideas communicated throughout the day in a soft cocoon of expectation and waning sunlight as the thinkers packed up their belongings and prepared for the next day. Anna walked past the doors of her colleagues, some darkened and others with light beaming through frosted glass windows. Even after years of working side by side with them, she was still highly satisfied that the search committee had recognized that she would fit well with so many other exceptional names in the field.

Turning left to head towards University Drive and home, Anna contemplated what was waiting for her at 349 Bristol Ave. She knew Sean's job often allowed him to work from home, but some element of his work schedule nagged at her whenever she examined it closely. The explicit problem was indiscernible. He had good reviews from his firm and his paychecks came regularly and without issue. Sean would chat with her about what he was working on as they ate their dinner together, and it all seemed mildly interesting but not necessarily challenging. And yet Sean would often spend parts of the evenings and weekends working on certain projects and begging off spending time with Anna because of impending deadlines, barking at her if she intruded upon his workspace or his thought processes with her requests.

Her husband's displeasure and the backlight of the computer screen on his face: such a pairing had occurred so frequently over the years that Anna now connected the two in a visceral sense. Both triggered her defensive instincts, such that her heart would race and her teeth clench tight at the hint of sarcastic annoyance in Sean's voice or the aura of blue-tinted light glinting off his stubble-strewn jawline. When they were first married, despite or perhaps because of the lingering shadow of her mother's illness, Anna would lay in bed at night thanking God for her husband. She would sink into their new queen-size bed with his warm body like a monolith laid out to protect and encase her in the night. Now, in her darker moments she would walk home and match her mental cadence to her footsteps: *I-chose-wrong*. Right-left-right. *I-chose-wrong*. If Sean had been working diligently out of a sort of brilliance, Anna could have been more forgiving. But she knew what Sean earned and how often (that is, never) he had been promoted by his firm, which meant that his work ethic was not a mark of talent but only of mediocre thoroughness. And Anna couldn't accept that his middle-class initiative trumped what she had to offer him.

Walking quickly through campus and crossing into the residential streets of town, Anna's thoughts lapsed back to Sean's defense of his master's thesis. It had occurred the same year as her doctoral defense, which had taken her a total of only four years, master and doctorate combined. In his program, part of the defense was public and open to anyone who chose to attend. Of course, most often the attendees were just the friends and family who wanted to show support, but sometimes esteemed faculty or curious undergraduates would sit in out of interest. Anna could no longer remember the focus of

Sean's thesis, but she did recall the question and answer session that followed his presentation. Sean's thesis topic had apparently captured the interest of one of the more famous faculty members in his department, Dr. Eleanor Jameson. She was rarely seen outside her office, where she held court with her prime selection of graduate students and post-docs, and it had caused quite a stir when she walked into Sean's presentation, her gray hair parted on the side and swept back into a tight bun at the nape of her neck. Anna had watched as Sean took in Dr. Jameson settling herself into her seat with a pad of paper and a pen. He had closed his mouth tightly around his teeth, such that you could no longer see his lips, and his thin six-foot frame stood at rigid attention. As he ran a hand through his shaggy brown hair, Anna had seen his nerves taking over. *Oh God*, she thought, *please don't screw up.*

The wind was picking up as Anna worked her way towards the park by the local elementary school. Cutting across it reduced her commute time by five minutes and sometimes afforded her an opportunity to see young families playing with their children on the swings or to glimpse babies in their strollers as their older siblings came down the slides. When the park was full, she marveled at the kaleidoscope of color created by the mix of children's jackets, hats, and gloves. So many people at the university wore the requisite black or navy blue that the transition times between classes transformed the campus into tracks of mottled bruises as students and faculty traveled between buildings. On this frigid day, the park was empty and Anna crossed it alone, her mind still fixed on that day four years earlier.

Sean's presentation had gone surprisingly well, and Anna had sighed in relief that his nerves seemed to calm down once he began to go through the slides he had rehearsed so many times at home. A brief question and answer session was next, and then the public forum would be over and Sean would retreat with his committee members for further deliberation. The floor was opened for questions, and Sean fielded a few from fellow graduate students that clearly were asking out of politeness and encouragement rather than trying to foul him up. Anna silently thanked them in her mind.

A Flash of Red

Then, Dr. Jameson raised her hand and before Sean could even indicate to her, she spoke in her characteristic commanding voice:

"Earlier, you referenced Koolhaas's work on the Seattle Library. Could you explain how his work has informed your own perspective on the future of architectural design?"

Anna had heard Sean discuss Koolhaas before at home and with some of their friends at dinner gatherings. It didn't seem to be a hard question, but she held her breath, waiting for Sean's reply.

Clearing his throat, Sean began, "I think it is now well-accepted in our field that Koolhaas represents the epitome of modern architectural thought and pushes all new architects to consider how to reconcile our need for modern visions with the inevitable lag in making those visions a tangible reality." Anna cringed. He'd pronounced epitome as *ipi'təʊm*, with a long -o and silent -e.

Sean continued after that, but Anna could only focus on the snicker she had heard escape Dr. Jameson's mouth after Sean's foul-up of the word. *No one else is hearing a word you say, Sean*, Anna thought. *Just stop talking.*

When Sean finished, he instinctively looked to Anna, but she avoided meeting his gaze. She was worried her embarrassment would bleed through any attempt she made at a reassuring smile. Sean passed his thesis defense, and that evening Anna had planned a celebratory dinner of roast chicken, mashed potatoes, and cherry pie, one of Sean's favorites. She laid the table with their wedding china and lit some candles to soften the atmosphere. When Sean came home that evening though, he made it clear they wouldn't be celebrating together.

"Thanks, honey, but I really need to start on these revisions."

Sean filled a plate, briskly kissed her on the check, and took the food into the office. Anna put a little food on her plate and was about to head over to the office as well, thinking she could at least keep him company while he worked, when she heard the lock on the door click. Anna spent the evening on the phone with Joyce, her oldest friend, listening to the comforting words on the other end of the line between her own sobs.

As she came out the other side of the park and saw the glint of setting sunlight on the front windows of her home, the sting of Sean's rejection over four years ago still felt raw to Anna. She took a deep breath, righted her satchel again on her shoulder, and headed towards their home's front door, hoping, but not expecting, to feel warmed once she was inside.

Sean

It was approaching five o'clock, and Sean knew Anna would be returning home soon. Zipping up with his left hand, he closed down the windows on his computer with the other. Sean sat for a moment and gazed through the blinds onto their front yard, still bleak in the last gasps of winter, and fought the familiar turbulence. The pleasure always dissolved so quickly, leaving behind sadness in its place.

Sean stared at the blank computer screen, thinking of how he could use a variety of instruments to measure his marriage: the accumulation of years, cycles of reconciliation, periods of dejection. His periods of online abstinence were one such tool. They were like the deep notches in the basement wall of his childhood home that showed how much he had grown, or not grown, each year: Anna's breakdown in graduate school the year after her mother left, when they first started trying to get pregnant, when Anna told him why they couldn't get pregnant. Smaller life events could trigger the same abstinence: Anna's gentle attention to his needs in bed one morning, pride over his wife's attempts to help a struggling student, even the tender brush of their hands against each other could lead Anna and Sean to follow their clear path towards mutual happiness. But it never lasted. He always failed eventually, not because he didn't want Anna, but because she didn't want him, because his attempts to adore her did not measure up to her standards. His last attempt to be that good husband was now far behind them, back when they had first moved to Bristol Ave. almost four years ago.

When Anna barged into the office the night of Lena's arrest, Sean hadn't been working. He had been at honeyboxjunket.com. Not out of displeasure with Anna—they had tried a few new things earlier that afternoon. He just needed a little extra release, and she was making dinner. He couldn't explain why he hadn't gone after her, except that he had felt he couldn't afford to leave himself unfinished. He had no idea how serious the situation was, Sean reminded himself anytime he thought about that night. Sean liked to believe that, had he realized, he would have rushed alongside Anna to help her. If honest with himself, though, Sean knew he couldn't be sure.

He remembered Anna calling from the hospital that evening, recounting what had happened and telling him that her mother was sedated and they were thinking of placing her in residential treatment for a period of time while doctors assessed her response to medication. Could he do some research online about treatment centers and then come to the hospital with a change of clothes for Anna? Yes, he could. And he had done exactly what was asked of him, without any distractions to prevent him from persevering. Sean had continued being the supportive husband for the next several weeks as he, David, and Anna, had visited facilities and had eventually settled on Pembroke Farms, an institution only an hour away that specialized in the residential care of psychotic patients. He had been there for Lena's official diagnosis of *schizophrenia, first episode, acute phase*, a diagnosis Anna would repeat out loud for weeks afterwards as if in disbelief. He had helped as much as he could during Lena's transfer from the hospital to Pembroke, and had been there to hold Anna as she cried. They had watched as, with each visit, her mother slipped further away from them in a haze of different medications that sprouted more problems than they solved. And he had remained there for her over the next several months, holding her hand, caressing her hair when she cried, telling her everything would be okay while the hope of recovery slipped further below the horizon until everything was dark and shapeless.

But none of that had been enough, Sean thought, shaking his head slightly from side to side and reveling in his distorted reflection on the computer screen. *You agree, don't you?* Sean asked his reflection, and the nebulous head nodded back at him. She always wanted more.

He stood up from his chair and moved into the hallway, heading towards the kitchen. Sean opened a bottle of wine, pouring a large glass. Looking at the clock, he decided he'd go back to his desk and watch for Anna as she returned home from work. He thought for a moment about peering into the fridge and starting dinner before Anna came home, but determined it wasn't worth the effort. Instead, before moving back to his office to wait, he opened the refrigerator and pulled out a package of split chicken breasts and the gallon of milk. Sean dumped their contents down the garbage disposal, using the milk to help slush the slippery half-carcasses down the drain. The packaging he took out to the industrial-sized suburban garbage can on the side of their home. And *voila!* His sleight of hand was complete. At first, these little tricks he pulled had brought on a guilt stronger than Sean had ever felt. This deep into his marriage, though, Sean was on the edge of feeling like she deserved it. And that made him hate himself even more.

* * *

"Hello?" Anna called from the front doorway. Sean was on his second glass of wine now, and he felt himself suppress a burp as he tried to call back from his office. He'd kept the shutters entirely closed this evening.

"Hey," he finally managed.

Anna stepped into the close room and brought the smell of the outdoors with her. With her windblown hair and pert nose, Sean thought she could pass for a fairy, but prettier. He considered saying so, but decided instead on grabbing the box of tissues on his desk and holding them out for his wife.

"Your nose is running, honey."

Anna's chin dipped for a moment and he saw her calculate whether to grab the tissue and wipe her nose in front of him or walk out of the room to clean herself up in private.

"Oh, thanks. I'll be just a second."

A Flash of Red

While Anna was in the bathroom, Sean shut down his computer and headed to the kitchen to wait for her. She emerged, her hair smoothed and face freshly washed.

"Gorgeous," Sean smiled at her. "How was your day?"

Anna was already rummaging in the refrigerator now, starting to prep their dinner. "Fine, busy. You know."

"No, I don't. Tell me about it—dinner can wait."

Anna poked her head over the refrigerator door, not closing it yet. "Well, we were talking about De Clerambault's syndrome."

"Sounds French," Sean interjected, offering a wink that Anna didn't seem to notice.

"Not really. It can affect anybody. You know, mental illness doesn't limit itself to one culture over another."

"I know, I was just—"

"Although," Anna added, "there is some interesting work on culture-bound syndromes. You know, ones that manifest—show up—in specific contexts as a result of cultural mores. Norms, I mean."

"How interesting." Sean walked over to the refrigerator. "What's for dinner? I was hoping for chicken tonight. Maybe with that nice cream sauce you make."

Anna smiled up at him—she always appreciated when he showed an interest in her cooking. "Well, you're in luck—"

She turned her attention back to the contents of their fridge, a frown marring her lovely face. "I could have sworn…"

"Oh, well, if you forgot to pick up the ingredients, don't worry. I'll eat anything." Sean swallowed the rest of his wine in one satisfied gulp.

* * *

Sean awoke the next morning with the next two days stretching ahead of him, completely unscheduled and rich with potential. He shifted in bed, savoring the extra space created by Anna's regular weekend visits to her parents, and then headed downstairs to make himself coffee and a light breakfast. Passing by the kitchen table, Sean picked up Anna's note and read it with a pang of compassion mixed with resentment.

As Sean turned the coffee maker on, he gazed out of the window of their kitchen and caught a glimpse of the sunlight reflected by the elementary school's playground slide. Holding his wife's beautiful stationery in his hand and feeling under his thumb the indentations of the word "love" carved into the cardstock, Sean found himself transported back almost a decade to another playground.

* * *

In the spring of his sophomore year, Sean's landscape architecture class had been assigned the task of designing a new playground for children. The pack of students, foggy with fatigue in the early morning sunlight, traversed across the common from their building to the university's daycare center. Sean could feel the wetness of the spring dew settling on his sneakers as he headed towards the building and he arrived slightly annoyed that he hadn't taken the sidewalk. Why were undergrads always cutting corners?

His class was taught by Prof. Suparmanputra, a burly Indonesian man with wild curly gray hair and skin the color of toasted almond. Sean loved his class, if only to hear Prof. Superman's (as his students affectionately called him) resonant voice roaring on in his exotic accent about the advantages of living fences and green roofs. Eschewing the standard PowerPoint slides of many other professors, Prof. Superman's preferred lecture style was to scribble wildly on the board to emphasize whatever principle he was covering, ultimately ending each class sweaty, spent, and covered in chalk dust. One day, Prof. Superman had been so enamored with his lecture on the unforgiveable sin of abandoning history for current design fads, he clapped his hands together to highlight the final point of his lecture, smiled like a man who had just seen the waiter bring his food after a long and hungry delay, and then turned to collect his things, absentmindedly wiping his sweaty chalk-dusted hands all over the seat of his pants. Sean, not wanting his professor to walk across campus in such a state, approached him and quietly mentioned that he might want to freshen up in the restroom before heading out.

"What's that, Kline?" Superman had boomed in his apparently immutable voice.

Sean discreetly stated again that the professor might want to freshen up before leaving the building.

"Dammit, boy, I can't hear a word you're saying. Speak up!"

Exasperated and regretting his choice to try and help, the words left Sean's mouth before he had a chance to parse them into something more polite. "Professor, you have chalk all over your ass."

Stealing a glance at the professor, anticipating a berating, Sean saw Superman's shoulders begin to shake. He was laughing.

"Well, Kline, it's not the first time I've managed to mess myself in public!" The professor clapped a hand onto Sean's shoulder. "I do appreciate your concern, but next time just spit it out, man." And with that, Superman strode off to his next destination, firmly ensconced from that moment onwards as one of Sean's favorite professors.

The day Sean met Anna, Superman had been extolling his students on the transformative power of landscape, much like the transformative power of childhood.

"Each child has the potential to grow into an amazing or a decrepit human being, much like any landscape we touch can be transformed into a Versailles or a retail parking lot. So, for our next assignment, we will marry these two potentials. Can you create a playground that will help transform a child's exterior, and likewise their interior, worlds for the better? I hope so. Now get to work!"

Sean and his fellow classmates were unleashed onto the playground. Each student had been given a schematic of the playground's current setup, so baseline sketching wasn't required. Sean headed over to the small red playhouse that resembled a miniature one-room school house, intending to sit inside and begin marking out his ideas for modifications. When he crossed the threshold of the entrance, ducking his head to fit inside, he saw the house was already occupied.

A slight, blonde woman was sitting next to a little boy of about three years old who appeared to be nearing the end of a crying bout. Gazing back, Anna's blue eyes conveyed clearly her request for some privacy. Sean moved back out into the sunshine, calling a quiet, "Excuse me," over his shoulder. Not expecting a reply, he was pleased to hear her call back, in a slightly deeper tone than he would have initially expected for such a petite woman, "We'll just be another minute." Sean stood outside, admittedly intrigued by the conversation occurring within. As he waited, he considered the quick glimpse he had caught of the woman, remembering that she was wearing khaki shorts in a longer style than was typical of undergraduates and that the shoulders exposed by her sleeveless shirt had each had a constellation of freckles.

"Okay, Kevin, let's rehearse it one more time. When Jeremy comes by you and calls you stupid, what are you going to do?" Anna's voice was expectant.

"I'm going to walk away," Sean could hear the little boy reply in the high-pitched tenor of childhood.

"And if you feel so mad that you want to kick him, what can you do to calm down?"

"Count to five."

"Very good. Let's practice. One, two, three…" Anna and Kevin recited the numbers in unison. As the two of them emerged from the little house, Sean saw Kevin give Anna a quick hug around her legs before running back into the center's building. Smiling to herself, she looked around for a moment before noticing Sean standing nearby. "It's all yours," she gestured with her hand to indicate the open doorway. She was almost back at the building when Sean finally got up the nerve to say something.

"That was really nice, what you did there. You're really good with kids."

Anna had looked a little startled at first, as if unsure how to handle the compliment. "Thank you."

A Flash of Red

* * *

The coffee maker gurgled unattractively and Sean realized he'd added water but forgotten the coffee grounds. The resultant "coffee" that filled the carafe was one shade lighter than dishwater, not that he'd know really. Anna did all of the cooking and cleaning up afterwards.

Sean wondered, looking at his hands, when he had last touched her. When had he last traced the gorgeous curve of her ass, bowing in and out like the body of a stringed instrument? He had made her vibrate once, just with the soft touch of his fingertips. When was the last time she had welcomed that touch? *Way too long ago*, the answer echoed inside his head. And with it also came the ache Sean had begun to feel too ripely, despite his self-medication. He needed his wife.

Anna

Saturday mornings were difficult. Whereas the week provided clear demarcation for how to spend her time, the weekends were malleable and offered multiple pathways of opportunity. The possibilities—pursuing new hobbies, cleaning her home to an immaculate state, revisiting her marriage in various forms—left her overwhelmed. Even though Sean's weekends were regularly, though not always, filled with his own professional deadlines, a pattern begun in graduate school, Anna still found herself languishing without clear guidelines for action. On weekends where she planned to visit her father, and in turn her mother, Anna welcomed the definitive structure to her Saturday and Sunday. She would wake early, careful not to disturb Sean. After showering, dressing, and eating her breakfast as quietly as possible, Anna would head out the door with keys and an overnight bag in hand before 7:00 a.m., a note left on the table wishing Sean a restful weekend with assurances she would miss him. The two hour drive from Winnetka to her father's home was easily managed. With her thoughts wandering as she drove, pinpoints of light on the surface of her mind would catch her attention, and like a hungry albatross catching the glinting of a fish's scales from above, she would dive down to retrieve the morsel.

Today, Anna's drive to her childhood home recalled for her the family trips to Niagara Falls, the long drive in the car rewarded with the most spectacular roar of water she had ever heard. She remembered the tinkle of the water coming from the hose in the backyard as her mother pretended to water the flowers, looking to catch Anna who hoped to get caught as she sprinted through the bushes to the maple tree in her bathing suit. She reminisced about sneaking into the kitchen only to find her father cupping her mother's buttocks in his hands, the two of them embraced in a kiss. It was hard not to examine each of these memories for symbols of her mother's future. It was hard for Anna not to examine her own life in the same way.

Her mind could flit from one childhood memory to the next, the majority of them so filled with happiness and security that the present state of her life seemed impossible to connect with her previous existence. After that night in August when her mother attacked Anna, all of their intertwined lives—Lena's, David's, Anna's, and Sean's—lay in a jumbled mess on the floor of their once sturdily built sanctuary.

In the end, Lena hadn't hurt Anna, aside from a few defensive wounds on her forearms. As David recounted the story later, Lena had become more and more agitated and incoherent over the previous two days. David was vigilant, attending to her and ensuring she wasn't alone, in the hope that it was just a bout of stress that would pass. When she had disappeared that evening from the house as David went to make her a cup of tea, he had panicked and called the police first, describing Lena's recent symptoms. It wasn't until the police indicated that they would send a patrol car over immediately that David had admitted to himself how serious the situation was. And then Anna had called.

Lena's screams alerted the officers and David, who had seen Anna's headlights as she parked by the house. Sweeping in from both sides, the intervening officers quickly subdued Lena and wrestled the knife from her hand, kicking it away into the boxwoods where as a child, Anna had played hide and seek with her mother.

Anna remembered her father crying on the front step, inconsolable, while their neighbors poured out of their front doors, standing on their tiny porches to confer with each other. She distinctly recalled, still with intense bitterness, that no one had come over to help. Staring around in bewilderment, Anna had not known what her role was. An advocate would have demanded to ride to the police station with her mother. A victim would have accepted the offer to stay overnight in the hospital for observation. Anna had been neither of these, but instead had sat down with her father on the front step and wept for the changes she saw rushing into her life.

* * *

As she neared the exit to her hometown, Anna began to prepare for the demands that she would face that day and the next. Somehow her fears of losing herself to the same illness that had captured her mother's mind were relieved by visiting Pembroke. Her daily life on Bristol Ave. seemed to include, more and more frequently, experiences that forced Anna to question whether her hold on reality was still firm. When she visited her childhood home, and likewise the fortress that kept her mother safely contained, Anna's mind ticked with precision. It was only once she returned home to Bristol Ave. that her anxieties reemerged through little reminders of her possible inheritance. She was certain she had bought the ingredients she needed for dinner last night.

Anna thought about a conversation she'd had with her best friend, Joyce, soon after her mother became ill.

"What do you mean, he didn't go with you?" Joyce was appalled.

Anna could hear the clatter of silverware in the sink on Joyce's end of the line. Her friend was a compulsive multitasker, a trait she herself had probably passed onto Joyce, Anna thought as she put down the rag she had been using to wipe the front windows in their apartment.

"Joyce, I just rushed out. He didn't know what was going on. He was working." Despite her lingering hurt over this incident, Anna also hated when anyone criticized her choices, even if it was her best friend.

"What kind of asshole just sits there while his wife goes searching for her missing mom? Really? He doesn't deserve you." The sound of rushing water punctuated Joyce's words.

"You can't judge him based on one situation. That's not fair."

"Okay. How about his toast at the wedding? You put so much time into your poem, and all he had was one measly sentence?"

A Flash of Red

The background was quiet. Joyce must have finished the dishes. Anna had loved Sean's toast. Simple, just like Sean. Later he had showed her the inscription matching his toast on his wedding band. Although she would have preferred a little more detail for the audience to see how powerful his feelings were for her, she still loved how sincere he had looked when he spoke.

"I loved his toast—doesn't that matter?"

"Of course it does. Sorry. I know I shouldn't be focused on this, with your mom and everything. I just wish I was there for you, you know. And it makes me mad that your husband wasn't. Isn't. So what can I do to help?" Her voice shimmered across the connection.

"Just listen. And tell me everything's going to be okay."

"Everything will be okay, sweetie. And if it isn't, then I'll make it okay, somehow." After years of friendship, Joyce's verbal poultices were molded to perfection. And Anna knew her friend meant every word.

* * *

She should have called Joyce last night, Anna thought, instead of spending the night crying in her bedroom alone, while Sean put a big project "to bed" down in their home office.

Yes, it was easier in some ways to spend her weekend with her father, and less so her mother, than with Sean, but these visits brought with them their own despair. Anna clicked her blinker to move into the exit lane, knowing and yet uncertain of what lay ahead.

Perhaps to Sean, or to someone else who had not visited her family for an extended period of time, the state of David's home and hygiene would have been surprising and appalling. The Lichner family had always been attentive to the care of their home and to their own appearance, and Anna attributed her own polished demeanor directly to the models provided by her parents. Pulling into the driveway now, the boxwoods were clogged with carcasses of ragweed and dandelion. The bushes themselves had taken on a hirsute quality, with patches of leaves extending out over the pathway in unregulated clumps. From a distance, the three bushes resembled shaggy-haired dogs, offering their ears and noses for a rub by passersby. Anna hated them.

Anna parked in the driveway and headed up the path to the front door. She noticed that the pathway had not been shoveled, but the snow had melted as a result of the sun. The telltale outlines of icy footprints still remained where the postman and her father had pressed down the snow. Using her key to enter, she pushed the front door open into the stagnant aroma of body odor and microwaved Salisbury steak.

"Dad," Anna called as she hung her jacket on a hook by the front door. Surveying the living room, she saw the furniture remained in the same place and, despite dust and tracks of mud on the once pristine carpet, it was still free of clutter. This was a relief to Anna.

"In here," she heard her father call from the kitchen, eternally the gathering place for her family, when it was gatherable. Anna knew what to expect behind the swinging saloon doors popular in homes when she was a child. The counters were cleared, if not truly clean. No dirty dishes were piled in the sink, but the trash was overflowing with plastic utensils and empty cartons of Swanson dinners. Meeting her father's tender gaze as he assessed her health, happiness, and any detectable changes to these since the last time he had seen her, Anna blinked and looked away. She wiped her face with her hand, and then returned a smile. If he saw her cry, the veneer she had struggled so hard to create would split down its seams.

Coming in close, she hugged her father, smelling the pungency of his flesh and feeling the encrusted nature of the burgundy cardigan he was wearing. The collar of his button-down shirt was stained with dried sweat (*He's been sleeping in his clothes again*, Anna thought), and the bristles of his patchy beard scratched against her ear. But it felt so good to be held.

"Hi, Daddy! How're you doing?" Anna asked, pulling away from their embrace.

A Flash of Red

"Oh, fine. Just fine, sweetheart. Want some coffee?" It was their little ritual. David would make coffee and they'd sit down and talk. David loved hearing about his daughter's life.

"Perfect. I'll just go put my bag upstairs. I'll be right back."

Anna watched as her father turned to their ancient, yet enduring, French press. It was still pristine. As she listened to her father setting the kettle to boil and opening a fresh bag of coffee beans to grind before placing them in the press, Anna was certain that a fresh pint of cream was waiting in the fridge for her. Although her father avoided cooking, he had always treasured the ritual of making coffee for the people he cared about.

Heading up the stairs to the second story, Anna passed the 11 x 14 print of her on her wedding day, standing next to Sean with her parents flanking either side. Her father was so handsome in his dark suit that fit his lanky frame so well, clean-shaven with the same sandy-blond hair and blue eyes as her. They all looked so content, the smile lines around Lena's and David's eyes like quotation marks that bordered the joyful moment.

Little had changed from her last visit. In her old room, her bed was made up with the sheets she had slept in last time and the curtains were still clumped with dusty tendrils that fell from the ceiling. But sunshine streamed through the window and, in her pensive state of mind, Anna felt relief watching the dust particles dance in the beams of light. She washed her hands and splashed cold water on her face in the upstairs bathroom, noting the Sudoku book next to the commode with a smile. Looking to dry her face with a towel, she opened the closet door for a fresh one, making a mental note to switch in fresh towels for her father before she left.

Anna could hear the spray of the tea kettle, followed soon after by the satisfying whoosh of water as her father poured it into the press. Taking a step down the stairs, she paused for a second when she heard a tapping. The sound was coming from her parents' room. As she walked past the third bedroom, which had shifted over the years from playroom to home office, the tapping became louder. Once in the master bedroom, she identified the source of the tapping: a

70

female cardinal was seated on the window ledge with a sprig of bark from one of the neighborhood's many birch trees balanced in her beak. As Anna watched, she saw her tap against the window pane in a disorganized rhythm. She wasn't sure why the bird was trying to get into the house, but thought perhaps a little tapping from inside might encourage the cardinal to seek out a better place for nest-building. Anna strode over to the window and tapped the pads of her right index and middle fingers against the glass, in what she hoped was a friendly message to move along. In response, the cardinal paused and turned her head cockeyed such that Anna could see only the bird's right eye gazing up at her. Dropping the white bark on the ledge, she flew away.

The strange interaction clung to Anna as she moved to leave the room. Having turned to her right, she couldn't avoid glimpsing her parents' bed, which was perfectly made on what was once her mother's side. David hadn't touched Lena's bedside table since she left, and her reading glasses continued their silent vigil atop the books Lena had been reading prior to her illness: Faulkner's *As I Lay Dying*, a favorite of both hers and Anna's, *Shakespeare's Sonnets*, and Pielmeier's *Agnes of God*. On her father's side, the sheets were tumbled and, moving closer, Anna could see dried rings of perspiration emanating outward from the depression left in the mattress by her father's body. She would need to wash the sheets as well.

Back down in the kitchen, Anna settled into a chair at the table while her father brought over the tray of coffee, sugar, and fresh cream along with two sparkling white coffee cups.

"So—" David leaned across the table towards his daughter. "How are you? How's Sean?"

"We're fine. He's busy with work—you know. Always a deadline looming." Anna managed a smile. "How about you, Dad? What's new?"

As soon as she had asked the question, Anna regretted her choice of phrase. Her father had retired from his accounting firm after Lena's illness, and had relied on his pension and Medicare to help allay the costs of Lena's institutional care. To the best of Anna's knowledge, David spent his days watching television, rereading his favorite books, and visiting Lena several times a week in anticipation of her imminent return home. After Lena was hospitalized, the inevitable distancing of friends and acquaintances had occurred without much fanfare. In typical Midwestern fashion, their neighbors brought a slew of casseroles for the week following their visit from the police, only to then immediately begin avoiding the Lichners. That was how it was in Indiana, Anna noted ruefully—emotional debts were repaid by leaving Campbell's soup casseroles and taco bakes, after which the outcasts were ceremoniously avoided for the audacity of allowing tragedy into their lives.

The one exception was David's childhood friend, Colin, who had known David since grade school, and his wife, Grace. Anna knew Colin and Grace stopped by to visit at least once a week, and often invited David over for dinner, insisting that David take the leftovers home to reheat for supper the next day. When she replaced the cream in the refrigerator, Anna saw two neatly wrapped foil packages affixed with Post-it Notes in Grace's distinctive script, denoting the proper reheating instructions, nestled among the prepackaged foods David favored.

"Not much, not much. Your mom sends her love. She looked really good when I visited yesterday. Really..." Here, David searched for the right descriptor. It was a common occurrence when anyone tried to describe Anna's mother.

"Really...focused." David's eyes lit up when he hit on the right word. "She should be coming home soon."

Anna bristled at his father's optimism, but knew better than to try and convince him otherwise. David regularly imagined, and sometimes initiated, plans for Lena's imminent return home, often with disastrous emotional and financial effects.

"Hmm...I was planning on visiting her later after you have your shower. Are you up for the drive?"

David halted the ascent of his coffee cup. A redness spread from his cheeks down his neck, but he didn't mention his embarrassment out loud.

Anna added gently, "Mom always loved you clean-shaven."

"Of course, sweetheart," David took the coffee cups to the sink. When he moved upstairs, Anna stood up to wash the dishes. She would do the laundry later that evening.

* * *

Both David and Anna were quiet in the car on the drive to Pembroke Farms. Turning right into the estate's long drive, Anna was once again impressed by the physical welcome the institute offered, despite the misnomer embedded in its name. Pembroke Farms was not a farm in any regard, but an institution for the mentally ill that boasted over ten acres of manicured and fenced-in grounds and a drive lined by ancient ash trees. When in full leaf, these trees offered privacy to any car or ambulance as it made its way from the road to the main care house. In this final month of winter, Anna thought, the trees instead resembled skeleton acolytes beckoning visitors onward. Pulling into a parking space designated for visitors, Anna took in the strong brick façade and welcoming wraparound porch of Pembroke Manor House.

Built to resemble an exaggerated version of a 19th century Midwestern farmhouse, the manor house presented to the visiting public an exterior imbued with folksy wisdom, from the rocking chairs on the porch to the flowing white curtains with blue embroidered hems gracing all twenty front-facing windows. Inside, Anna already knew, great pains had been taken to camouflage the modern institutional efficiency practiced in the care of Pembroke's patients without actually hiding it. All of the doors in the institution had locks and windows which allowed inside actions to be observed and monitored, but the doors were beveled and notched to create appealing dimensions for the eye to scan rather than a typical institution's flat prepubescent entryways. Corridors were separated by locked doors and demarcated by ward numbers, moving from the less intensive Ward 1 to the most intensive Ward 3. The traditional linoleum flooring and acrylic signage were absent, replaced with repurposed wooden floorboards from razed local barns and hand-carved signs reminiscent of Mennonite woodcrafts denoting the Lord's Prayer, the words carefully crafted in script and adorned with facsimiles of grapes and other fruits of the field. Anna knew it cost a fortune to keep her mother here and, not for the first time, she wondered how much her father sacrificed in his own daily life in order to maintain this level of care for Lena. Walking up the steps, Anna took her father's arm, quickly brushing a few flakes of dandruff from the shoulder of his fresh shirt.

David and Anna entered through the broad oak door, signed in, and affixed their visitor passes before being escorted by a nurse to the visiting area for Ward 3. If Lena had been in Ward 1 or 2, they could have walked outside, chatting in the slowly reawakening garden and feeling the comforting crunch of the gravel path shifting under their steps. For Ward 3 residents, though, visits were limited to supervised indoor meetings. As she heard the now familiar clicks of keys turning in locks and doors closing tightly, Anna saw the nurse discreetly settle his heavily muscled body into a straight-backed chair directly across from where Anna and David were sitting on a plush linen couch. The nurse avoided eye contact, focusing his dark eyes instead on the pale sunlight streaming through the curtained windows. As Lena was guided into the room, Anna thanked him silently for his tact.

It was clear that effort had been made with Lena's appearance. Her hair was freshly washed and vibrantly red as ever in a ponytail, with her gray streak making a pronounced division down the middle of her skull. She was wearing a light blue tracksuit Anna had helped her father pick out last month during one of her visits; they were allowed to provide clothes for Lena as long as they were fastened with Velcro or elastic. The nurses escorting Lena eased her into a sturdy molded plastic chair at a forty-five degree angle to David and Anna's position on the couch. In prior visits, both staff and family had learned that Lena responded best when not encountering her visitors head-on.

Stealing a glance at her father, Anna saw him instinctively reach out to touch Lena as she settled herself in the chair. Although the medications Lena was currently prescribed, as with all previous medications, worked only intermittently to mitigate the cognitive effects of her illness, they somehow consistently managed to hijack Lena's control over her own body. Lena's hands routinely shook and her motor coordination was impaired, making bumps and bruises a common side effect of her attempts to navigate her environment unaided. With David's gesture, Lena glanced up for the first time and took in her husband and daughter sitting in the room.

Over the years, Anna had become accustomed to what was about to follow. For one suspended moment, Anna saw Lena's facial muscles relax into the comfort of recognition. *It's worth it, just for that.*

"Hello," Lena said.

"Hello, darling." Moving towards Lena to take her hand, David flinched as she quickly crossed her arms and wedged her hands deep under her armpits.

Anna already knew this visit wouldn't last long.

"Darling, darling, daring dear. My darling daring dreary berry bear." Lena's voice was soft and urgent. She sat up straight in the chair, flinging her head back to scan the crease between wall and ceiling behind her. Left to right. Left to right.

"Hi, Mom," Anna said calmly, quietly. She deplored the overloud voice used so often with mentally ill individuals. "We brought you a few treats."

Anna hesitated, boxes in hand, before passing the ginger cookies and Earl Grey tea bags to one of the two nurses flanking Lena's sides. Lena's hands remained secured under her arms, her gaze still fixed behind her. This had happened before during their visits with her mother. Sometimes she was calm and focused, and their conversation would flow almost normally. Those visits were hardest afterwards, with her father planning for an unattainable future as soon as they closed the car doors to drive home. On other days, like today, Anna had learned it was best to end the visit quickly, to avoid agitation and pain on both sides.

Anna touched her father's arm to indicate it was time to go. David, though, was not yet ready.

A Flash of Red

"Lena. Honey. Tell Anna how much better you're doing." Looking at Anna, David stood up and pointed towards Lena accusingly. "She was much better this week. We talked about you, about our friends. We made plans for when she was coming home."

David was beginning to look frantic, his hands flailing wildly as he spoke. As Lena remained fixated on the wall behind her, David appealed to the three nurses in the room.

"Tell her—please! You saw us. We were talking about taking a second honeymoon." The nurses looked on, their faces kindly impassive. Of course, Anna thought, they'd seen this all before.

David sagged, exhausted and bereft. "She's almost ready to come home."

Something about this final statement caught Lena's attention. Flipping her head back towards him, she leaned forward enough to catch hold of David's wrist.

"Home. Home is where the heart is, and the heart is gone. I destroyed it with my mind." Lena's voice carried across the air in the room, barely above a whisper.

The nurses, knowing the inevitable end to this scene, began encroaching on David and Lena. Husband and wife were intertwined in a macabre embrace by then, David weeping quietly while Lena touched her nose to his as she spoke, her arms wrapped around his hips.

"My mind can destroy your heart." And then, as the nurses gently pried Lena off of David and took her back through the doors, Lena gave a sidelong glance towards Anna. "Tap, tap, rap, trap on the window plane, I can make your pain."

With her final utterance, the door clicked shut behind Lena. Anna watched her figure retreat down the hallway, her tracksuit matching the embroidery on the door's curtains.

76

Part II
Sunday - Tuesday
March 19 – March 21

Anna

Driving home on Sunday, the clouds were rich, corpulent. The bright reds and pinks of the late March sunset created a gentle hue on the rolling underbellies of the clouds. Anna felt her mouth water when she gazed at them, and realized that she was thinking of cotton candy.

In college, the movie theater closest to campus had been a run-down but historical building that still featured red curtains around the screens and brass poles with velvet rope separating the ticketed from the non-ticketed customers. Anna and Sean went there on their first date. She had accepted Sean's abrupt invitation on the playground quickly, mainly because she had been trying not to seem surprised. She could count on one hand the number of times she had been asked out by a relative stranger (even since becoming an adult, the number hovered around four), and the last thing she had expected after prodding that little boy (she thought his name had been Kevin or Kasey—something with a K) back into the daycare center was to have an attractive stranger invite her to dinner and a movie. Sean had been and still was so incredibly gorgeous. Tall, sleek, and rippled, that day he had stood with a confident set to his shoulders that made him seem even taller than he was. His smile had a sharp edge to it, like he was a leading man in a Harlequin novel. To Anna's eyes, he was almost too pretty.

If she had anticipated his invitation, Anna probably would have declined with the claim of an imaginary boyfriend. She disliked boys who clearly knew they were good-looking and seemed to expect acceptance from any female they chose. Anna typically walked around campus with a slightly irritated look on her face, especially when she was walking alone. Whereas her friends might smile at cute boys as they passed by, exchanging fleeting sparks of sexual energy as they approached each other only to shift into separate worlds again, Anna averted her gaze and kept her mouth pursed. Anna preferred to seek out a boy she wanted and had deemed worthy of her attention. She'd pursue until he relented. For the most part this had been successful, including with her senior prom date, although Billy was the reason she had avoided pretty boys since then. He had been a great date and had helped her settle her slightly ambiguous popularity level finally in the upper tier of the school's ladder, but subsequently tried to push his advantage on her one too many times on the ride home.

But then there was Sean, asking her to go to the movie theater across from campus for a matinee and then out to dinner for burgers. And she had been caught so off guard that her typical off-putting manner was beyond her reach. So, she had accepted.

When they arrived at Haulden's Cinema, she couldn't believe it still sold cotton candy, and Anna was delighted to get a billowing cone of it (she had insisted on paying for herself, not wanting to be obligated to Sean. The theater was attempting to market itself as a place for cinephiles and elitist students by only showing classic films. That Saturday, Haulden's was screening Hitchcock's *Vertigo* on Screen 1 and Wilder's *Some Like It Hot* on Screen 2. Sean and Anna, not surprisingly, opted for Screen 2.

Anna remembered sitting in the theater next to Sean, who had been such a gentleman—opening doors and protesting that he should at least be allowed to buy her ticket since he had invited her (Anna steadfastly refused)— that Anna wondered whether he would change tack once they were seated in the darkened, nearly empty theater. To her great satisfaction, though, the entire movie passed without him even trying to hold her hand. They had sat side by side, both laughing at the exact same jokes in the film, until the credits were finished rolling on the screen. Then, Sean had held Anna's coat out for her to ease into, and they had walked companionably out of the theater and down the street to the local diner, which Sean had assured Anna served the best burgers in town.

Anna switched on her left blinker as she moved into the passing lane to get around a lumbering minivan and thought how naïve she had been in that theater, impressed with Sean's physical restraint.

They hadn't made love until their fifth date. They had gone to a county fair near the university, and they rode the shabby amusement rides and walked the midway for hours, enjoying each other's jokes about the strange food items (fried Oreos! Pig's feet on a stick!) and the equally colorful fair employees. At one point, they'd started counting the vendors' teeth. Anna got to 25, Sean only to 17. Total.

She had loved his humility back then; his constant assertions that she knew better, she should pick, she was the best. He liked what Anna liked. He wanted what Anna wanted. She hadn't seen the rough texture this type of deference breeds on its underside. Not at the beginning, at least.

After the fair, Anna knew she wanted to give her virginity to Sean. She knew it with certainty—this man deserved her. As Sean turned the ignition in the hand-me-down pick-up truck he'd apparently inherited from his father, she suggested that they return to his single dorm room. How Sean had managed to get a single so early in his undergraduate life was beyond Anna, but she was very thankful for it that night and for many nights afterwards. Eventually she would wish for the interruption of a roommate's knock or the jangling of their keys in the lock. Something to end their transaction, so that Anna wouldn't always have to be the one to say "No, not this time." But that would come later, after Sean's passions had been laid down in front of Anna like a holiday meal for her to enjoy, each of his desires packaged with care. All Anna could do then, after he had opened himself to her scrutiny, trusting that he would be loved, was fight her urge to be sick. And yet outside the sessions of physical intimacy, Sean remained his amazingly ardent and submissive self for such a long time that her love for him grew into a permanent structure in her heart.

A Flash of Red

The mundanity of sex in college life annoyed her. She was always overhearing someone talking about fucking, or putting dicks in her or him, and cock-blocking. It was like the entire youth culture had a big phallic growth on its brain. Fucking was such a non-issue that Anna had found in the past that most men she dated were expecting "to fuck" or "be fucked" on the first date. Like it was required reading or something. And it would inevitably involve half their clothing being on, rushing to find the proper holes and gangways, and often times ending without even so much as a kiss on the mouth passing between them. Although Anna had avoided these disasters of self-respect in her own co-ed life (her virginal status being well-marketed and maintained), the embarrassments her friends had shared had scarred her nonetheless. Now more than ever, she demanded romance and appreciation before she unveiled her tender insides. She would be won, not defaulted upon.

And at this point in their relationship, Sean had won her with Olympic energy. He had listened, asked questions about her interests and passions, treated her like the treasure of his life. And she was growing to love him. Anna felt it was the right time to change her sexual title, and that Sean would be the ideal recipient.

That first night, they had made love like they were in a movie, Anna's preferred tableau for sexual acts to begin with. Sean undressed her with painstaking detail. He knew she was inexperienced, and although he had seemed surprised when she first indicated her plans for that evening, he had quickly shifted into what Anna had assumed was a process planned in his mind, revisited and adjusted many times to a state of perfection.

Each button and zipper was unfurled with slow and almost anguished patience and his hands moved over her body with sensual dedication. His lips found hers immediately, and then slowly moved their way down her neck and collarbone. Each part of her body had tingled, vibrating from his thorough perusal. And with his penetration into her, which came only after they had locked their gaze and, his mouth upon hers, he had breathed into her his question, "Now?"

Sarah K. Stephens

Anna was unable to make a noise, and instead showed her utter permission by thrusting her hips into his sturdy v-shaped frame. It had been slow, tantric, and magical. Even the lighting had been perfect—the soft glow of Sean's desk lamp the only illumination in the room. Anna had been impressed that he knew to avoid the stark glare of the ceiling's fluorescent lights.

And although Anna knew in her intellectual core that such devotion could not be maintained indefinitely, she had hoped that it would last for a while—a few months, even years—before they began to make love a bit more mechanically, their roles easily identified, their pulse-points and climaxes easily achieved. In hindsight, Anna thought that she could have handled that eventuality better than the reality that instead followed.

A few weeks after their first time making love (Anna had made it clear to Sean that the word "fucking" would not be part of their relationship), Sean had shifted his weight upwards from laying on top of her and, taking her breasts in both hands, placed his penis between them, asking if it was okay. Anna, not wanting to be a selfish prude and believing in Sean's total adoration of her, said that it was. He loves me, she'd thought. With that, he had begun to rub himself vigorously between her breasts, squirting oil onto them from a bottle Anna hadn't noticed sitting next to his clock on the desk abutting his bed. Anna lay motionless, appalled at what she was experiencing. But this was the man who caressed her and appreciated the smallest details of her body, tracing the small strawberry-shaped birthmark on her hipbone with his finger for minutes at a time. The same man who listened raptly when she spoke about her interesting women's lit lecture and made her smile when she found him reading a copy of Betty Friedan while waiting for her last class to end before meeting for dinner. Although she was fairly certain he wouldn't understand the book, she'd noted the gesture. He loved her, and she could meet him halfway.

Anna's wedding rings caught the weak midwinter light, and she reflected not for the first time how much she would have preferred to choose her own engagement ring.

A Flash of Red

Yes, he loved her, and she loved him, but then they got married, and her mother became sick, and graduate school came with all of its stresses and pressures, and Sean started to become—Anna wasn't sure what the best word was to describe it. Distracted? Uninvested? Lazy? The accumulation of life piled up around them, and Anna's revulsion became harder to control. She was surprised that she had such a defined weakness, but indeed it was there, lurking inside her. And inevitably, her weakness grew gangrenous and began to stink, its decay finding its only exit through her mouth. When Sean pushed her head down towards his lap as an unspoken request for a blow job, one Anna that had learned should include a quick release of his shaft as he came so that his viscous seed could decorate her face, Anna had said that she would rather they made love and looked into each other's eyes.

When Sean flipped her over in order to penetrate her rectum, with her grabbing his balls and moaning for him to "double team her," Anna demurred, saying that she felt like anal sex was giving her health problems—she'd been having some bleeding. And lastly, when the ever-present bottle of lube was used to allow Sean to place his entire fist inside of her, Anna asked for him to stop. "I feel more turned on by you when you only put one or two fingers inside." In reality, she was thinking that she wasn't turned on at all. This was the gentler option, though, and at the time, Anna felt Sean deserved that.

* * *

After the emotional tumult of the weekend, Anna looked forward to a quiet night on Sunday. As she pulled in the driveway that evening, Anna allowed herself to believe for a moment that Sean would provide the reunion she had imagined so many times before: a broad smile evoking sincere satisfaction in her presence, a physical embrace that sunk into relief at the return of one's partner, as if shrugging on a favorite sweater. Anna entered through the garage-side door, aware Sean would know she was home as a result of the noise the garage door itself made in its ascent and descent. Walking through the door into the far side of the empty kitchen, Anna sighed quietly to herself and moved upstairs to begin unpacking the few items she had brought with her.

On her way, Anna glanced through the open door to the office and saw that it was empty as well. She mounted the steps, taking them two at a time as she anticipated sinking into the scalding water of a bath and cleansing herself of the disappointments that trailed behind her. As she entered the darkened bedroom, her eye caught an unexpected ribbon of red color flashing from the walk-in closet. Frightened to see movement in the empty room, Anna crept over to the closet door. As it did every time Anna couldn't connect the outside world to her inner reality, her heart began to beat an insistent cadence of fear. Just when she had come to the conclusion that her final lucid thoughts were making their stalwart departure, she heard Sean's voice emerge from the closet.

"You're early. I'm not ready yet." Sean's voice was sheepish, coming from the confines of the closet.

"What are you doing in there? Do you want me to leave?" Anna's reply, despite her diminished fear, still managed to be accusatory.

"No, no, just —give me a moment." Anna sat on the bed with her coat and shoes still on as she waited for Sean to emerge.

After another minute, the door from the closet swung open, revealing Sean naked except for a pair of silk boxers adorned with miniature bull's-eyes Anna had bought for him when they first married ("I always hit the right spot, don't I?" Anna had said, taking him in her hand after Sean excitedly put them on.) She hadn't realized he had saved them. One long-stemmed rose was between his teeth. He looked delicious, Anna thought, gazing over his tight abdomen. But that hunger in her had been replaced by another months ago, years ago. Loving Sean with her mind and loving Sean with her body had always required two different sets of wires in Anna's brain, one to translate the adoration he had once regularly shown her in their daily life and one to suppress her discomfort with his sexual desires. Although in the past she had been able to operate on a parallel circuit, feeding both pathways with the same energy source, she couldn't entangle them anymore.

As Sean walked over to take Anna's hand, he turned the light on in the bedroom, revealing "Welcome Home" spelled out in red rose petals across the bed. Anna forced herself to smile, letting Sean guide her out of her jacket and blouse and then lying down submissively on the bed as he cradled her feet in his hands and took off each shoe one at a time, kissing her arches as he did so. Anna cringed, thinking how he would want to kiss her lips next and how filthy her feet must be after the drive. *Please stop. Please stop.* The words flashed in her head again and again, as he eased his weight onto her, as she felt his hardness push against the thin material of her pants.

"You look so beautiful," Sean cooed, gently touching the edge of her ear with his lips.

"Thank you." Anna's words and body remained stiff. She hoped Sean would notice, but despite Anna's inner wishes, he persevered.

"I can't wait to be inside you," he whispered, locking eyes with her. "I missed you so much." His left hand reached down to her pants and began unfastening the button and zipper.

He's not going to stop, Anna realized, her mind, face, and body panicking, and so she knew what she had to do.

"I can't do this—all I can think about is how you can't give me a baby." Anna spoke the words, her voice almost sultry in its whisper, and watched as Sean's face shifted from anticipation to what could only be described as shame.

Sean paused for a moment, his body poised over hers, before lifting himself off the bed, turning quickly around to grab his plaid fleece robe off its hook and heading downstairs without a word. When Anna heard the familiar click of the office door, she knew it was over.

Anna stood up, carefully dispatching her discarded clothing into its proper place, and moved to the adjoining master bathroom to run a bath. She had navigated the situation to her desired outcome, but sinking into the scalding water she felt more powerless than she had under the weight of Sean's body. Not having noticed the warning signs, Anna now saw that she had become embalmed in her carefully constructed life.

Bard

Turning the knob on the radio off, Bard sat quietly at his desk. He knew that many of his peers preferred the slim multifaceted technology that incorporated phone, e-mail, internet, and games, but Bard remained drawn to the old aluminum-cased AM/FM radio his grandfather had used when first surveying land purchases in Kentucky. He had been listening to a program on public radio, one of the recent crop that attempted to combine empathic reporting with cutting edge social and scientific issues. This show had devoted itself to detailing a current court case. A *Chicago Times* reporter, Tom Halsley, had garnered significant public support and sympathy when his young family had been gunned down outside their home after his series of exposés on a Midwestern heroin syndicate were printed. Although the reporter had lived, it had been assumed that Halsley was the primary target and had only escaped by chance, having left for work earlier than usual that morning for an emergency editorial meeting he had called. Now, Bard learned from the broadcast, new evidence resulted in Halsley being under investigation for murder. It seemed the heroin syndicate was a fabrication, the articles serving as a cover to help explain the planned shooting of his family, which it was alleged had been carried out by a murder-for-hire team engaged by Ms. Sofia Carbone, Halsley's twenty-something nanny.

Bard turned off the broadcast after the reporter droned over the dolorous background music that "Ms. Carbone's aversion to sharing her lover with anyone else led to the tragic deaths of Halsley's beautiful wife and two young children." *As if the death of his family would have been more forgivable if Halsley's wife had been overweight and pock-faced,* Bard thought. Checking the time on his watch, he rose to grab his coat and bag. He had arrived home after classes for a brief reprieve, but now he was expected at a group meeting for his critical thinking class, one of the general education requirements thrust upon undergraduates in the hope that they would develop reasoning skills. Before leaving, he once again checked the syllabus for his course with Dr. Kline. She did have office hours on Monday afternoons. He had yet to decide what to do about the information he had come across recently, but knew any decision could not be made without first seeing Dr. Kline again.

This Monday was warmer than usual for March, and Bard noted that some students had switched already to sandals and shorts from the more bundled selves they had presented that morning on their way to classes. Sunshine was another intoxicant to undergraduates, Bard observed, leading to poor choices in self-care and unwise couplings. He pulled the collar of his pristinely tailored overcoat up to shield his neck from the still-cool breeze. Solid in his figure, Bard preferred a tapered European cut to his coat. The nipped-in waist created a pleasant pressure on his abdomen.

Today, his group meeting was to be held in Guildford Hall, the building adjoining the library and used for studying at one point or another by most of the students at Ambrose. Appraising the outside, Bard could understand why. Although Ambrose University was a private institution, its academic credentials and pedigree were undeniably "nouveau intelligence," and it self-consciously sought out opportunities on the grounds to demonstrate that its academic worth was comparable to that of the deeply rooted Ivy League institutions. Guildford Hall was one such attempt. Its outer walls were constructed of grey limestone; a variety of columns, fantastical creatures, and Latin phrases were carved into the structure. Ivy had been strategically planted around the borders of the building years ago, and now an impressive phalanx of leafy green climbers extended across the north- and east-facing walls of the building. The inside was equally contrived. The reading room which served as the main public area for the building, was filled with twenty long, rectangular oak tables, with nostalgia-inducing green-shaded lamps affixed at regular intervals to light the room. A deeply stained wood paneling covered the walls and, much to Bard's amusement, inlaid bookshelves with a random assortment of leather bound books could be accessed by a sliding ladder.

The plush red carpeting helped to hush the voices of the students congregated in the room. Although some students sat alone among piles of books and their laptops, the majority of occupants in the reading room were in groups of three or four, talking quietly among themselves while they pored over their conjoined papers. Bard scanned the room before recognizing his assigned group. Daniel Pugh sat hunched over the table, his wiry arms and slicked hair giving him the appearance of a Kafka-esque creature. Jolene Sands was wearing what Bard now recognized after several weeks as her typical Monday outfit: a thick orange turtleneck sweater with pilling on the sides where her hefty arms rubbed while walking, and low-riding jeans without the necessary belt. Finally, Bard turned his gaze to Phebe Cotsworth, her curly black hair adorning porcelain skin and deep blue eyes rimmed in long black lashes. To Bard, Phebe was a consistent reminder of how beauty can corrupt. Much like St. Catherine, Bard figured Phebe's meeting with God would undoubtedly disappoint on one side.

Without looking up, Phebe spoke first, her voice frying at the end of her observation. "You're late, Bard."

"Sorry, everyone," Bard replied. "I stopped for reinforcements." Setting down his load of cardboard Starbucks coffee cups and pastries, Bard undid the buttons on his jacket and settled down next to Jolene.

Looking somewhat appeased, Phebe continued, "Okay, we really need to get this presentation organized and condensed. I don't understand why we're still disagreeing to begin with."

"Because you're essentially taking a classist position. Just because Parker was the lowest in rank on the lifeboat doesn't make his murder defensible." After their first group meeting, Bard had deemed Daniel the strident one.

A Flash of Red

Their assignment was apparently a well-known case in the field of ethics. The Lifeboat Case, as Bard and his classmates had read in their primer for the project, involved four shipwrecked seamen left floating in the Atlantic Ocean in a small lifeboat. After several weeks with limited food and water, two of the men, including the ship's captain, decided to sacrifice the cabin boy, Richard Parker, to sustain the three remaining survivors until a ship rescued them. The third man, Edmund Brooks, adamantly dissented, although he still ate parts of Parker's body after the boy had been killed. The question posed to the British government, and also to Bard's class, was whether the killing of Parker was ethically pardonable.

"Yes, but the decision to kill Parker wasn't because of his class. He was the weakest and likely to die anyway," Jolene contributed.

"But Parker was only the weakest to start because he received the worst rations—you're not seriously arguing that cabin boys and captains ate the same food?" Daniel again. In an earlier meeting, Bard recalled glimpsing the torn lining of Daniel's coat and the name Evan Pugh inscribed on the tag, the way mothers tended to label children's clothing before heading off to camp.

Speaking for the first time, Bard offered his own opinion. "One person sacrificing himself for someone else is supposed to be noble, right? But that's only true if they sacrifice themselves willingly."

Bard glanced around the group, trying to see if they were following along. Jolene was halfway through a chocolate croissant, Daniel was staring red hot holes through Phebe's forehead, and Phebe was scanning the side of her Starbucks cup. Bard assumed she was looking to see if the macchiato was made with skim milk.

"So, was Parker willing to be eaten by everyone else? That seems to be the main question." Bard added this, hoping to move the conversation forward.

"We have no way of knowing that," responded Phebe, finally taking a sip from her coffee cup. "And I don't see how it's even a consideration. Parker's death saved three other people. Done—end of story. He's a hero."

"So now we're using an algorithm." Jolene said. "Killing someone is okay as long as it saves three people? What if it only saves two? Or just one? And does that mean killing two people is only okay if six or more people are saved?" Phebe glared at her across the table. Clearly, it was no longer girls vs. boys.

Jolene would not be discouraged. "We aren't calculators. It's absurd." She was waving her arms in the air now, her face approaching the same tint as her sweater.

Bard was surprised to find himself enjoying the discussion. He especially relished seeing Phebe, a girl who he'd intuited operated under the parentally-anointed belief that she was perfect, wrestle with the idea that she could be wrong.

After a long exhaled breath, Phebe apparently decided to concede. "I see your point, guys," she said as she took another sip of her coffee. "Let's go with Daniel's idea. Can we start dividing up the sections of the presentation? If I leave now, I can still make it to my 3:00 p.m. Pilates class."

If surprised, Daniel and Jolene hid it well as they stood up and shifted around papers, listing off the sections of the assignment piece by piece. As Bard strode over to a nearby garbage can to throw away his coffee container, he happened to glance back over his shoulder. He saw Daniel and Jolene, heads bent together over the materials, and Phebe, phone raised discreetly at the edge of the table. Leaning over to see what had captured Phebe's attention, Bard saw the perfect framing of Jolene's crack aligned with Daniel's hand-me-down jacket.

* * *

Walking from his study session to Dr. Kline's office, Bard's gaze settled on the fouled snow on the ground, more gray than white in the low light of winter. Walking the paths across campus, Bard passed by at least a dozen young women in the unofficial uniform of campus: long puffer jackets in black with fur-lined hoods. He couldn't understand why young women,

89

finally outside the constraints of high school and experiencing their first real opportunity to be an individual, chose to look like everyone else. Bard tried to picture Dr. Kline as an undergraduate and wondered what she had worn. The image he conjured wasn't wholly clear, although based on the unique style of coat she wore now, he was confident in guessing that she hadn't blended in as a student herself.

Passing one pack of young women, who were distinguishable from each other by whether their jackets were belted or not, Bard overheard one say in her tinny voice, "Oh my God. He sounds so pathetic..."

And it was that word, pathetic, that whipped his mind backward. After their mother had left, it had become his older sister's weapon of choice.

Bard could remember her using the term as a chisel to their father's wounded heart: "This dinner is pathetic—we would never eat anything this awful if Mom were here." Or worse. "You're so pathetic, Dad, that's why Mom left. To get away from you."

Bard knew Rosie was gentler to her friends, but only to a point. "Come on, Darlene! You're such a pathetic skank. Just let him do it."

And Rosie refused to address Bard directly. Instead, she'd comment to the room or dinner table in general when Bard came in. "What a pathetic fag of a brother I have. No wonder Mom couldn't stand to be here any longer."

Their younger brother, Henry, escaped Rosie's assaults at the cost of being entirely ignored by her. Stared through, Bard thought, as though he were only a fog wafting through the scenes of her life.

After a few months, the entire family had deemed Rosie to be intractable and she was left to do as she pleased. Bard, his father, and Henry had all retreated from Rosie, as if her words might infect them with her hatefulness. None of them had the strength to stand by her, or the insight to see through her abrasiveness. Now, with years and miles separating them, Bard could see that Rosie had only been working to defend the soft and tender self that their mother's absence had left revealed. But at the time, Bard had offered Rosie no charity of his heart. Then, just when they all thought Rosie would ruin the family with her exploits, Rosie had decided to reinvent herself. Even now, Bard was unsure which version he preferred.

Turning his gaze upward, Bard found himself standing in front of Klingersmith Hall. Adjusting his coat and bookbag to smooth out any dishevelment from his commute, Bard climbed the stairs towards the front entrance and Dr. Kline. Pulling the door open, Bard made a mental note to call his sister.

Anna

Anna purposefully scheduled one of her office hours on Monday with the knowledge that students rarely begin their week in earnest until Tuesday. As she walked down the hallway from the conference room towards her office, Anna went through her mental list of tasks to take care of in the next hour. Turning the corner into the corridor for her office, she quickly reassessed her to-do list when she saw Bard sitting in the standard issue 1960s-era chair placed for waiting students. She was startled to see him sitting quietly with his own thoughts. Over the last two or three years, Anna had become so conditioned to the sight of people spending their moments alone in front of a screen that Bard's reflective posture made her slightly, though not unpleasantly, unsettled.

"Hello, Bard—here for office hours?"

"Yeah, I was going over stuff this weekend and had a couple more questions." His voice with its soft lilt sounded warm to Anna after her awful weekend, like a balm placed over an aching wound.

Anna fiddled with the door's old lock and, with practiced dexterity, opened it and gestured to the table where they had sat previously. She settled herself in a chair, absent-mindedly smoothing the crease in her right trouser leg as she crossed it over her left. "What can I help you with?"

"I've lost the handout you gave us on the different axes of diagnosis. Do you think I could get another copy?"

Without having realized she'd steeled herself for his question, Anna let out a relieved gurgle of laughter.

"Sure. I know these things can get lost in the shuffle. Let me run down the hall and make you a copy. I'll be right back."

A Flash of Red

Anna grabbed the original from her lecture folder and walked down to the mail and copy room four doors down, not bothering to wonder why Bard hadn't asked for the worksheet earlier in class. The handout had been given to her by Professor Karling, who had taught the abnormal psychology course before Anna had taken it over, and was now enjoying emeritus status and retirement. Taking the original out of the copier tray, Anna admired its longevity. The text had the distinguished lilac hue of the ditto machine. Anna decided it'd be prudent, as long as she was here, to make some extra copies. Just in case.

It was while Anna stood there, ticking off the counter on the copy machine in her mind—*21, 22, 23*—to the noisy shuffle of the copier itself, that she realized what she had done. Grabbing her copies and the original, Anna walked back to her office as quickly as decorum would allow, her palms already beginning to sweat through the fresh papers as she attempted to keep the appearance of calm. When she passed through the threshold of her doorway, she saw Bard sitting patiently at the table, his fingers laced together in a solid mound on the fake cherry-veneer. She handed one copy to Bard, and stole a glance at her desk as Bard studied the form. The box was open on her desk, but from their vantage point at the table it appeared nondescript, like any other box of copier paper, even with the lid off and its contents seemingly ready to spill out in silent revelation.

"Thank you," Bard said, rising to leave. Pulling on his coat and picking up his leather satchel, Anna noticed the black glimmer of Bard's phone sticking out of the side pocket. *So it's not that he doesn't own one*, Anna thought. He just shows self-restraint.

Closing the door after Bard was safely down the hallway (other ambitious students could knock, Anna decided), she immediately went over to her desk and assessed what Bard may and may not have seen. She had begun filling the box a few years ago, during a period of loneliness so intense that her daily life seemed bounded by the opaqueness of industrial strength trash bags, impenetrable and rotten. She and Sean had begun trying to get pregnant after he signed the paperwork on his job at Baker and Bigwell. Eighteen months in, they had hit an impasse. Sean insisted they should let it "happen naturally" and Anna wanted to seek medical intervention. Back then, Anna had assumed his reluctance originated in cowardice, a fear of being revealed as less of a man. Anna had always recognized Sean's faults and enjoyed how she could use them to her advantage, but she hadn't predicted the other side effects that tagged along.

What began as thoughtful, supportive discussions about their options degenerated over time into guerilla warfare, each of them bringing up their side of the argument when the other least expected it. It would come up when they were out to dinner with friends, each of them seeking out support for their perspective on the issue and instead obtaining awkward silence. One would mention it after a bout of laughter over a funny anecdote from work, with the apparent hope of clinching concessions through shared joviality. It could even happen during sex, with the belief that one intimacy could transform into another. And so one day, as Anna was sitting slumped in her office chair filled with the ambivalence she now felt towards going home, she had decided to start a collection. A collection of joys. Eschewing the decorative tendencies promoted on online daily living sites (there was no fucking way Anna was going to make a Sunshine Box, where you "collect the rays of hope for your future self," complete with sunbeams and smiling celestial orbs embossed on the outside in glitter), Anna chose an empty cardboard box with no label aside from the paper company's generic logo. This box would be utilitarian, a toolbox for her days when regret and despair were winning. Pastels, Anna felt, were not an option.

The first object she had placed in the box was a picture of Lena and herself that her father had given her. She and Lena were standing in front of the school's brick entryway, which stated "Clarkston Middle School est. 1943" in recessed letters, both of them smiling with their arms wrapped around each other. Years ago, when Anna was still in high school, she had spent "Take Your Daughter To Work" day with her mother at the middle school where she had worked for over two decades. Despite the obstinacy that had run rampant in her teenage years, Anna had reveled in the respect shown to her mother by colleagues and students alike. Her mother was in charge, commanding the battery of almost-teens through their most difficult years. Anna had kept the picture in the shallow side drawer of her desk until she had added it in the box.

Over time, a variety of joyful detritus had accumulated. There was the pair of bright pink baby mittens she had found at the school playground one evening on her commute home, nestled into the icy snow beside the picnic tables. The morning after Sean had ruined Joyce's one and only visit to their home, Anna had added a picture taken of her and Joyce at a high school dance—homecoming their junior year—both dressed in an excess of sparkles and bows and smiling brightly for the camera. And the book of baby names she had bought at the used bookstore, with penciled notes from previous expectant parents denoting names to avoid (Adrienne—"No! Hated that kid in school") and to consider (Penelope—"Penny for short!"). All twelve issues of *Pregnancy* magazine, with dog-eared pages of strollers and cribs she'd wanted. And then, there were the brochures. The easy privacy of the internet had allowed Anna to request pamphlets for a variety of programs, ranging from French Language courses that required moving to Paris for six months, to learning artisanal cheese-making in Ireland at a year-long internship. The common thread between the programs was that participation would require a move and separation.

Anna had taken the box out of the bottom of her filing cabinet that morning when she had arrived and had performed the same ritual she had sought solace in again and again: handling the items, one at a time, picturing what her life would be like if she could actually use them, and then carefully placing them back in order. Out of respect to her first two additions to the box, she always kept the mittens and the photograph on top.

After going through the contents of the box, Anna had turned her attention to the tasks of her professional and personal life, which were all now essentially encompassed in her e-mail inbox. First, she had paid the monthly bills via their respective online interfaces. Next, she had uploaded a few letters of recommendation. Finally, Anna had sent off a series of e-mails that reflected her irritation with recent discoveries. Not having anticipated any students coming to office hours, Anna had left the box out when she realized she was late for class. An undergraduate program meeting had followed. By the time she had returned, Bard was already waiting for her and she had forgotten that it was still out.

For the second time in less than a week, Anna wondered what Bard knew about her life.

Bard

His visit during office hours told Bard more than he could have hoped. Knowing that the copier was down the hallway, Bard had initially planned to check out the photos, certificates, and notes in Dr. Kline's office while she was away in the copy room. If he could gain a better understanding of her needs, he could mark out his next steps. Signs of a satisfied existence would tell him to back off—that her husband's online activities were not a symptom of a greater malignancy, but rather a minor mutation in an otherwise healthy organ. Bard could back away, however uncomfortable that may make him, at least confident in the knowledge that Dr. Kline was a recipient of the dense love she deserved.

After she had left, Bard noticed the open cardboard box on her desk. Compelled to begin there in his rapid overview of the room, Bard stood up from the table and peered into the open container. What he saw was unequivocal. Feeling slightly ashamed but also unsure of how else to proceed, Bard reached into his side pocket, retrieved his phone, and snapped several pictures of the box's contents. Knowing he had just become privy to Dr. Kline's inner wishes and regrets, Bard sat back in his chair and waited for her to return. There was no need to review the outer enamel she posted to protect herself from the world: blazingly vivid wedding photos, certificates of accomplishment, expensively framed photos from trips abroad. Bard knew all of this was camouflage. The contents of the box, even in his quick glance, told him that.

Sitting calmly while he waited for Dr. Kline to return had been difficult. Bard was anxious to get back to his computer and examine the photos in greater detail. The whole prospect of being invited to see deeper into Dr.

Kline's life excited and aroused him. She had left the lid off of the box on purpose, Bard was certain of that. Otherwise, she would have maintained the membrane of privacy she tended so skillfully and put the lid on before leaving. Dr. Kline wanted to share her inner pain with him, and this made Bard feel incredibly special.

Now, back at his apartment after his afternoon classes, Bard plugged his phone into his computer and opened the photos in full size. The pieces were snapping together, each one confirming his instinctive response as they found their proper coordinates in his mind. The baby mittens were obvious, and on their own not entirely damning of Sean. Looking at the spines of the magazines though, Bard read in pixelated clarity *Pregnancy,* sequential months over two years ago on the issues. His heart stumbled in his chest, pumping in syncopated beats. *She wants a baby. Desperately wants a baby.* If he was leaping to conclusions that aligned with what he wanted to be true, Bard was unaware of it.

The picture he found more puzzling: was the woman her mother? The physical resemblance wasn't striking, although their pose suggested intimacy. Zooming in on the frame, he noticed the photo's backdrop. When Bard entered a search for the school's name, he came across its website along with a cache of links to old newsletters for the school. *I need to narrow this down. Think, think.* Mentally returning to Dr. Kline's office, he tried to recall the names on her diplomas and chastised himself for his cockiness in thinking he didn't need to examine them. The letter "L" floated in his mind, but nothing more came immediately. Bard used the exercise he had taught himself when he was a boy trying to impress his mother with his memorization skills. When he felt an idea on the edge of his consciousness, he would begin counting back from 100 by sevens. By the time he hit 58, the refocusing of his mind almost invariably brought the idea back into sharper relief. Today, the trick proved as effective as ever. By the time Bard hit 72, the name was staring him in the face. Although Dr. Kline's married name was used on her higher level diplomas, her undergraduate degree had been awarded to Anna Lena Lichner. Assuming that she may have been named after her mother, Bard again ran a basic search on the keywords "Clarkston Middle School + Lena Lichner." The results, from his perspective, only strengthened how he already felt about Dr. Kline.

Expecting a faculty directory listing or a PTO page to lead the list of results, Bard instead found the link to a news article in the district's local paper. Clicking on the link, which cried out in lurid blue font "Principal Assaults Daughter after Student Suicide Attempt," Bard read the brief article detailing Lena's arrest, with a quote from one of the arresting officers stating, "The alleged suspect seemed disoriented at the time of the encounter. She repeatedly threatened to harm us with her thoughts." The article speculated that Lena's degraded mental state may have been due to a student's recent suicide attempt at the school where she worked as assistant principal. A photo of Dr. Kline, looking exhausted and embarrassed, was featured with the text. Dr. Kline stood next to a shadow of a man described in the caption as her father, David, as they entered the hospital where Lena was being cared for. The final sentence stated that the Lichner family was seeking private care for Lena and that her daughter, Anna, would not be pressing charges.

Pushing his chair back from the desk, Bard tried to calm the cacophony inside of him. Pain is what he felt, stark and terrifying, but relief was married with it. *We understand each other,* he thought. Bard felt the future was full of promise.

* * *

Bard enjoyed attending the five o'clock weekday mass at the largest Catholic church in town, St. Anthony's. One advantage of living in a university town was that the churches were often desperate to bring in the youth contingent, and would regularly offer services at times identified as ideal, or at least less bothersome, to students. Ambrose University and its surrounding area boasted a unique schedule of religious services offered on a daily basis. The schedule included the following: 1:30 p.m. mass on Sundays at St. Anthony's, 3:00 p.m. Tuesday praise service at the Baptist church on Maple Ave., a noon service on Saturdays at St. Michael's Episcopal church, and study groups at the local mosque and temple, both at 8:00 p.m. on Mondays. A buffet of options for religiously-questioning youth in search of answers. And except for the Baptist praise service (blonde, buxom girls in low-cut shirts) and the mosque study group (serious young men and women with a passion for debate), the only other attendees besides Bard had been part of the wash and set crowd: old widows and widowers looking for redemption, solace, or love. Bard had attended each of these services, searching, as it were, for a way to strike a balance between his mother's past and his future. He wanted to know which religious practice would connect him to God without also auctioning off his mind as penance. To his bemusement, he eventually settled on the Catholic services, the draw of familiarity once again proving more powerful than most things in life.

His own relationship with the church was complicated. His mother's devout faith ran like a river through all of his memories of her: seeing her in her Sunday dress and mantilla while he held her hand during the Lord's Prayer, smelling her perfume in the hallway as they prepared to go to vespers on Saturday evening (she always dressed for church, even if it was just a preparatory service and not a sacramental one), watching her intent gaze as she examined the priest during his sermon. Bard had thought of his mother as someone who could really stare into another soul, her dark brown eyes focused on the abyss at the center of a person. As a boy, it had been his mother's gaze that had made him feel completely seen. When his mother's illness began to make itself known, Bard had worked hard to avoid remodeling his memories. It was so tempting, though, to see her devotion, her focus in her faith, as a harbinger of his mother's eventual removal from reality.

The priest at St. Anthony's, a Father Cleary, kept weekday masses to under an hour. The sermon today, as always, was brief and uninventive, following the same lines as all sermons: be kind to others, trust in God, help fund your church with good deeds and good money. Bard proceeded up the narrow aisle of stone flooring, flanked on each side by wooden pews, to the front for Communion. As he passed returning communicants in the pews ahead of him, he saw one mousy middle-aged woman reach into her purse and pull out hand sanitizer upon returning to her seat. There were also Catholics who refused to sip from the wine cup, taking only the wafer out of some fear of contamination from the other communicants. Bard had no worries there.

Anyone who wasn't an idiot knew that the prayers of the service brought about transubstantiation, transforming the wine and bread into God. And God, Bard knew, was perfect in every way, thus offering antibacterial protection to all of His communicants.

After receiving Communion, Bard returned to his seat and recited his prayers of thanksgiving as his mother had taught him to do. Kneeling on the pads affixed to the pew, Bard kept his head upright and his eyes fixed on the large wooden statue of Christ on the cross, the final station, while he whispered the words to himself, "What has passed our lips as food, O Lord, may we possess in purity of heart…" His mother had always loved that prayer.

Through his adolescence and now into his early twenties, Bard's relationship with God had changed significantly. His attendance at mass, along with the rest of his family's, had declined gradually after his mother's institutionalization, until they had become the classic paradigm of middle-class disinterested Catholics: "C & E-ers," Christmas and Easter Catholics. Even then, his father would hustle them out of church as soon as Communion was finished under the pretense of avoiding the traffic congestion after the service, but Bard knew his father could only stand so much before he needed to remove himself from the familiar sights, sounds, and smells that were an intricate part of his memories of his wife's saner and, later, her deteriorating days.

After leaving for college, Bard's interest in religion seemed to be set at a low heat, simmering below the surface of his daily life and popping up through the unbounded pathway of his loneliness at night, when he would read. It remained there, subterranean to his consciousness, until one day when he was on a flight home to Kentucky for the winter holidays his sophomore year. Bard had flown many times and was a well-adjusted and comfortable flier. Several other members of his family, his father included, detested air travel and honestly believed that stepping onto an airplane was essentially making a formal and ticketed request to die a painful and fiery death. Hence, Bard's necessary trips home and his unvisited existence at college. His father had never seen, nor likely would ever see, the campus of Bard's chosen undergraduate university.

That day, Bard had boarded the relatively small plane, two seats on each side of the aisle, and had quickly found his seat overlooking the wing.

A Flash of Red

Having spent the previous week up late each night studying for final exams, Bard had intended to sleep through the two-hour flight. Resting his head in the nook between his chair and the fuselage of the plane, Bard felt he must have fallen asleep almost instantly, as he could not remember the take-off or the first hour of the flight. He did remember waking from a sound sleep to a nightmare landscape: the passengers surrounding him floated out of their seats for a few seconds, and then fell back into them for a moment before the next lurch of the plane came and the cycle repeated itself. Dancing in front of his eyes were the gauzy carcasses of the oxygen bags that, as flight attendants monotonously intone at the start of every flight, deploy when cabin pressure is lost. Struggling to catch his nervous system up from his haze of sleep, Bard looked for the flight attendant. He knew that if she was calm, everything would probably be okay. He had finally found her sitting, strapped into her seat, with the oxygen mask affixed to her face so tightly that red marks were appearing in her cheeks. Her eyes were wide and unblinking, as if she couldn't see the chaos in front of her. Bard had been certain of one thing at that moment: they were going down.

He scanned the faces of the other passengers in the tiny jet: a young mother reassuring her children, holding them to her chest, trying to stay calm while her hands visibly shook, an elderly couple holding hands with their eyes squeezed shut, a man dressed in a business suit vomiting into the aisle. Bard was fully awake now and his internal systems had caught up with the current maelstrom. He was deeply afraid and all of the physical symptoms of his fear were showing: his body was shaking and his vision blurred. He found himself needing to blink repeatedly before his eyes could focus. His mind was a jumble of images and thoughts and he was barely able to suppress the scream of primal fear that wanted to escape from his chest. His bowels had turned to water and for a few brief moments his fear of death was subsumed by the fear of defecating in public. Afterwards, he found it interesting that public humiliation was more concerning to him than death itself. For Bard, this fact seemed to affirm the ludicrous emotional landscape of humanity, like the oft-quoted fact that more people are afraid of public-speaking than of dying.

The plane was now no longer jumping up and down, but was listing towards the cockpit, such that Bard's seat in row twenty was at a forty-five degree angle to the front of the plane. Absurdly, in his panicked state, Bard's mind floated back to all of the blow 'em up movies his brother, Henry, had forced him to watch back in high school. Each of them seemed to have a plane crash of some sort and the pilots would always intone the same thing, "Prepare for impact," just before the big fireball explosion lit up the screen. Bard waited to hear the three words come across the loudspeaker.

Many people reach for rituals as they prepare for death, and Bard was no different. Remembering the prayers his mother had taught him as a boy, Bard began to recite the Rosary. *I believe in God, the Father Almighty, Creator of Heaven and earth...* Bard could feel his pulse slow slightly with each refrain of the Creed, his mind finding a calm despite the turmoil around him as he moved into the Lord's Prayer. And when he came to the part that stated, *Pray for us sinners now and at the hour of our death,* Bard's peripheral vision noticed a movement outside the window that had previously only revealed clouds. He looked out.

To his amazement, he saw the face of a woman. She had olive skin, warm dark eyes, and wore a blue hood with a red cloak over her shoulders. Her arms were outstretched as if welcoming a frightened child into her embrace. The woman's face was set with a calm serenity and Bard felt soothed immediately after meeting her gaze. He continued reciting the Rosary, this time out loud, as he kept his eyes fixed on her. With each line, the plane moved slower and slower, as if the pace of time were slackening. With each line, the plane steadily moved back to its original level orientation. The fearful faces of his fellow passengers became calm and welcoming, and the children who were crying were comforted.

Then Bard felt the plane's wheels hit the tarmac, heard the engines reverse their thrust, and eventually felt the plane roll to a stop. Bard had not moved his eyes from the window, but was unable to pinpoint when the vision of the woman had disappeared from his sight. She simply faded back into the clouds. The pilot came on the intercom and announced that they had made an emergency landing in Columbus as a result of rudder malfunction and loss of cabin pressure. He stated that it had been a true emergency, but that thankfully they were now safely on the ground. The plane had been grounded until thorough inspections had been made, and all passengers had been rerouted through other flights.

When he had finally arrived safely home in Kentucky, Bard had gone to the family library to search through the extensive collection of religious literature his mother had collected haphazardly from old bookstores around Lexington. She'd at first purchase them, supposedly, for their pretty front matter or for their colorful reprints of icons and famous religious art. Eventually, though, she had started hoarding them with a feverish intensity. By the time Bard's mother had left, she had collected multiple volumes on the saints' lives and miracles, and books with artistic depictions of the history of the Catholic Church. The weighty bodies of his mother's obsession had been left behind to rot in their house, under the doctors' recommendations that his mother would benefit from a forced separation.

It was while paging through one of these volumes, searching without any real direction, that Bard had seen a painting of the "Intercession of the Virgin Mary." Looking back, he felt that this discovery amid his desultory search for information was an indicator of Her blessed intervention. In the painting, the Virgin's arms were outstretched over an ancient battlefield, her blue hood and red cloak shimmering in the fading light of early evening. Bard had read in the image's caption the long list of places where the Virgin had emerged to protect those threatened by war or illness or death, a list as diverse as her power: Blachernae, Niagara Falls, Mexico City, and on and on.

Bard had been a believer ever since.

Fr. Cleary had retreated through the paneled wood door at the back of the Sanctuary. The service at St. Anthony's was over. Bard checked his watch: 5:45 p.m. *Weekday efficiency.*

The pews were emptying of their assorted mix of weekday congregants as Bard stood to leave as well. The back of the church boasted a small shrine for the Virgin Mary, her ceramic statue surrounded by four rows of glowing red votive candles. All but three candles were already lit. Instead of leaving immediately after the service in his usual rush, Bard hesitated as he passed the small statue, her blue and white robes bathed in red light.

Bard had kept his miraculous rescue and his newly blossoming faith a secret from his family. He was aware that his new interests mirrored his mother's too closely not to trigger worried predictions from his father or siblings. Admittedly, it had worried him as well.

His mother's obsession had served as a caution to Bard, so he'd limited his faith to the cerebral. He would memorize facts about the saints—St. Gemma wore a hair shirt made of goat fur; so did St. William—and find a certain satisfaction in his ability to recite them back. His favorite was St. Luke, the most feminine of the Gospels. Bard enjoyed committing scripture to memory, much like his mother had once encouraged him to memorize other literature when he was younger. His attendance at mass was an opportunity to receive the sacrament and complete the necessary tasks for salvation, the completion of a spiritual to-do list.

But now, things had changed. Dr. Kline had said so herself: *Genes are not your destiny.* If he wasn't bound to become his mother, why should he continue to keep God at a distance? Why should his faith be limited to only an academic pursuit? No, Dr. Kline had offered Bard the freedom to let God hold his heart in His hands. With such guidance, Bard could let his faith inform his actions more than ever before.

With that in mind, Bard knelt down in front of the glowing light.

Sean

He had known his attempt to reignite something long lost in his marriage was a fool's errand, and yet he had done it anyway. He had let himself get nostalgic.

On both Monday and Tuesday morning, Sean ignored the lunch bag on the counter, clearly laid out in place of an apology. Instead, he bought overpriced sandwiches at the hipster café down the street from his office. It was either that or Subway. He hated the pretentious kids littered throughout the café, dressed as if they were mentally ill group home residents on a community outing. Girls wore short volleyball shorts paired with aggressively long cardigans, while boys suctioned themselves into ankle jeans and sculpted ever more manic hairstyles. Everyone, of course, wore black thick-rimmed glasses.

He returned to his office today reeking of hummus and beet greens, having ordered one of their vegetarian options. Settling into his chair, Sean reviewed the items in his e-mail inbox that had arrived while he was out. Newswires and interoffice e-mails were the majority of them, and Sean dealt with each message in chronological sequence, dispatching them with a quick nonchalance. He replied, deleted, and moved messages to their appropriate storage place with succinct automaticity and little interest. Sean found the need to write a response to someone sitting in the same building as him incredibly tedious. The final message in the queue, though, jarred him from his rote method. The subject line read "DesdeMOANa." His stomach wrenched, the acidic bile of his fastidiously healthy lunch rising in his throat. He was so careful, Sean thought. Or at least, his mind added, for the most part.

A Flash of Red

Clicking on this message, Sean stared at the screen and reread the lines three times before he began to realize what it might be telling him. The message read:

Why, we have galls, and though we have some grace,
Yet have we some revenge. Let husbands know
Their wives have sense like them. They see and smell
And have their palates both for sweet and sour,
As husbands have. What is it that they do
When they change us for others? Is it sport?
I think it is. And doth affection breed it?
I think it doth. Is 't frailty that thus errs?
It is so too. And have not we affections,
Desires for sport, and frailty, as men have?
Then let them use us well, else let them know,
The ills we do, their ills instruct us so.

Sean looked at the sender: DesdeMOANa69@hotmail.com.

Sean read through the lines again. He pasted the quote into an online search engine, and soon the results showed him its origin. It wasn't even Desdemona that was quoted from *Othello*. It was Emilia, Desdemona's friend. The site offered a translation of the Shakespearean dialect, which Sean resentfully read over, not having encountered any Shakespeare since high school. Emilia was instructing Desdemona about the humanity of women, the harm husbands can inflict upon them, and, in a moment of internet poignancy, "that husbands should treat their wives well, or else risk their wives' retaliation."

And then Sean saw it, in the signature line of the e-mail where the redundant addressee information is offered in grayed-out type. It read "Never trust the Internet, Sean." He knew then it was from Anna.

To confirm his suspicions, he logged onto their shared MasterCard account and reviewed the last cycle's statement. Anna handled the credit card bills. Stupid, he had been so stupid. And there it was, staring back at him. March 1, 1:00 p.m., Sexy Minds: Oozing IQ, $33.45. Sean had expected, naively, for the name of the company to be discreet. He could imagine Anna's discovery as she scrupulously reviewed the bills throughout the month, and her subsequent online investigations leading to the sites that catered to this particular form of IQ enhancement, followed by her own excavations of his computer's history while he was out of the house. Sure, Sean had a password on his computer, but he also knew how easily passwords could be hacked. Especially by someone you loved.

He could picture Anna laughing, wondering if Sean would even understand her veiled threat. Maybe she was counting on his ineptitude to allow her to harass him online without him even realizing what was happening. Was it the length of his silence this time? Or was it that he had refused to sleep in the same bed with Anna for the first time in their marriage? Something he had done had finally ripped off the last remaining thread holding their two hearts together. Every cruel, nasty, wretched thought he had ever had about his wife now spilled down his throat and into his gut, sitting like a glistening puddle of oil in the hot churning of his stomach. *Belittling. Petulant. Martyr.*

He closed his internet browser and picked up a proposal for a new Martin's Super Market. Pretending to review the specifics of this newest box store to arrive in town, which was a generic assemble-by-numbers construction anyway, Sean contemplated the shift this e-mail ushered into the structure of his marriage. He knew that he had in part carved into the foundation himself. He had not known, though, that his treatment of Anna would mushroom out into this cloud of anonymous accusations and veiled threats. Could he go home tonight and tell Anna everything, and follow that with a thoughtful discussion about their marriage and how they could fix it?

That would require a confession and an apology from Sean, and he could only provide a sincere one if he knew that his relinquishment would be mirrored by Anna's admission of her own frigid, inadequate love for him. *Even then, where would they be?* he wondered. Anna would demand that he give it up, his online support system, and Sean would demand that the void be filled with Anna's nonjudgmental affection. Sean had little confidence in either party holding up their half of the bargain.

He thought he had done everything correctly. He had prepared thoroughly for Anna's return on Sunday evening. There were the rose petals, the romantic lighting, he had even worn that ridiculous pair of underwear Anna had bought for him when they were first married. He had touched her, caressed her, making explicit time for foreplay rather than just getting to the ultimate sensation he knew they both wanted. And just as he had lain there, looking at his beautiful wife, thinking how lucky he was to have her and that all of his tricks needed to stop because she was worth it, he had seen it. She'd winked.

Anna had suffered from a nervous spasm in her face since she was a child. In better times, they'd joked about how even someone as perfect as Anna needed to have something a little misaligned. When Anna felt anxious, the right side of her face twitched up, as if she were winking. She had it under control for the most part now in her adult years, but once in a while it reemerged. After her mother's incident, it came almost constantly for a few days. Anna had been mortified. The last time he had seen Anna's tic was when he had stolen her office keys, had helped her look in various places in the house, and then had discreetly put them back in the key bowl in the front foyer. He'd suggested they look there one more time, since he hadn't checked that spot yet. And of course, there they were. Anna's face gave its involuntary twitch when he held up the keys, which had been sitting at the very top of the bowl in clear view. He knew it had been cruel, but he also knew she wouldn't have the energy anymore to nose around Sean's activities that day and, admittedly, he had been rather indulgent that afternoon.

Sean couldn't believe that all of his romantic efforts on Sunday had made Anna feel so uncomfortable, so anxious. And when she had accused him again of being less than a man—"you can't give me a baby," she'd said—he'd felt the familiar lurch of despair in his chest. Such a well-chosen "can't"— *Anna had always been good with words,* Sean thought.

Because, of course, it was his fault, his inadequacy, his imperfection. His wife was immaculate, except for that little twitch. And even that, Sean had found endearing, like a tiny blemish that highlights the otherwise utter smoothness of a gemstone.

He needed to reply, and then he needed to go home and pretend. His fear that his most secret weaknesses would be revealed and his despair that his wife hated him would all need to be hidden. If she exposed him, the people orbiting their life—his co-workers, their friends, her father, his father—they would all oscillate between pitying him and loathing him, neither of which made Sean more of a man.

Sean knew everyone knew about porn, looked at porn—but Sean had also seen the press conferences with the pale and sorrowful men in dark suits apologizing for their online "indiscretions." He knew that awareness and tolerance were entirely different things, and if Anna knew how much he depended on his online support system to get through each day, and if she decided to spread his vulnerability around their little world, then he would be ruined. No one would ever look at him the same again. He'd just be "The Pervert." So, Sean realized, he would have to go home and act like nothing had happened. Or, the thought occurring to him suddenly, he would go home and become the perfect husband he had once been. If Anna was punishing him for his distance and distraction, maybe he could slow down whatever plan she had by playing into her desires.

This decision filled Sean with a rush of energy. Moving from the pose of pensive concentration he had adopted at his desk while mulling over the shitstorm of his life, Sean remained seated and scratched the wheels of his chair quickly across the vinyl carpet protector in his cubicle. The cadenced clacks against the hard plastic always strained on his nerves, and today he could feel the hackles on his neck stand up as he sped across the two feet of surface to his computer.

Clicking reply, he wrote to DesdeMOANa69@hotmail.com:
To Whom It May Concern:

A Flash of Red

Go fuck yourself.
Sincerely,
SJK

After hitting send, Sean felt surprisingly calm. He picked up the next proposal to review, but his mind was elsewhere.

* * *

Sean knew exactly when and why he'd clicked on the offer. Although he knew the program would be more than likely worthless, desperation had pushed aside his rational thought with the impossible promise of an easy solution.

The day before, he and Anna had met another couple for dinner. Having left all of his college friends behind when they moved for Anna's job at Ambrose, and preferring the unconditional support he found online to the possible rejection he might meet in any new friendship, Sean found himself regularly attending dinners with guests chosen solely by Anna. Sheila and Andy Stump were typical academics from Anna's neighboring department of sociology. Sean had never quite identified the difference between sociology and psychology, although he didn't dare admit this to Anna. In private, Anna often went on about Sheila and Andy's work being just an ugly doppelgänger of the studies executed by the psychology department's research faculty. Sean felt it could perhaps be because the sociology department required faculty to run a research lab and to teach, whereas Anna's department offered the luxuriously separate tracks of teaching faculty and research faculty, but he never offered his opinion in front of Anna.

Sean and Anna had met Sheila and Andy several times before, and over the years they had become decent acquaintance-friends. They would meet for a dinner of good food at one of the overpriced restaurants near campus and Anna, Sheila, and Andy would talk shop while Sean sat nervously by and tried

114

to smile at appropriate times and look interested. He hated going to these dinners, as they mainly entailed him being ignored for two hours while he gnawed at an overpriced and overcooked steak, but Anna seemed to love them.

So, there he was. The dinner had gone well so far, with much discussion over the sociology department's new head and the potential for one particularly cantankerous psychology professor to finally retire. Sean knew vaguely of both circumstances thanks to Anna's comments over their dinners together, and he felt capable of nodding in all the right places and doing the "active listening" Anna had instructed him in when they had first become a couple. "I only know you are listening if you nod your head and give me little verbal encouragements, like 'hmm' or 'uh-uh.' Otherwise, I think you're just wondering when I'm going to stop talking." She had said this sometime during their first months of intimate lovemaking, and Sean had wanted to please her as much as she was pleasing him. He had noted her instructions accordingly, and practiced the skill with care. Now, even though his interest in pleasing his wife had dulled, he could still actively listen with the best of them, although admittedly his mind often wandered away from his camouflaging gestures of interest.

It was during one of these moments, over their salads (which were always à la carte; Sean preferred a restaurant where the salad came *with* the dinner rather than adding seven dollars for some overdressed spinach leaves that cost forty-five cents to slap together) that Sean caught a comment from Sheila.

"Really, we ought to have some sort of test for instructors. You know, something that proves they can actually *do* their job."

Sheila was overweight, with smooth pale skin that already hung a bit loosely at her jowls, and a broad crown of dark curls that sprang from her head with enthusiasm. As usual, she was dressed in loose yoga-y pants and some type of flowing shawl-like shirt, Sean guessed as a way to mask her weight. One ephemeral sleeve of her turquoise top floated in the air and almost caught fire in the table's center candle as she gestured for emphasis with her next statement. "I'm serious," she said, apparently laughing at her own brashness.

"You don't know how many times I've heard about adjuncts teaching our poor unsuspecting undergrads that Margaret Mead was right. It's criminal! How'd they pass their comps?"

"They probably didn't," Anna said. "These adjunct faculty are just warm bodies. I wouldn't be surprised if we started seeing people with only a BS filling in."

"—BS indeed!" Sheila interjected. The entire table burst out laughing. Except for Sean.

"I actually heard about a lecturer last year," Anna added conspiratorially, "who literally spent each class reading definitions from the textbook!"

"I'll do you one better," Sheila leaned across the table, her large cleavage puckering the tablecloth. "Three words: group project, peer-graded."

Anna gave the expected appalled gasp. "Ick. But technically, that's four words."

"Touché! I'll bet you passed *your* comps."

Of course Anna did, Sean thought. In fact, he remembered she'd taken her comprehensive exams a semester earlier than planned, just, well—just because.

Andy sipped his wine, looking thoughtful. As thin as his wife was round, with a prematurely bald spot creating a tonsure of drab brown hair, Andy looked the typical disheveled professor. Sean had always enjoyed Andy's sense of humor, their shared love of adolescent jokes unearthed at their first dinner when Andy had sat down in his chair and accidentally made the most obscene sound as his pants rubbed against the vinyl of the seat. The group of four had stared at each other in awkward silence for a beat, until both Andy and Sean burst out laughing simultaneously.

"I better stay away from the cobb salad," Andy had added, only making Sean laugh harder while both of their wives rolled their eyes. Andy was an outlet of humor for Sean during these dinners and Sean watched with hopeful attention as Andy cleared his throat to speak. Unfortunately, the conversation only got worse for Sean.

"What we need is a shibboleth. Like telling the Gileadites from—whoever it was—I forget. That other tribe. We could cut interviews down to one question. Results would be unequivocal!"

Sean was nervous about the track of this conversation for many reasons. The wind-bagginess of it was grating, as was the assumption that the four of them were entitled to judge the merits of others. But most importantly for Sean, he had no clue what *shibboleth* meant.

"That's perfect!" crowed Sheila.

"What is?" Andy and Anna both asked at the same time. Sean was busy pulling out his phone, hoping that the wireless internet would be fast given that it was close to campus and students (rich students, but still students) frequented the restaurant they were at and would undoubtedly require decent Wi-Fi to entertain themselves while they waited for their food.

"Unequivocal! That's perfect. We could ask applicants to define it."

"Sure, but—and not to be a bore or anything—but *technically* that isn't a real shibboleth." Anna's voice wheedled out across the table.

"Right, right," Sheila replied. "Too much creative license with that one."

"Perhaps heterogeneous? Or quinoa?" Anna tossed those two offerings into the ring effortlessly.

"Hmm, maybe. What about you, Andy? Any ideas?"

"How about epitome? My students always get that one wrong."

"As in, 'Your class is the epitome of brilliance, Prof. Stump!'" Sheila said.

"Precisely!"

Sean dropped his phone on the floor, the sweat from his palms slickening the surface of its case. He could see the site for the online dictionary loading as his phone clattered to the ground by Anna's fashionable black heels.

"Oh honey, did you drop something?" Anna asked as she reached down to retrieve Sean's phone, her tone edged with a hint of annoyance that he had been messing around on it during conversation. Despite Sean's own clumsy attempt to grab it himself, Anna hoisted it up from the floor, glancing at the screen as she did so. And there, displayed in crisp black lettering against a generic white background was the entry from the online dictionary Sean typically referred to:

Shibboleth*

noun shib·bo·leth \ˈshi-bə-ləth *also* -ˌleth\ : a word or way of speaking or behaving which shows that a person belongs to a particular group
*Merriam-Webster Dictionary

Sean tried to meet Anna's gaze, to smile, maybe share his uneasiness with her through a little laugh and self-deprecation. But Anna's face was rigid, her gaze already up and on their dining partners before she had even given Sean his phone back.

A little too abruptly, Anna asked Sheila, "So how's your 415 class going this semester? I heard they tried to give you two hundred seats with just the one TA again."

Sean sat sullenly for the remainder of dinner, wishing that his wife had been confident enough in him to have made a joke of it. To have shown off how her competent, gifted husband didn't know what shibboleth meant, and how ridiculous the entire conversation was. But instead, she had deflected the attention from him and avoided exposing his ignorance.

On the car ride home, neither of them spoke. The next day, Sean bought the kit.

Anna

Anna arrived home early on Tuesday, her arms sagging under the weight of her groceries. The chill in the house mimicked her own marital ice age, Sean having avoided her since Sunday night. She wasn't sure where in the house he was sleeping, but she had woken for the last two mornings to find his side of the bed placid and cool. Both nights she had eaten her dinner alone, having come home to a shuttered front window and a locked office door. Even her knocks and perkily false inquiries of "How was your day?" were ignored. So she ate her portion of dinner, left a plate for her husband, and went to bed. In the mornings, he was already gone, having apparently showered in the other bathroom, dressed, and left before she was conscious. The dishes from the previous night's meal were cleaned and put away, but Anna discovered her offerings from the night before in the trash, uneaten. Her initial reaction had been that Sean knew she deserved better.

Leaving work promptly after her final meeting for the day, Anna had come home, grabbed their car, and driven across town to the Whole Foods market. As graduate students, they had developed a habit of shopping at Martin's, which offered double coupons and cheaper produce in exchange for their simpler infrastructure of metal shelving and industrial linoleum floors. Even as young professionals, Anna and Sean still leaned towards its economy, although occasionally they would venture to Whole Foods when in need of a dose of luxury. She selected all of Sean's favorite foods, loading her cart with juicy dried dates, rounds of soft, fresh cheeses, and cartons and cartons of fresh strawberries—Sean loved strawberries. When they had first been dating, Sean had taken her strawberry picking at a farm on the outskirts of their university's town. He had eaten two strawberries for each one he put in his basket, and by the time they retreated to the stand to check out with their burgeoning lodes he looked like an overgrown toddler, flushed in the face with a halo of strawberry juice circling his grin. Anna loved his smile.

She had bought three grass-fed, organic beef filets (two for Sean, one for her), fresh asparagus for the side dish, baby arugula and goat cheese for the salad, and a few bottles of wine to help ease the tension. Strolling past their section of fresh bread, Anna selected a spinach and garlic fougasse along with three baguettes, still warm in their thin paper sheaths. By the time she made it through the candy aisle, her cart was full, with long, luscious bars of dark Lindt chocolate topping off the accumulated goods. Before heading to the checkout, she had one more section of the store to visit—one she had markedly avoided but now sought out as a sign of her dedication to the task at hand.

She would win. If it meant conceding some of her physical armor, so be it. At home in her kitchen, Anna opened a bottle of Borolo and poured herself a large glass—liquid courage, she thought, trying to place where she had heard the phrase. Vonnegut? Or maybe it was one of those Bridget Jones novels. Either way, she was going to need it.

Sean and Anna had not made love in six months. For most couples, a drought in sex was brought on by the entrance of children into the household, rather than the absence of them. Without the hope of successfully becoming a mother, and with Sean becoming more and more distant, what was the point in tolerating Sean's fantasies? It had finally become too difficult each month to receive the stark reminder that she was only an approximation of a woman, the message literally written in blood against the pristine white of the toilet bowl. It was when she looked down between her legs and started seeing messages written in her body's remorseful waste (*Bad, No, Wrong*) that she halted her sexual life and, she assumed, Sean's as well. Now, her period came with no judgment. There was no opportunity to make a baby, so she couldn't be blamed for the absence of one.

When Sean and Anna had first decided to start a family, their future had shimmered again. It was June, Anna and Sean both had their degrees and steady jobs, and they were settling into Bristol Ave. It was the perfect time. They huddled in bed in the morning after making love, and engaged in the daydreaming of all expectant couples. What would he or she be like? Who would she take after? Names? "Anything but MacKenzie," Anna said, thinking of the nastiest, most popular girl at her high school.

They wrote their likes and comments into the baby name book Anna found second-hand. It seemed like the first month was spent in whispered embraces, gently reassuring each other that they would be good parents. Anna certainly would find out she was pregnant in a few weeks.

But she hadn't, and the months went by. Sean was remarkably cheery, telling Anna it was normal for it to take a few months for couples to conceive. When six months had passed, he ordered *Pregnancy* magazine for Anna, hoping it would cheer her up and help her realize that most women needed to be patient before getting pregnant. It didn't. All of the glossy pictures of thin woman with inexplicably large bellies shrouded in yoga outfits and empire-waisted dresses praising the benefits of gluten-free diets, whole-fat milk, and honey for conception, along with breathing exercises and various coital positions to improve fertility exhausted Anna. These women represented what she wanted to be and, as was becoming clearer and clearer with each passing month, would never become.

As the tension inside her mounted with failure after failure, Anna scheduled appointments without Sean. The first step, Dr. Mason told her, was to test the would-be father's sperm. Anna knew Sean would be too skittish to provide a sample on his own, but Anna also knew he had certain preferences and she took advantage of them. She hid the collection cup behind her box of tampons in the closet while she cleaned up her face, and then rushed out for a supposed early meeting to drop off the sample before it got cold. They tested Sean's sperm and the results, which Anna had been certain would offer a simple solution housed in her husband's failings, were clear. Sean wasn't the problem, but luckily, Sean hadn't been there to hear that.

Then the focus turned to Anna and the issue was finally diagnosed. Somehow her body had tricked itself into thinking that she didn't want to be pregnant, as if she was on the pill, Dr. Mason explained. Anna had liked Dr. Mason from the start: full-bosomed and motherly, curly dark hair, a penchant for batik prints and clunky wooden jewelry, a mother for would-be mothers, guiding them to the promised land of strollers, Diaper Genies, and prenatal yoga. But even Dr. Mason couldn't fix Anna, and now Anna harbored a small stone of hatred for her too.

It was all wrong. Anna had never failed at anything in her life, and she could barely admit this failure to herself, let alone to anyone else. When Anna gave Sean her version of the news from the doctors, Sean coped by retreating to his work, diligently logging hours in their home office, but remained adamant that fertility treatments were off the table. "I'm not a lab rat," he'd said. Adoption was out—Anna had shared too many scary stories with Sean from articles in grad school about reactive attachment disorder and foster care's malignant effects—which left them clinging to the bare threads of their marriage as they faced a childless future together. Anna had taken up a few new hobbies (French cooking, scrapbooking, memorizing bird calls), discarding each one in turn until she was left watching *Sex and the City* reruns, telling herself that it was okay, that other women couldn't get pregnant either. And so life had marched on, their friends routinely getting pregnant and celebrating at baby showers that Anna inevitably ended up organizing and sitting through with a glazed smile, scratching indentations into her hand with her nails.

Not being granted nature's fickle permission to start the next part of her life had left Anna vacant and, if she were honest with herself, embittered. Sometimes, she allowed herself to hate these women, her friends, who kept telling her how wonderful pregnancy and motherhood was and how to stop worrying, and "It'll happen when you least expect it." She wanted to slap them on their jowly cheeks, bloated from the fetus' hormones. And sometimes, she allowed herself to hate Sean. More than sometimes, she admitted. He didn't understand her despair. Just like with her mother's illness, he was incapable of any more than just parroting responses she had taught to him, hugging her with rigid arms, fixing his gaze across the room rather than on the nape of her neck. Once she had laughed when he finished his routine.

"I'm glad you're feeling better," Sean had said, his sarcasm crouching behind his gorgeous dimples.

"I feel so loved in your arms," Anna had deadpanned, staring at him fixedly, waiting until her husband broke his gaze first.

Not really the breeding ground for a luscious sex life, Anna noted, sipping at her wine. Today, though, this didn't matter. She needed to reestablish their physical life, if only superficially. She wanted him to think everything was fine. Anna took a slug of wine, tied on her apron, and took out her sharpest knife. This wasn't going to be easy, she thought.

* * *

As an only child, Anna had grown up knowing that she was special and that her specialness deserved to be acknowledged. Her childhood was littered with examples of her parents' confirmation of this. She wasn't a spoiled child—Anna had always argued to herself that being special and being spoiled are really two different things. Anna had no problem with hard work, with putting forth effort in order to achieve desirable outcomes. From winning runs in softball to high grades in school to commendations in college, Anna knew she could achieve it all if she put in the necessary time and focus.

No, she wasn't rotten, but she was gilded. From a young age, Anna felt her ideas were important and transformative. People should listen to her, because she was keener than the next child. Than the next adult, even. Given the right level of compliance, she could mold anyone into their best self.

A Flash of Red

When Anna was a sixth grader, her science teacher had begun a section on evolution. Mr. Romano had diluted Darwin's ideas in the hopes of making them more approachable for the children.

"If I tied my left arm behind my back for the rest of my life, never using it, then did the same to my children, and my children's children, etc., eventually my family would stop having left arms. If it's not necessary, it's eliminated. *That's* survival of the fittest."

The class nodded in acknowledgment, dutifully writing down Mr. Romano's example. Everyone except for Anna. Even with her rudimentary understanding of cells and DNA, Anna felt a correction was warranted. Ever the rule-follower, Anna raised her hand and waited to be called on before asking her question.

"Mr. Romano, how does tying your arm up change your DNA? That's how our bodies change, right—when our DNA changes?"

Mr. Romano blushed slightly. Anna decided he wasn't accustomed to being questioned by his students, especially about these finer points of scientific theory. He reiterated his point, this time giving the example of the appendix and how, now that it had no use, humans would eventually be born without it. This second attempt did not appease Anna any more than the first one had, but she put her hand down, wrote the example in her notebook, and stayed quiet for the remainder of the lesson.

That afternoon during study hall, she went to the school library and retrieved a book summarizing Darwin's ideas, along with those of a few other major scientists from the last two centuries. She took copious notes, brought them home, and presented them to her parents at dinner. She explained how her science teacher was misconstruing Darwin's theory and that her attempts to seek a correction in class had just led to further expansion of his wrong interpretations. With Anna on the verge of frustrated tears, David and Lena sat in quiet fascination as their daughter discussed her concerns.

"I don't understand—*he* was wrong! What if everything I'm learning in his class is wrong?"

Exchanging a glance, David and Lena each took one of Anna's hands and assured her that everything would be okay.

"Don't worry, sweetheart," came her father's soothing voice as he moved from across the table and wrapped Anna in his arms, accidentally brushing his mustache against her ear and neck as he nestled her into his chest. "Write it all down in a letter to Principal Matthews and then Momma and I will go have a meeting. We'll get it all figured out."

A month later, Mr. Romano was teaching gym and health class, which at that time in America's public school system was the windowless basement apartment of the teaching hierarchy, and Anna was engrossed in the lessons of her new teacher. Dr. Maria Dunkirk had been poached from a community college by the school for the sole purpose of teaching sixth grade science once a day.

If she could eliminate an incompetent teacher when she was just twelve years old, Anna told herself, then she could certainly fix her marriage. Years and years of baggage might lie behind her and Sean, but Anna had always had a gift for forward-thinking. She'd leave the past in the past tonight, and then Sean would have to as well.

By seven o'clock the table was set with their wedding china, the candles were lit, and she had dressed herself impeccably. Her hair was swept up in a simple chignon, with the dangling diamond earrings she had picked out as Sean's wedding gift to her, and a clingy green sheath dress that nipped in at her waist and hit just below her knee. The dress's silky fabric was cut and gathered to accentuate her tiny waist and slim hips. Sean disliked it when Anna dressed raunchily (she recalled a failed attempt at crotchless panties and a short jean skirt, waiting for him to come home when they were first married), and preferred her in classic feminine pieces. Despite his unconventional carnal preferences, outside the bedroom, tasteful clean lines were most readily approved by her husband. Anna sat down at the table and waited, having set the food in the oven to warm until Sean's arrival. She drank another glass of wine, her third now, but who's counting? The wine went down warm and smooth. She knew what Sean needed and she was ready. In the meantime, she would take her own advice and call Joyce.

Anna's best friend in high school, and still, Joyce D'Orsay was pedestrian in her looks despite her exotic name. Broad nose, pale frizzy hair the color of dirty Ivory soap, and a nasty underbite that she had corrected with extensive orthodontia work when she was an adult, Joyce had presented herself as the perfect project for Anna. An outcast throughout her middle school years, the decision by her family to move from California to Indiana the summer prior to her freshman year was met with complete support from Joyce (and her three equally socially-challenged brothers.) A fresh start.

Joyce's arrival at high school was perfect in its timing. Anna's best friend from elementary and middle school, Adrienne Brower, had decided the summer preceding ninth grade that she and Anna were just not a good fit. They had grown apart, they were moving in different directions, they would still be friendly. Adrienne had blossomed over the summer from an awkward string-bean figure into a womanly form, her breasts, nose, and arms finally finding harmony with her figure. And with her physical transformation came a change in confidence as well. Adrienne no longer sought out Anna's advice for clothes, homework, books, or boys. She had even begun to teach a few things to Anna, suggesting a different haircut to better complement Anna's heart-shaped face. At that time, pixie cuts were all the rage, and Anna was determined to follow suit. When Adrienne tried to talk her out of it, suggesting an inverted bob instead, Anna had pursed her lips and quietly mumbled, "That looks better on square-jawed girls, like you."

So when Joyce arrived, eager for acceptance and ready to morph however necessary to fit into her new social group, Anna sought her out before second period was over. Anna was accepted and respected, having a well-worn niche in the group of uniquely smart and polished girls and boys at the school. They weren't the most popular, but did offer solid footing on the social ladder. Anna could offer Joyce a secure fenced-in yard of social acceptance and sincere friendship, as long as there was the unspoken understanding that Anna would always be a little better than Joyce, the smarter, prettier, more adored half of their dyad.

Despite its importance to the happy functioning of their friendship, this last rule of engagement remained obscured to Anna and Joyce, like the mucky dung-colored bottom of an ardent glacial lake. If disturbed, the beauty of the lake became marred by the stirred-up undercurrents of mud and silt. If it remained untouched, then perfection and contentment were preserved. Both girls, and later women, saw their friendship as a great safeguard in their life; a saving grace in times when everything else had become ripped and tattered. And their friendship was an emblem of female intimacy and love, with Anna and Joyce offering consistent comfort and love to each other throughout the years. But the rule of engagement persisted—that whereas Anna's friendship was revelatory to Joyce and constantly pushed her towards a better self, Joyce's friendship with Anna was solely confirmatory, making Anna only more like herself rather than allowing her to grow into someone better than where she had begun.

Joyce was now married with no real interest in having children anytime soon. Anna's high school encouragements had buttressed Joyce's academic pursuits, leading her into AP calculus, AP physics, and a discovery that she had a gift for seeing numbers (Anna preferred to think of herself as the observant, writerly-type). Anna had only a vague idea of what Joyce did for a living now, but she considered Joyce's accomplishments in the foreign land of financial matters and her friend's self-assurance as a grown woman one of her greatest achievements. Joyce wore primarily well-cut, outrageously expensive business suits and had her hair styled and regularly dyed a warmer shade of honey and hay at a world-class salon. She was a self-possessed and happy woman, married to a dull but sweet mathematician; Anna knew she still thought of her oldest friend as an essential cog in her life's many intersecting wheels.

The waiting plus the wine, were beginning to wear down Anna's optimism. When her call connected with her friend's familiar voice, she felt lucky. She'd caught Joyce on her commute from the financial district to her brownstone in Brooklyn—often the two women had to resort to an exchange of voicemails as they worked towards twin professional achievements: CFO for Joyce, full tenure for Anna. Even though she made more money than Anna and Sean combined, Joyce remained true to her middle-class roots and always took the subway to work. Joyce picked up on the second ring, as she was walking from the station to her home.

"Hi, honey, what's up?"

"I am sitting in my best dress, with dinner cold, waiting for Sean to get home. We had a big fight."

"Okay, spill." Anna could hear traffic in the background. She could picture Joyce walking down the street, her sensible and expensive heels clicking the sidewalk as she moved along in her broad stride.

"We had a fight on Sunday. I came home from visiting Mom and Dad—exhausted—and he was waiting here, naked. I just couldn't do it. And now he won't talk to me."

"How many days has it been—three? And all because you came home from visiting your *mentally ill mother* and weren't in the mood? I don't see what there is to apologize for."

Anna loved how Joyce could vindicate her with one quick response. Of course, Anna hadn't given her all of the details: the sweetness Sean had shown in his preparations for her, Anna's nasty remark to end it all, their six month drought. All of that would have been too incriminating. Still, the fact remained that his timing had been awful. And now he was shunning her, while she was trying to make up for it every damn day.

"Made any gestures of good faith?" Joyce was still in corporate mode, it seemed.

"I've made him dinner and packed his lunch every day. I come home and knock on his office door, but he keeps locking it and won't open it when I'm around. And then I just eat alone and go up to bed. I have no clue where he's sleeping at night—the couch isn't made up."

"Probably in that office nestled up to his computer." Joyce sucked in a breath. "There's something weird going on there. Remember when I came to visit and tried to use it to check my e-mail? He had a total meltdown, shouting about his privacy and all of his important work stuff getting ruined."

Anna did remember. Joyce had visited her and Sean once. On what would turn out to be her only visit, Joyce had asked to use a computer to view an attachment her phone wouldn't download in her e-mail. Anna was using her laptop for a few work tasks, so she suggested Joyce go in and use Sean's computer. As Joyce booted it up, Sean rushed in from the living room, where he had been watching something on TV, and snatched the keyboard out of Joyce's hand. He demanded to know what the hell she was doing and why she felt the need to snoop around his work computer. He worked with sensitive material, damn it. He had stood there, his left hand shaking slightly as he pointed at Joyce, and had waited until she left the room. Then he threw the lock and yelled out that he would be working into the evening. Joyce left the next day, after profuse apologies from Anna and an icy silence from Sean. That day, Anna had booted up his computer, but he had already put a password on it.

While she was speaking to Joyce, Anna wandered into the office. She drew the blinds and sat down in the office chair, looking for signs of whether her husband had slept in the room for the last few nights. Everything was neat, orderly. Post-its on Sean's monitor indicated various reminders for work projects: "Remember—Call Jameson re: mock-up" "Print DJM asap." She opened his bottom right drawer and saw, obscured by a sheath of loose grid paper, a blue box with a familiar title. It read: *Oozing IQ: The #1 IQ Booster for Men.* On the cover was a professorial-looking man, perhaps a bit too young for the status, who was reading from an open book while a group of young co-eds with short plaid skirts looked on, some of them sitting with their legs spread, others waiting expectantly on bended knees.

"You're right," Anna said to Joyce. "Something's wrong with Sean and that computer."

Sean

Before facing his wife at home, Sean needed a drink. He wasn't the sort of man who visited bars, and as a result he was unsure where to go. Luckily, living in a college town afforded him a variety of options, ranging from pseudo-Irish pubs to posh lounges with oddly shaped furniture to the one gay bar in town. Mainly he wanted a dark hole in which to be absorbed for a period of time, a stool to sink into and be swallowed whole. He chose Marty's, which from the outside was an ugly squat building. It was two blocks from his office and on the way home. Marty's still used the neon-signage that was popular back when Sean guessed quaaludes and polo shirts with collars flipped up were also a statement of trendiness. It could be safely assumed that trendiness would not be the status quo inside, and Sean felt it would offer the best option for him to wallow without having to overhear undergraduates discuss philosophy and politics in self-important tones while they chugged Jägermeister.

Sean pulled open the cheap aluminum door and immediately saw it was a good choice. Dark, with the damp floral fragrance of disinfectant, the bar was small and discreet. A dart board hung on the wall, an old 13-inch TV, with its heavy backside, was nestled into the corner of the ceiling at the right-hand side of the bar, and only three townies, solitary islands, sat at the heavy oak slats separating bartender and customer. The TV was tuned to one of the NCAA pre-game shows, the steady stream of the announcers' comments murmuring across the quiet room, seemingly soothing the men like a water-feature would in a fancier locale. In March, almost every public space in Indiana was filled with the drone of basketball dribbling and March Madness paraphernalia.

A Flash of Red

The three men were evenly spaced along the bar, and the only remaining seats were in the gaps between them. One man wore scuffed Florsheim shoes and a cheap suit that was too large in the shoulders; he was messing with his phone while he nursed a large glass of brown liquid Sean had never learned to distinguish. Poor man's businessman. Sean figured he probably worked as a teller in one of the low-level banks that seemed to be popping up in town like mosquitoes after a rain. The next guy worked construction, Sean surmised, his scuffed boots exposing their steel toes and his sleeveless Budweiser T-shirt streaked with sandy-brown dust. He was, with no appreciation of the irony, drinking a Coors. The last man, furthest from the TV, was slim and well-kept, with stiff blue jeans and a flannel shirt tucked into his waistband. He wore stiff motorcycle boots with a shiny polish and thick rubber soles, his formal posture mimicking their rigidity. Sean sat down next to him. He reminded Sean of his father. Or of how his father once was.

Sean's mother had died when he was fifteen, leaving his father to collapse into himself and then expand into a new grotesque version, like an iteration of a dying star. His mother, Colleen, had doted on both Sean and his father, Darryl. His childhood had been a happy one, filled with family dinners and vacations out west in their camper. His parents were always affectionate with each other, and rarely fought. Being an only child, Sean was secure in his role as the main fixture of their lives. They ladled out their unconditional love in heaping spoonfuls, and he dutifully did his chores, brought home good grades and sparkling reports from his teacher, and excelled in the various little league sports they suggested he join. The interchange of mutual affection and Sean's unquestioning compliance lasted until his freshman year of high school.

That year, Sean's adolescent brain fell into the predictable pattern of realizing that his parents were human, and therefore no longer worthy of his adoration. At the dinner table, his mother's reminders to eat and to sit up straight "like his father" slowly crawled under Sean's skin and added to the itchy irritation already caused by excesses of testosterone and sexual frustration. Her requests to help her with the weekly routine of laundry, floor-scrubbing, and general housework began to be met with insolent comments about her appearance, her wheedling voice, and her lack of intellect. All of these were typical of the teenage need to seek freedom and push against childhood's restraints, but Sean had not known that his mother's well-tended garden of contentment was incapable of surviving such a sudden drought of adoration.

Slowly and insidiously, his family inched closer and closer to a precipice that none of them seemed to be aware of. His verbal lacerations of his mother began to seep into the tethers holding her to her husband. Sean could hear his parents at night, in their bedroom, his mother intermittently crying and shouting, his father's hushed tones trying to soothe her. In the mornings, his father would sit him down, the scent of his aftershave astringent in the cool morning air, and talk to him before leaving for work. Darryl owned his own machine shop, which necessitated that he look like the boss without really looking like the boss. Over the years, his uniform had become crisp jeans with a tucked in button-down shirt, denim or cotton in the summer, flannel in the winter. Sean had grown up thinking his father's hair was his best feature, thick and brown with a wave gliding through it. He always wore it well-trimmed on the sides, with more length brushed in a side part on top. As an adult,, Sean had come to appreciate less tangible parts of his father even more.

Gently folding his hands on the table, coffee cup nestled between them, Darryl would speak quietly and firmly with Sean about the importance of respect, the value a man should have for all women, especially his own mother, and the need to honor the code of a gentleman. His father was a good man, and Sean wished he had internalized his rules when he had the chance.

Back then, though, Sean's virile state had blinded him. All he could see was himself, right there in that moment, wanting to be free and grown up and without a keeper. And so he'd patiently listen to his father, nod his head and promise to do better, and then take the next chance he had to let his mother know that he wasn't hers. That she did not control him.

Hindsight is always so unforgiving and Sean could look back and see the signs clearly posted, red and yellow and orange in their palette of emergency. *Warning: She starts drinking before 9:00 a.m. Caution: Your mother now smells. Attention: She doesn't leave the bedroom. Emergency: She stopped talking a week ago.* As a teenager, all he could see was himself.

Sean settled at the bar and began nursing his drink. When the bartender asked, Sean simply said, "What he's having," and pointed to his bar mate, knowing full well a real man, his father's man, would know the difference between scotch and bourbon.

"Hell of a team this year," Sean said, pointing to the screen and trying to make eye contact with his father's doppelgänger. Perhaps hoping for a companionable chat, an invitation to pour out his sorrows, even maybe ending with a fatherly pat on the back. Sean's reminiscences had made him delicate.

"Fuck off," his companion said, before rising and moving to another stool across the bar.

* * *

The evening went as hoped. Sean discovered he was a decent actor, although the years of miming his wife's preferred responses should have told him that already. When he arrived home, Sean had already prepared himself for the role: repentant, besotted husband. Finding Anna in the office on the phone with Joyce (who he really actually liked, although he was certain she hated him thanks to Anna's one-sided confidences about their marriage), Sean pretended he hadn't heard her previous comment, reached for her waist, and pulled himself close to her. Anna was visibly flustered. As she stumbled through the end of her conversation with Joyce, Sean began stroking her hair and planting gentle kisses across the surface of her right collarbone. When Anna hung up, he enfolded her in a mammoth embrace, her face pressed into his chest, and whispered over and over again, "I'm sorry, so sorry."

Her nose was pressed into his sternum, bending it into an odd L-shape that made her look disfigured. She burrowed further, like a rodent, as if she wanted to climb into his sweater. Sean knew she could feel his hardness. He felt righteous—she wasn't the only one who could fake love.

He eased her back from his chest and gazed into her eyes with gentleness. "I saw all your work in the kitchen. It looks delicious."

At that point, something cracked inside of her and tears began to stream down her face. "Ssh, ssh…don't cry. Everything's fine." Sean took her face in his hands and kissed her tears. "Don't cry."

"I'm just so glad you're home," Anna responded, and Sean, despite all of his subterfuge, was still struck by how beautiful she was as her mouth stretched into a hesitant smile.

"I am too," he replied. And for the finishing touch, he took her hand in his as they walked to the kitchen, brought it to his lips for a kiss, and, resolutely gazing into her eyes, said, "I love you."

Part III
Wednesday - Sunday
March 22 – March 26

Sean

Had it all been a mistake? Sean asked himself. Could he have gotten it so wrong? He was pouring a cup of coffee in their kitchen, recalling the rather adventurous and creative session with Anna in their bedroom this morning. He could feel the chafing at his neck and groin from so much recent friction. He felt like a fucking teenager. He felt like he was falling in love.

He and Anna had made love the night of his apology. Sean had initiated it, thinking it was important for him to embody the typical male who expects physical satisfaction after an emotionally intimate exchange. Anna had been pliable to all of his advances, and their physical responses to each other were intense and gratifying.

Afterwards, Sean and Anna had lain together, her finger stroking his left thigh. And then she had risen from the bed, naked and rouged with sex, and had gone to their bedside table. Opening the second drawer, she'd pulled out the bottle and foil wrapper, not saying a word, and handed them to him. He'd felt himself recover instantly. When they had been younger, they could repeat their climaxes three or four times in quick succession if he used a condom for the first few times. As Anna strategically draped herself across his groin, Sean's mind cleared itself of its earlier worry and paranoia to make room for a solitary word: *Yes!*

In the subsequent days, Anna had continued to act like her old self. She wanted him. She needed him. And he gave himself willingly. Sean had not felt so adored by his wife in years. And with each acquiescence, each bend and moan and "yes, again," a fading light in Sean's chest began to brighten. He remembered how good it felt to make Anna happy.

He liked writing her notes. When he saw her place each one deliberately in a folio nestled in her underwear drawer, where he knew she kept all of the letters and cards from him, he felt intensely good about himself. He liked touching her, not just sexually but also tenderly. Sean didn't realize how enjoyable it could be to hold Anna's hand as they took a walk around their neighborhood, Anna catching his gaze as they spotted something ordinarily beautiful (a lilac bush, a returning robin, a female cardinal with twigs in her beak) and smiling. Inexplicably, his part as the loving husband was becoming less and less a role to be played, and more a natural instinct. By the third night, the pain of Anna's betrayal had begun to be replaced with another emotion: doubt. Maybe he was wrong, Sean thought. Maybe that e-mail was just from some punk intern at an IT company playing a prank. Or the e-mail could have been intended for someone else; another Sean with similar extracurriculars and e-mail user-id. He hadn't received any further e-mails since his reply, so perhaps the sender had realized their mistake.

The weekend had flown by in a haze of happy domesticity. Anna had decided to finally paint their upstairs spare bedroom a non-nursery color, and she and Sean had spent their Saturday contentedly poring over the sample paint swatches from the hardware store, driving to pick up the paint, and slapping on several coats in their old high school t-shirts and matching battered jeans. Pizza, a nice full-bodied red wine, and a variety of positions followed their day of hard work. He had only had to sneak off once or twice for a little "me" time. It had been a nice little Saturday.

Bard

The late hours of Sunday found Bard exhausted yet agitated, and unable to sleep. He had spent the last several nights awake, out much later than he had planned. At first, he'd wanted to avoid approaching Dr. Kline at her home. He didn't want to scare her and he also didn't want her husband to be aware of their budding intimacy. He wasn't hoping to catch a patch of nipple or curve of a sacrum. He was collecting the stations of Dr. Kline's life, cataloguing them in his mind to help build his courage. So he had compromised himself, just a little. For her sake.

In his mind, he thought of it as field notes. Before you could change a culture you needed to understand it. Before you could understand a culture, you needed to study it. And he needed to change the Klines.

It wasn't difficult to conceal himself. Dr. Kline lived in a house flanked by a copse of trees on either side. It was an older neighborhood, with mature arboretums at the disposal of any voyeur. Given Dr. Kline's incandescence, Bard wouldn't have been surprised to learn that other students had stood in the same places he had, hoping for a glimpse into Dr. Kline's life. Of course, Bard's motives were far more altruistic, he told himself. All of the hints in her office had helped him know something needed to be done. Now, just a few more assurances and he would know what his next step should be.

The first night, Thursday, Bard didn't know what to expect—whether he would hear angry voices, slamming objects, or loaded silence. He didn't know if he would peer in or just listen. When he arrived though, what he discovered frightened him.

A Flash of Red

Crouched underneath the side-facing window of the first floor of the Klines' home, Bard buried himself in the copious needles of the pine trees and was thus able to wait in rather reasonable physical comfort. He could be certain no discovery would occur—the footpaths through the swampy yard of their home that appeared as the earth was defrosting showed much activity around the front and side doors, with no trace of interest shown for this lonely face of the house.

As Bard crept into his position, he noticed that the windows were closed against the bluster of March's winds. The house was dark and at first, Bard thought that it might also be vacant. And then he heard them. The shrieks were violent, piercing, and undeniably female. Being a novice in the art of lovemaking, his knowledge came only from peripheral experiences: descriptions in novels, comments from classmates, a scene in a film. None of these prepared him to listen to Dr. Kline's frightened gasps and cries as her husband abused his wife's matrimonial compliance. It continued for over an hour, at which time the riot finally subsided. Then Bard distinctly heard the torrent of rushing water. He could picture Dr. Kline hobbling to the bathroom, quietly shutting herself inside, and finally finding comfort in the pelting downpour of the shower. He prayed that she had locked the door.

At first, Bard wasn't going to return. He spent the next day examining what he had learned, asking himself if it was enough. Finally, he determined he needed more. He couldn't defeat an enemy that he didn't understand, and he couldn't risk losing. For her sake. So he went back, night after night. It was torturous, listening to the mistreatment of a woman he so admired. Going through the garbage and finding so many greasy remnants of what she had undergone made him gag. *How could a man do such terrible things to his wife?* he wondered.

By Sunday, Bard had been exhausted trying to keep up with his classes while simultaneously completing his nocturnal rounds. Seeing Dr. Kline in class on Friday had been awful. He could see the bruises on her neck, the sunken shadows under her eyes. He couldn't pay attention to the information she so gallantly provided despite the horrors she had experienced each night. All he could see was how thin her wrists were. How easily she could be broken.

Finally, Sunday night arrived. The same symphony of atrocities were heard at the Kline house that evening, but something differed in the stillness that followed their "coupling," if you could really call it that. From his perch at the side of the home, Bard could see into the bottom floor of the house. The previous nights, the first floor had remained dark and uninhabited. This night though, Bard caught the glimmer of bluish light flickering into existence. He knew it couldn't be Dr. Kline—she was up above camouflaging her tears. Creeping up to view the inside of the house better, Bard could see the husband's sleek profile through the open doorways of the first floor rooms of their home. He was in what appeared to be the room they assigned as the office. He was signing in, clicking, reaching down into his lap. That was when Bard knew he had seen enough.

Part IV
Monday – Thursday
March 27 – March 30

Anna

The crimson carcass' purpose was unmistakable, left on their doorstep like an offering from an overzealous feline. It was clear to Anna someone wanted her to have this. Anna could have believed the poor creature had flown into their window and fallen, stunned and concussed, to the ground to die, but the throat of the cardinal had been ripped open. Nothing else on the bird had been touched.

She had noticed it when she stepped out to lock the door behind her as she left for work. She was surprised Sean hadn't mentioned it when he had left a half hour earlier, although admittedly she knew that he was otherwise preoccupied. It had been a very different weekend from the previous one. Everything she had wished for him to say, to do, for so long was happening. He had been almost perfect. Still, she'd mention the bird to Sean, just so he knew she took care of it.

And the sex, Anna thought as she stooped beneath the kitchen sink to pull out a fresh trash bag. Sure, she had had to compromise herself a little, but God—it was worth it. She was doing things she had never done before, or hadn't done for years, with her body. She wanted to be wild for him to the point of distraction, and he wanted to be amorous, and together they molded themselves back into the relationship they had once had. She scooped up the carcass, using the trash bag as a glove, and then flipped the bag over to cover the bird. Anna walked over to the trash can and gently placed the bag inside. Closing the lid, Anna's mind was on Sean.

A Flash of Red

When Sean had arrived home the night she spoke to Joyce, Anna had been ready to take on in private the role of penitent wife. She was to blame, she was wrong, and she had deserved to be punished. Anything to avoid failure. But it seemed that wouldn't be necessary.

There he was, holding her and saying everything she had ever wanted to hear and touching her just as she wanted to be touched. The waves faded, the words receded from her thoughts. In their place, a shining beacon, a lighthouse in shallow waters, lit up her body from her head to her groin. She was illuminated, energized, ready for action. Her heart, much like her legs, opened on command to welcome her prodigal husband home. Sometimes she felt so much for Sean that she was certain it couldn't hurt just her. That he must feel it too.

After washing her hands at the kitchen sink, Anna paused by the refrigerator for a moment before finally grabbing her keys and heading out the door.

Sean

For the first time in his marriage, Sean felt totally in control and was determined to have it stay that way. After the weekly staff meeting, he sat down at the computer, coffee cup in hand, ready to tackle the day's tasks with efficiency and focus, and he realized that in his spent state he had forgotten to write a note for Anna. Sean thought about calling her at work to give her a real-time version, but he decided not to risk interrupting her schedule of classes and meetings. Instead he decided to slip one under her plate before dinner that night, so that she would see it when they cleared the table. She would like that, he was certain of it. Refreshing his screen to try and get through his tasks sooner rather than later, he marveled at what a difference a week could make.

In his inbox, Sean saw the user-id pop out from the sea of banal office e-mails: DesdeMOANa69@hotmail.com. The subject line read: "You can't fool me." Time stamp: 10:12 am. There it was again, the bilious surge in his gut rising hot and acidic. He tasted metal in his mouth. Sean clicked on the e-mail to open it:

> *There is no terror, Cassius, in your threats;*
> *For I am arm'd so strong in honesty*
> *That they pass by me as the idle wind,*
> *Which I respect not.*

There was no other text included in the e-mail. Reading the passage, Sean immediately knew where it was from: Shakespeare's (again, Shakespeare!)

A Flash of Red

Julius Caesar. Sean had read it his freshman year of high school and remembered this passage. His English teacher had required each student to write an essay about its meaning. He could still picture Ms. Collins, in her starched gray hair and nubbly blue cardigan, standing in front of the class outlining the prompt for the essay: "Having conspired to kill Caesar, what is Brutus now conveying about himself in this speech to Cassius?" Sean had earned an A on the essay—he remembered that. He had written how Brutus thought that he was untouchable and that, despite the terrible things he had done, his actions had all been justified and his power remained absolute. Therefore, threats against him were unfounded and meaningless. Not surprisingly, the essay had been written before he lost his mother.

Staring at the words glowing on the computer screen, Sean wondered what Anna would have done if he had failed in a more egregious way, like not saying "I love you" during sex or not complimenting her on dinner, instead of just forgetting to write a note. He had fooled himself, there, for a little bit, thinking she still loved him.

Sean wrote four letters in reply and hit "send." As he headed home early for the day, to his online companions and his sleek polo sweatshirt and the partially closed shutters, he thought about how the word "cunt" was currently hurtling across the ether into DesdeMOANa's inbox.

Anna

Anna had only a few tasks to do in preparation for her remaining lectures that week. Thankfully, her office hours were quiet. As the clock ticked past the hour, Anna closed the door and set about her next item of business. She had decided to clean out the box, her trousseau of failures. She removed the lid and began first by clearing out the *Pregnancy* magazines. They all went into an opaque plastic bag, and then into the trash bin. Same with the other parenting and baby paraphernalia. The nursery was painted over. It was time to move on.

The picture of her mother she placed on her bookshelf in a place of honor. It was also time to stop hiding. It was essential now, more than ever, that she start being brave. And the brochures—they might prove useful soon. She packed them into her satchel to take home.

Anna reached for her jacket and headed out the door. Tonight, her steps would be punctuated with a mantra markedly different from her past constitutionals.

The cherry buds were blossoming on the trees as Anna traversed the blocks separating her from her husband. The smell was intoxicating, sharp and bright as Anna breathed in. Pink blossoms clung to the boughs of the trees, dusted the squares of grey concrete sidewalk, and swirled in the gentle breeze that caressed Anna at her back. Spring had finally arrived and Anna was swimming in it. She stood under one tree for a moment, her arms spread out in her still-winter coat, and spun for a moment. Gazing upward, she reveled in the spinning parabola the view offered of the world: sky, clouds, treetops, pink streaks of petals. She felt untethered.

When Anna stopped, she had to steady herself for just a moment before moving forward. She was at the corner next to the elementary school playground, which was edged with large yew bushes to provide a boundary between the sidewalk and the school parking lot. Then she saw them.

Anna put her hand over her mouth, trying to keep the vomit from spilling out of her throat onto her chest. She didn't count them, couldn't stand there long enough to get a real assessment. But Anna believed after her initial bewildered survey that there must be at least twenty, strewn in a checkerboard across the bushes. Red, brown, red, brown, in rows and columns. Their beaks were all pointing southwest, towards Anna's home on Bristol Ave. Cardinals, male and female. Like the cardinal this morning, all of their throats were torn open. Anna reached out with her other hand to touch one. She stroked the feathers. They were soft and tender, like a child's eyelashes on your cheek as they kissed you goodnight. She ran the rest of the way home, to Sean.

Sean

When Anna arrived that evening, Sean knew even before she came through the front door that something was wrong. Showtime, he thought.

"Sweetheart, what is it?" He looked at her closely; he had never seen her so overwhelmed with fear, not even when her mother was at her worst. Then, she had been determined, focused. Now, she seemed to be flailing, her emotions careening off her in arcing tangents of pure terror. He wondered if it was all a show, a way to distract him again from the destruction she was orchestrating against him. If so, she was even more talented than he had imagined. If he hadn't received that e-mail earlier, he would have plunged down into the depths of this trauma with her, grasped her and paddled them both to the surface to catch their breath and find sanctuary. His heart would have beat double time until he knew she was feeling safe, even as he knew he was partly to blame. But he had received that e-mail earlier, and everything was different.

Sean took in her blue eyes, her red twitching face streaked with tears and sweat, her fingers repeatedly going into her mouth, then out, in, out, blood starting to prickle the tops of her cuticles.

"Anna! Talk to me. Are you hurt? Did somebody try to hurt you?" *Not that he cared*, he told himself. Not that he cared.

She finally spoke, the words spilling out with the taint of stomach acid, as if she were about to vomit. "Down by the playground. They're all there. There must be twenty of them. Somebody killed them."

"Killed who? Killed what? Talk to me!" Sean's voice cracked on the last word. He was getting into the spirit of things.

"Birds. Song birds. All they do is sing, and someone killed them for it." She spit the words out, mucous streaking through the space between her face and his and then falling on the carpet in indiscernible droplets.

"Maybe it was a cat? Or something else?"

"No, these were…" Anna seemed to search for the right word. "Arranged. All their beaks were going the same direction." She locked eyes with him. "Toward our house. Like someone knew I'd walk by and see them."

Sean had had just about enough of this bullshit. He wasn't about to let his wife play the martyr card again. "But who'd want to hurt you? I'm sure it's something else and you're just—" It was Sean's turn now to search for the proper, inoffensive word. "—misinterpreting."

Now she wasn't just frightened, Sean could see. Anna was getting angry.

"You don't believe me, do you?"

She had retreated from his arms to the corner of the hallway where the front door was open. She looked trapped, her eyes darting around the hallway, focusing on the crease between wall and floor, between wall and ceiling. Never meeting Sean's gaze.

"I found another one this morning, you know!" She was hurling the words at him now. He needed to be careful. He'd gotten too reckless there for a few minutes.

"Another what? Another bird?" Sean approached her, his arms held out with his palms up, like you would approach a frightened child. Or a peevish wife.

"Yes! Another *bird*." Anna recoiled from him. He needed to change tack.

"Okay, sweetheart. Just— I want to help. Where's the one from this morning?

These little verbal strokes seemed to calm Anna and her shoulders relaxed slightly as she replied, "I picked it up and put it in the garbage."

"Do you think we could go look at it? I just need to see what we're dealing with here. Then we can figure out what to do." Sean was careful to put emphasis on the "we."

Anna nodded her head wordlessly and then put her hand out for Sean to help her to her feet. He graciously obliged. Grabbing his coat and slipping his shoes on, he moved with her solemnly out the front door, down the walk, and to the right side of the house where the industrial garbage cans resided as they awaited their weekly processional to the curb and back. Anna stood by, looking anywhere but at the garbage can, as Sean lifted the lid to peer inside.

There was the black garbage bag, plumped up in the middle and cinched at the top. Prodding it open gingerly with his thumb and forefinger, Sean peered inside the bag. It was empty.

"It's not there," Sean said. Anna's face morphed as Sean looked on: shock, doubt, anger.

"It should be there! It was on the front step with its throat ripped open and then I picked it up and put it in there—I *know* I did."

"Here, let's go down to the playground." He began walking towards the street, his hand placed on the small of Anna's back, prodding her forward.

* * *

It was strange, Sean thought. Strange that, in the moment when he and Anna rounded the corner of the street and saw the plain, unadorned yew bushes, his mind turned to his father. Darryl was a stoic man, a man's man. After his wife had killed herself, Darryl quietly went about making the funeral arrangements, then the memorial arrangements, and then retreated into a cocoon of brown liquor and easily digested food. Sub sandwiches, Twinkies, pasta from a can. Hops and Hostess reigned in their household. For the first few years, while Sean was still in high school and still reliant on his father for some forms of care, the change was easily written off as the effect of no longer having a woman's touch in their lives. This was despite the fact that Darryl had always been the one to maintain the quality of their living conditions via fix-it projects and clear-out exercises.

A Flash of Red

The house became filthier, with the detritus of life building up on surfaces: unopened mail, dirty dishes, unwashed clothes, unfinished bottles of soda and beer strewn about. For a while, Sean liked how the house he occupied took on the trappings of the day after a wild party—the smell of stale alcohol, unwashed bodies, and rotting deli meat. It made the house feel fuller and livelier than it had in a good while. After a year or so, though, this fullness started to become burdensome and made itself known in the expanding girth of his father's body. The weight of their situation, Sean called it. Sean became reluctant to let anyone, friend or stranger, into his house. And Darryl became reluctant to leave.

As the years accumulated and Sean moved further and further from his place of origin, Darryl accumulated as well. Eventually, his grief ballooned him into a three hundred pound man who required a scooter to move around the house and an oxygen tank to help him breathe. He developed type 2 diabetes and was able to go on disability soon after. The checks were enough to get him through the month well-supplied with beige, shrink-wrapped foods, and to pay for a nurse to come to the house once a week to check his insulin and oxygen levels. He hadn't come to Sean's wedding, citing his deteriorating health, and Anna had only met Darryl once when she had insisted upon it during their engagement. Anna had told Sean she wanted to see where he grew up, meet the man who had raised him. She insisted it would help her love Sean even more, to understand where he came from.

The meeting had gone well at first. Sean had telephoned his father a week ahead of time to tell him that Anna wanted to meet him. Sean had called his father when they became engaged, but their contact had been rarer and rarer over the years. When Sean and Anna came for their only visit, Sean hadn't seen his father in over two years, having spent most of his holidays at university for a variety of made-up excuses: research assistantships, jobs at the library, a senior thesis to finish. Sean honestly had had no clue what to expect when they pulled up to the split-level ranch he had grown up in.

The lawn had been mown recently and the wheelchair ramp that Darryl's insurance had helped install was freshly stained, although the flower beds were full of weeds. The brown shutters on the house were all still affixed, and the windows were framed in fresh white curtains from the inside. It was a nice touch, and Sean was hopeful as they walked up the path and knocked on the front door. He heard the whir of his father's scooter through an open window as they came closer. Darryl opened the door with a forceful movement, and the air from the outside and from the inside of the house mixed into a eddy of smells that washed over Sean and Anna: deodorizer, cut grass, sweat, and laundry detergent. Darryl stood up to greet them, although it was difficult for him. He shook Sean's hand and gingerly hugged Anna before retreating to his scooter and ushering them into the living room, past a portrait of Sean in high school, one of his mother from a Glamour Shots photo shoot a few years before her death, and a posed wedding photo of Darryl and Colleen at the altar on their wedding day.

It was clear the house had been cleaned after a long period of filthiness. White discolorations on the blue carpet suggested food and human stains that had not been cleaned up promptly and then had been scrubbed with vigor sometime the previous week, Sean guessed, to create a semblance of fastidiousness. The surfaces were clear of dust, food, and dirt. Sean could see the curtains were new; the crease fold was still obvious. They must have been pulled from their packaging a few days or hours ago and hung by his father (or some unidentified helper.) And the couch appeared to be a recent addition as well. In standing, Sean and Anna both could see the sales tag sticking to the foot of the sofa's back leg. Sean could imagine the old couch, pristinely firm on one side, sagging and u-curved on his father's preferred end. Sean pretended not to notice the tag, and sat down with Anna as Darryl offered them iced tea from a pitcher on the polished coffee table.

Darryl was wearing a clean, freshly pressed denim shirt along with khaki pants with elastic built into the waistband on both sides. Sean caught a hint of Old Spice aftershave and noticed that his father had carefully shaved his face, including in the folds of flesh collected under his jaw and chin. Sean was touched by the trouble his father had gone to. Looking over at Anna, she seemed just as affected, her eyes soft and welcoming.

They exchanged the small talk of family who had not seen each other in a long time: the weather, school, health (which Sean knew not to ask his father about, but which Darryl was always concerned with for his son), a few names of common acquaintances that had remained in their social circle, wedding plans.

Darryl's voice had a rasp at the back of each syllable, as if his palate were made of sand. Sean knew that Darryl saw and spoke with few people. His voice, like the rest of his body, was uncalibrated from lack of use. Always, such a stoic man. A man's man. Whereas some men would rail against the world, his father's grief hung off him in silent vigil, as a testament to his love for Sean's mother.

After the common pleasantries, their conversation had trudged into an empty void. Darryl looked at Sean and Anna expectantly. Sean felt the unspoken pressure. They were the ones brimming with joy and hope on their way to imminent matrimony. They should carry the conversation. Sean had warned Anna away from a few subjects (Darryl's health, the accident, his anticipated inability to make the trip for their wedding), but was himself embarrassed at his loss for words. It was Anna who picked up the thread, unknowingly tying knots in the process.

Her eyes were soft as her hand sought out that of her future father-in-law, which was like a welcoming pillow to her well-manicured fingers. Fixing her blue eyes on Darryl, she'd said, "So Mr. Kline, tell me all about Sean."

Sean saw his father shift in his seat. Darryl cleared his throat and moved his gaze from Anna to a bleached spot on the carpet directly in front of the couch. Food stain, Sean thought. Or hoped. Sean knew what was coming, had heard it many times since his mother's death. Sean had heard his father recount it at the memorial service for his mother (closed casket; family picture circa five years earlier blown up to grotesque proportions sitting on an easel nearby), and then

154

later on the phone to various distant relatives who were unable to attend the funeral. By that point, it had been almost perfect in its delivery.

"Sean was the greatest gift to our family. His mother Colleen," Darryl paused for a moment, as if caught out of breath, "prayed and prayed for years to have a baby. We had just about given up when, just like that, she was pregnant and then nine months later, there was Sean. He was the most perfect baby, and most perfect child. He's always made us so proud." Here Darryl paused to look up at Sean and Anna together, meeting their gaze with a tenacity Sean could not remember seeing in his father's eyes for a very long time. You have to believe, it seemed he was telling them. This must be true.

"When Colleen passed away"—Sean's father always spoke of his mother's death in this euphemism, as if she had just walked down the street one day and forgotten to return—"we were all so stunned. She had had so much to live for. Her health, her garden, her job at the hospital—she was a medical assistant at St. Mary's." Darryl would insert this detail for audiences who hadn't known Sean's mother.

"And, of course, Sean. Colleen and Sean had always been close, ever since he was a boy. Like two peas in a pod." Darryl chuckled to himself.

Sean remembered that Darryl hit that mark every time. He must have practiced conjuring up some memory from Sean's childhood that wasn't tainted by the family vandalism Sean inflicted later on; he and his mother making cookies in a flour-dusted kitchen, or playing in a pile of leaves, her rich black hair glinting in the sunlight. Sean had always known his mother was beautiful, even before he knew what beautiful was. It was an effective addition to the story and made the affection between mother and son that Darryl described tangible; it left a taste in your mouth of lemonade and Toll House cookies.

"So if you want me to tell you about Sean," Darryl continued (that phrase was added in for Anna only), "all I really have to say is that Sean was the light of his mother's life. Whatever else may've led to her accident"— Darryl never called Colleen's death a suicide, and somehow his local connections had helped ensure her death was ruled an accident—"Sean and I know that nothing could've pulled Colleen away from us without her putting up one hell of a fight. 'Scuse my language."

Darryl nodded towards Anna. It was another inflection he had added over the retellings, his concern for minimally harsh language only emphasizing the type of family they were and the veracity of his words. And then, as Sean already knew, came the finale.

"The only sense I've ever been able to make of it is that God needed another angel in Heaven, so now Colleen's with Him." It was at this point that the narrative usually stopped, followed by hushed words of agreement from whoever was listening. "Of course, she was a wonderful woman." "Yes, you were a happy family." "No, we can't imagine what may have caused the accident."

"You couldn't find a better son or a better man than Sean," Darryl had added that day, reaching out to collect Anna's hand in his once again. "He knows what love is."

* * *

Looking at the yew bushes, their empty green branches smirking back at Sean and Anna, Sean felt the same way as he had all those years ago. He knew his mother had killed herself because he had not been a good enough son. And no number of heartfelt stories or false memories from his father would change that fact. When his father had altered the sequence of events leading to his mother's suicide, recounting them to Anna in carefully practiced phrases, Sean had been amazed by his father's ability to alter the past so convincingly to the point that Darryl appeared to genuinely believe it. And now, his wife was lying to distract him from the same truth she'd discovered: he was not a good enough man. But this time, he wasn't meant to escape without being punished.

As he thought of what to say to Anna, who was now crouched on the concrete sidewalk and staring up into his face in what he knew was only a mimic of agitated disbelief, the thoughts of his father coalesced with his current predicament. Everyone he loved in this world lied to him, Sean thought. Not little white lies meant to smooth daily existence. Big, bloated, life-changing lies. Finally, Sean spoke.

"We'll figure everything out. It'll all be okay."

And Sean knew as he said it that the lie carried over his breath was of the latter variety. He reached down to take Anna's hand and lift her up for their walk home back to Bristol Ave., but he found no comfort in having joined the ranks of his father and wife.

Anna

After Sean and Anna returned from their search, Anna was distraught. Sean, to his credit, said all the right things. Verbally, he was so supportive. Loving, attentive. Even physically, he was perfect. Holding Anna, stroking her hair, her cheek. Textbook, if Anna had written a textbook of what her ideal husband would be in a crisis. Admittedly, her diary almost fit that description. Anna rarely wrote in it unless she was despairing about her life in some way, usually about her marriage. The pages accumulated, beginning with sparse entries of sadness and rejection a few months after her mother became ill during their first year of marriage, and the entries accelerating in frequency and intensity for the next eight years, reaching a fever pitch when their hopes for a family were decimated. It was a catalogue of how Sean was failing her as a husband. Anna knew some people would say it was unfair that she didn't keep a written record of their good days together, but she disagreed.

For all of his words and actions of love, though, Sean's face was different than before and any real comfort from his touch escaped her. His eyes, which she always felt were so warm in general, were mostly vacant, except for when she would reach out to touch him in return, caressing his cheek, stroking his forearm. In these interactions, Sean's eyes would pierce her for a brief moment before retreating again into the haze of emotion that allowed him to look through her. During that split second of transparency, Anna was afraid to admit what Sean reminded her of.

Like many children, she had held a fascination with reptiles when she was younger, around eight or nine years old. In her typical fashion, Anna had learned everything she could, poring over books from the library. One picture had transfixed her, and paging through the books she would find herself revisiting that image over and over, staring at it as if to memorize it, which she had. It was of a boa constrictor staring in what even young Anna saw as cold and calculated satisfaction as it squeezed a mouse to death. That was how Sean looked.

But despite her acuity in assessing her husband's failings, Anna's connection to reality was worn thin by that evening. She couldn't find an explanation for what she had seen, other than the obvious.

When she asked Sean if he thought she was going crazy, pleading in her mind to hear the soft tones of no come from his mouth, he had responded just as she needed. "No, sweetheart. It was just some sort of misunderstanding. Your eyes playing tricks on you." She had reached up to touch his cheek, cupping his chin in her hand in what she felt would convey tender appreciation. But his eyes. So sharp, cutting an incision with what? Pleasure? But maybe that was just part of her madness, as well. Paranoia that her husband hated her, wanted her dead, crushed under his weight.

Preparing for bed that evening, Anna could feel the hysteria creeping into her brain despite the half bottle of wine Sean had encouraged her to drink "to calm her nerves." "You've had a real scare, sweetheart." And then, reptilian eyes when she went to kiss him. Wild thoughts tossed around in her head. Sean had left the birds there for her to see. She had finally gone too far. He was retaliating, trying to get rid of her by putting her away like they had done to her mother. And then he could be the poor husband that everyone pitied. And brought casseroles to. And fucked. Was that why he had ordered that "program"? To make all of the suburban divorcées ooze for him once Anna was locked away?

Anna spent the night on the couch. Sean had excused himself for a half hour or so to check on some work issues in the office while Anna sat waiting on the living room couch, clutching her wine glass and trying to pay attention to the sitcom Sean had put on the television as a distraction for her. She couldn't follow the dialogue. All of the characters seemed to be shouting at each other, with intermittent guffaws coming from the audience at key moments. Their voices melded together in her mind, morphing into one mutated voice devoid of gender or age. It became background noise to the clutter in Anna's head until exhaustion and inebriation took over. Anna awoke in the early morning, alone on the couch, her glass of wine placed on the coffee table and a blanket covering her legs.

The next day proceeded in a similar fashion, with Sean dancing the steps of a doting husband caring for an invalid wife, his face never matching his feet. Anna drank too much and ate little. The fears in her head were constantly threatening to push through the barricaded door of her heart and prove just how dangerous her marriage had become.

On Wednesday, after two fitful nights and morning hangovers, Anna rose and moved through the house, the ambient sounds of morning murmuring through the walls. Leaves on the trees rustled, birds sang, cars started and eased down the street towards their destination. But the house was quiet. Anna saw a note on the refrigerator:

Didn't want to wake you. Left early for work. I love you, beautiful. Feel better.

Anna had to teach today. She had to function like a normal human being capable of higher level critical thinking. There was no room to detach from reality. She needed to stay focused. Keep the bad thoughts out. Let the good thoughts in.

She gingerly moved her body up the stairs towards their bedroom and the shower. Her legs and back were stiff from sleeping sitting up, and she cracked her neck from side to side as she approached the top of the stairs.

Dropping her clothes on the floor, Anna headed to the shower and turned the water on. Steam began to rise in the bathroom, making the air misty with humidity. Anna liked the way the world faded in the steam. Colors bled across edges, blurring objects into a pointillist image.

Anna spotted it between the lid and base of the laundry hamper. In the mist, the red dot caught her eye and drew her towards it. She needed to investigate. When she lifted the lid, the red dot floated up, wafting on the competing currents of warm and cold air in the brightly lit bathroom. Anna swatted at it with her hand, feeling the remnants of the wine and the beginning of a hangover. Her arm moved in slow motion in the mist as her naked body began to collect droplets of condensation in the moist atmosphere. She couldn't connect with the red dot as it floated until it finally seemed to decide to fall of its own accord, landing on the top of her right breast.

Reaching to collect it, Anna noticed a black smear separating the lid from the body of the laundry basket. With the indeterminate red dot safe in her hand, Anna stooped over to examine the basket and realized the black smear was the pair of pants Sean had worn the day they went to the playground. The top button clasp must have caught in the lid, leaving the right pocket protruding from the bin when Sean disposed of them, even as other clothes were heaped on top. This visual riddle solved, Anna returned her attention to the red dot. She moved it between her fingers, and its form shifted and melded with her touch, but the mist in the bathroom was robbing her vision of the clarity she needed, and Anna couldn't seem to identify what the object was, although she knew she needed to find out. Her racing pulse and shallow breaths told her that.

Anna decided to step out of the steamy bathroom into the cool, clear air of their bedroom. Moving from the cloud of steam, she emerged into the sunlit room, the bed neatly made and everything perfectly in order. Her vision clearer, Anna looked down with determination at the object in her hand. For a moment, it was as if she was still in the mist of the bathroom. Her mind and her eye couldn't seem to agree on what was in front of her, until her eyes seemed to take control and overrule her disbelief.

Sitting in the palm of her right hand, soggy and yet vibrantly beautiful, was a red feather.

* * *

Anna could barely think in class that day, but luckily the words poured out of her in a rehearsed monologue and only a few times did she find her mind drifting into the ocean of sorrow and foreboding that now awaited her in her quiet moments. The lecture was nothing new to Anna; she had covered the material many times before and could repeat the information with little attention devoted to it. If she had been less distraught, she would have enjoyed the irony in the topic: *Post Traumatic Stress Disorder.*

Was that what she was suffering from now? Or would soon? She had discovered in that one damning article of evidence that he couldn't muster the energy to dispose of properly, that her husband was going to great lengths to cruelly manipulate her. She was still unsure how he had managed to clean up the bushes before they arrived; an accomplice was the only option, perhaps her replacement, Anna thought. Her mind was a clanging maelstrom of terrible thoughts. *What other traumas lay in wait for her tonight? And the night after that? And that?*

And another thought surfaced above all of the rest: *What had she done?*

The manifestation of his hatred was so personal. The choice of the children's playground could not be coincidence; it resonated with their first meeting. Did Sean think these personal touches would help her believe that the depths of her mind were intruding on the ordered world of her sanity? And the cardinals. Anna knew Sean must feel proud of himself for being so discerning, probably sneering to himself, "See, I *do* listen."

One of Anna's most potent memories from her childhood was having lunch in the backyard with her mother, the two of them sprawled out on a red and white checked picnic blanket eating peanut butter and jelly sandwiches. It was a rare treat her mother would organize for the two of them during the summer months: sitting on a blanket, eating in the lush shaded grass of the big pine tree, lazily staring up at the clouds as they drifted overhead.

One time, Lena was telling Anna the story of how she had met David. Anna often requested the story and loved the way her mother would enhance certain parts: the detailed way she remembered what her father had been wearing (dark blue jeans with a crease down the middle, plain navy t-shirt without a crease), the atmosphere of the occasion (the rush of high school hallways, lockers slamming and students jostling to get to class on time), how he had saved Lena from a tardy notice her first day of high school. He had gently approached her and inquired if she needed help with her lock. Lena had been unable to get it unlocked and, as she described it to her daughter, had stood there on the verge of tears, knowing this was an inauspicious beginning to her high school career and wondering if her entire secondary education would be spent ill-prepared and running late. And then David had come, handsome and quiet, to save her.

Being an upperclassman, he was confident in his ability to fix the situation and once Lena told him the numbers, swiveled the lock open in "two seconds flat," as Lena would recount. Assured now of getting to class on time, Lena looked up into David's eyes and caught off guard by his handsome face, couldn't even form the words to say thank you. At this point in the story, Lena would try to mimic what it had been like, gazing lovingly at some random object and then stumbling over incoherent syllables until mother and daughter both broke down laughing.

That day, on the blanket outside, Lena came to that point in the story and just as she was about to stare admiringly at a sandwich or a blade of grass, a cardinal swooped down and landed on their picnic blanket. His crimson crest was raised, and he stood there quietly taking in Anna and her mother. Both had never been so close to a wild bird. Lena was so caught off guard in that moment that she ended up babbling again just as she had with David at their first meeting. For years afterwards, it had been Lena and Anna's little joke between themselves. One of them would see a cardinal (they were prolific in their suburban neighborhood) and quickly swoon, "He's so handsome!" To which the other would reply, "So why don't you marry him?" Gradually, their convivial give and take had died out as Anna moved on to college, marriage, and grad school, and, of course, it finally ceased to exist altogether once Lena was institutionalized. But Anna still recalled it as one of her favorite memories of her mother. And Sean knew that.

It made Anna physically ill to consider that after all the love and sex and promises and years together, Sean would turn on her and use the softest, most vulnerable parts of her to force her out of the life she had worked hard for, that she deserved. She had been right about his eyes; he was a predator programmed to seek out and feed on the weaknesses in others, even in his wife. She had known for a long time that his father's story about him being the perfect son, the sparkle in his mother's eyes, was a fabrication.

At their wedding reception, some of Sean's drunk high school friends, invited more out of sentimentality than actual sentiment, had cornered Anna during the latter part of the evening, when adults were flouncing around on the dance floor like unbridled show ponies who had forgotten their routines. Anna lacked any interest in participating, and had left Sean on the dance floor to seek the solace of a whiskey neat at the bar. A real drink. A man's drink, in fact. A drink that Sean never seemed able to discern, always telling the bartender "the same" after Anna ordered.

Pushing their sour-smelling breath and protruding beer bellies at Anna, threatening to spill their drinks on her pristine dress, Sean's friends (*Roy, Al, Doug?* She had forgotten their names, but remembered they were each one syllable and a pathetic cliché of blue-collar man-boys) had spoiled the quiet moment Anna had sought out by regaling her with stories of Sean's virile adolescence.

"The girls LOVED him," Roy/Al/Doug had said. She couldn't remember who was who. They were indistinguishable.

"Yeah, you're lucky to catch him. He's a wild one. Lot of notches in his—closet? Bedpole. Whatever the hell they say," said Drunk 2.

"That's why his mom died," Drunk 3 of their group chimed in impulsively.

This last exclamation caught Anna's attention, which had been wandering as she scanned the faces of her guests for someone to escape to in order to avoid this deluge of working-class machismo. She knew her husband was attractive. She knew she wasn't his first. What did it matter?

"What are you talking about? Sean's mother died in a car accident," Anna stated matter-of-factly, as these men were clearly idiots.

"Oh, you don't know?" Roy/Al/Doug said. "She was driving that night drunk off her ass 'cause her son hated her."

"My uncle worked in the coroner's office; told me the car smelled like a distillery when they pulled her out."

"Poor lady died of a broken heart." Clearly, Anna thought, all of the booze was making them sentimental.

At this point, the group of friends had stared into their drinks for a pensive moment. *What were they thinking?* she'd wondered. Were they sorry for dredging up old gossip at her *wedding?* Were they waiting for Anna to break down crying, or slap one of them? Or would they keep going and tell her she'd made a mistake—that Sean wasn't the man she thought he was?

Instead, one of the three looked up from his glass and proclaimed, "Shots!?"

Anna wandered back into the roar of the dance floor and found Sean in the crowd. As she approached him, the smile he gave her made her weak in the knees and she forgot all about his drunk friends and their gossip. *This* was the man she'd married. This kind and gentle man who doted on her and whose smile made her body vibrate all over. And she had forgotten about everything else. For a while.

As their marriage progressed, this alternate story of her husband would return to her in moments when he failed her. When he made stupid comments at dinner parties in front of her colleagues. When he didn't notice her haircut or the special outfit she wore just for him. When he retreated to his work and turned his back on her need to be loved, even when she begged for his attention. When he sometimes left his wedding ring on the bedside table for days without a second glance. Then the story would float to the surface, breaking open like bubbles of stench to pollute her thoughts: *He is cruel. He hates women. He hates me.*

But then they would reconcile. Sean would apologize. Buy her flowers (daisies, she loved their bright unassuming faces) although that became rarer with time. And these thoughts would retreat to the dark cobwebby corners of her mind, waiting to be resurrected when the next infraction against her occurred.

After the last few days though, it was like a spotlight had been turned on in her mind, revealing all of the dark and dusty thoughts she had pushed away about her husband and her marriage. It scared Anna to consider that she wasn't as special in Sean's eyes as she thought. It scared her even more that she may have underestimated Sean.

She realized thankfully that the ending time for her class was approaching. *Just hold on a little longer*, she thought. *Then you can deal with this in its entirety.* She glanced down at her hands, which she saw quiver slightly as she placed them in her pockets. The waistband of her slacks sagged as she pushed her hands in. Anna realized that she had lost weight recently; anxiety and preoccupation had stifled her usually healthy appetite. Her hipbones jutted out accusingly. She also felt her childhood tic coming back. As a girl, Anna had developed a habit of blinking or winking her eyes as a way of calming herself when nervous. By the time she was a teenager, Anna had come to control it, primarily out of social survival, but it returned to her periodically as a physical manifestation of stress. And today she was certainly stressed.

Gathering herself to push through the final ideas for the lecture, she glanced around at her students' faces. She felt naked in front of them, certain that they could see her agitation as clearly as they saw her wasting frame and bloodshot eyes. Even Julie, that poor girl who suffered so badly from social anxiety, saw fit to talk in class today. Anna was touched by the gesture of solidarity. She had once shared her own history of anxiety with Julie after class, offering what she hoped was empathy and encouragement. Her gaze fell on Bard, who had spent the class in his typical posture of dominance and confrontation, staring at her intently. That's one bright side, Anna thought, almost smiling before a bout of nausea gripped her again and her face twitched. At least she knew she wasn't going crazy.

Bard

Sitting in Dr. Kline's classroom on Wednesday, listening to her articulate pronouncements on the many failings of the human mind, Bard felt strong emotion well inside of himself. So much had happened in the last couple of weeks. Their relationship had progressed so far beyond where he had ever imagined it would take them. At the beginning of the term, Bard would never have suspected that he and this young, lithe creature would share the same dark smudge on their hearts. But it was true! She knew the pain of his loss, his ambivalence towards his mother, and his fear that he would one day follow her into an institutionalized hell. All because she must feel it too about her own mother.

And yet, Bard reminded himself, Dr. Kline was not only a victim of her mother's illness. No. She was also the victim of a selfish, degrading husband whose own perverse needs took precedence over the most basic and immutable need of a woman: to have a child. Bard admired her so much, wanting to remain in her marriage and keep the sacramental bonds intact, all while suffering each night, her cries for help ignored or interpreted as success by the monster she had married.

Bard felt the bile rising in his throat, and calmed himself with assurances that at least now, those cries weren't being ignored any more.

Just like St. Agatha, whose body was ravaged in order to keep her inner sanctity intact, Bard could see the signs of Dr. Kline's marriage in her strained figure more clearly now than ever. From Monday to Wednesday, Dr. Kline's face had changed dramatically. It now had the grey tinges of illness, her eyes sunken into her face and ringed by dark circles, as if the blood were no longer traveling to that particular organ in her body. As if she were tired of seeing the world clearly. Today, as she lectured on trauma and its effects on the mind and body, Bard could see her well-tailored pants were slung low on her hips and fastened by a belt that was pulled through one more notch than usual, the bubbling and bending of its normal sitting place revealing its new position. She is so strong, Bard thought, and yet even her strength cannot hide all that pain.

Bard realized that his musings had distracted him from Dr. Kline's lecture, and that he had missed her definition of trauma and stress. He would need to review that material in the text later. Or perhaps visit her in office hours to review it. She might even welcome that, he thought. A chance for them to connect face-to-face, rather than through passive gestures.

Focusing now on Dr. Kline's words rather than on her physical presence, Bard took in the information she was providing the class.

"Post Traumatic Stress Disorder, or PTSD, is a relatively new diagnosis. In the past, women who suffered the aftereffects of sexual trauma were called hysterics. Men who suffered similar symptoms, usually as a result of war, were described as shell-shocked, although certainly both men and women can encounter a variety of traumatic stressors beyond these few."

Here she paused for a moment, and Bard felt her eyes on him. Was it a message, he wondered. A mental placing of her hand on his shoulder. *I understand, Bard. I know what trauma is, and so do you.* The warmth in his belly grew, and he could feel a slight blush rising into his cheeks, as if he were a little boy again receiving a compliment from his favorite teacher. *I know what you have suffered,* her gaze seemed to say.

"The main symptoms of PTSD are both positive and negative, much like those of schizophrenia." Again, her eyes roamed to his. A gentle touch on his eyelids, his cheeks. He could almost feel her lips brushing his face. A motherly kiss. *It's okay. I know, but nobody else does. Your secret is safe with me.*

"Memory loss, blunted affect, and sleep irregularities occupy one side of the disorder. The other side presents itself in the positive manner—which, to review, refers to what?"

Anna scanned the classroom with her eyes, her brows raised in questioning scrutiny. Bard did not raise his hand. He knew Dr. Kline wouldn't have called on him anyway. She wouldn't want to attract attention. Julie, a milquetoast with limp chestnut hair and acne scars on her cheeks and neck, actually raised her hand to answer.

"It refers to the addition of inappropriate behaviors, rather than the loss of appropriate behaviors."

Julie's voice was squeaky and metallic, like a cheap tin bell ringing. Bard realized he had never heard her voice before today, as she typically slunk in and out of class without a word to anyone unless Dr. Kline stopped her for a moment after class. He could imagine Julie skulking through her classes, avoiding her roommate. A wraith that no one noticed, except for Dr. Kline. Even this pathetic girl, he reflected, Dr. Kline was able to help, and despite her own suffering, which in this classroom only he was privy to. Two words appeared in his line of vision and floated across the room in front of him: *Angel. Saint.* And he was not afraid, even though a few weeks ago he would have seen these phantoms as a sign of his own decline. No, he knew with certainty that these were divinely inspired, acolytes lighting his path to fulfillment. As he glanced up once more at Anna's weary face and shrunken form, a different word promenaded across the room, catching fire before his eyes as it traversed the space: *Martyr.*

A thousand pin pricks hit Bard between his lungs, forcing him to catch his breath. No, Dr. Kline could not be left in her glass house of a marriage, waiting for it to crash down and shred her to pieces in the process, leaving her rejected, defiled, and childless. He had delayed long enough. Now was the time for courage.

Bard scanned the room to see if his revelation had aroused the attention of his classmates, but they were studiously typing their notes on laptops in the clickety-clack style of automatons, writing down every word their professor said because they could not create a single original thought. Bard, of course, wrote all of his notes by hand. It was clear no one had noticed

Bard's spasm of insight. He looked up at Dr. Kline, who was now on the opposite side of the room. He locked his gaze on her as he so often did while she lectured. Just before she turned to move to another position in her lecturing circuit of the room, Bard perceived the minutest movement of her right eye as her glance fell on him and only him. *She approved*, Bard decoded.

* * *

Sitting down at his desk in his attic apartment, with a frothy cup of expertly made cappuccino steaming at his right-hand side, Bard entered in the user-id and password for DesdeMOANa69. It had been incredibly easy to track down Sean Kline's e-mail address. A brief online search of "Sean Kline + Winnetka + e-mail" had brought Bard to the employee descriptions of a local architecture firm and a smiling picture of the man Bard had seen in one of Dr. Kline's office photographs.

Bard's Hotmail account had boasted one message in its inbox yesterday. When he clicked on it, he had been startled by its brevity, but also amused by Sean's assumption that his interrogator was a woman. Shakespeare's female roles were often played by men, although Bard assumed Sean had skipped that English class. Or that semester.

Filled with purpose this Wednesday afternoon, Bard clicked the reply button to open a new message window.

Journey's end in lovers meeting.
5:00 p.m. Friday. Your place.
Repent what's past; avoid what is to cum.

Bard felt it a bit in poor taste to mix quotes from two plays, but the phrases were too perfect to omit. Feste and Hamlet would forgive him.

He clicked send, satisfied both with the message and his integration of his mother's lessons into this new crusade. He had time to prepare, and he would be ready. He hadn't saved his mother, but he would save Dr. Kline.

* * *

That evening, Bard called his sister.

Although they were not close, Bard ensured that he and Rosie spoke every few weeks because it was the proper, brotherly thing to do. They'd share their mundane life events and compare notes on the differences between a Midwestern college like Ambrose and a South Atlantic university like UNC-Chapel Hill, where Rosalind was studying business. Bard bemoaned the fact that his sister was growing up to become a member of the new proletariat, MBAs with too much money and not enough tact who spent their six-figure paychecks on soaring brick monstrosities without even an overhang to protect visitors at the front door (*Stay Out!* Bard felt those houses shouted to the street. *We're watching the game!*), high grade sex toys, and pornography to keep their marriages afloat despite descending penises and vaginal dryness. Bard should know, he made a good living off those peccadillos. No longer were families esteemed for their first edition copies of classic literature, their informed discussions of history around the dinner table, or the cultivation of exotic blooms in their loving, weathered homes. Now the marks of a refined life included impeccably stickered scrapbooks enshrining the thousands of pictures taken only of your own children playing in lonely formations in your pristine yard, and the accumulation of media devices that delivered formulaic visual content ever more quickly to your retinas. Bard hated the men and women enshrined in their suburban homes, never thinking of the needs of others, pausing their ingestion of prepackaged artisan dinners only to consider their next purchase on Amazon.

Therefore, it was only natural that Bard would approach any conversation with his sister with reluctance. All of Bard's siblings bore their own scars from their shared childhood, but Rosie's cut the deepest. And at the precipice of heroism, Bard realized he needed Rosie for the first time in his life.

Being the oldest, Rosalind had found it necessary to precede her siblings, along with her entire peer group, in all of life's achievements: academic accolades, menstruation, illegal substances, sexual discovery. By the time Rosalind had left for college, she'd seemed world-weary and ready for a quieter ascetic life. Bard had hoped she would use her move to another state and a new peer culture to reinvent herself into a woman of conviction, chastity, and purpose. But Rosalind had not followed such a path, instead becoming a hard-working, materially-obsessed woman, whose body was off-limits but whose credit card was always seeing action.

Rosalind bought with abandon: purses, duvets, shoes, electronics. Bard had only visited her apartment once, but had been dismayed to see a pile of unopened delivery boxes from Amazon, NET-A-PORTER, Sephora, and several other companies in the dark corner of her living room. Bard surmised it was the purchasing that offered the relief, not the wearing, using, or even unwrapping. He knew she needed help, but his sister's reliance on the material world left Bard unsure of how to offer anything to Rosie that she might actually take. And so, two nights before his life would change forever, Bard called his sister without any expectation of fortifying their relationship or endearing himself to her, but rather with the hidden agenda of using her to help someone else.

"Oh. Hi, Bard. I'm fine. Just getting ready to head to the store for dinner stuff. We're making pumpkin ravioli tonight."

"We?"

Bard heard some shuffling in the background, pages turning in a book propped against the counter. "Mario and I."

Mario. Bard didn't know Rosalind had started dating again. "New boyfriend? I thought you'd sworn off dating."

"I have. It's Mario Battali. You know—the Iron Chef America guy. I just downloaded his new cookbook on my eReader and we're spending the night together making a specialty dish from one of his restaurants in New York."

"Just to be clear, by 'spending the night together' you mean you and the cookbook?"

"And the ravioli, naturally. Now Bard, I can't talk too long. I have to get to the store for sage and European butter—hmm." Bard heard the swishing noise again. "And pumpkin puree and heavy cream. And semolina flour. Oh, this is going to be fun!"

"Rosie, if the book's on your eReader, why do I keep hearing pages turning?"

"Oh, this is so cool. I downloaded this app so that it would make a noise every time I click to the next page. It sounds really authentic. Just like a real book." Ungenerously, Bard wondered when the last time was that she had turned an actual page in a book.

"Sounds like a fun evening you have planned."

"Uh-huh. How about you? What are you doing tonight?"

"Not much, just catching up on work and school."

Bard did have a big project due in English, but he had been working away at it for weeks. He didn't like to rush things. Usually. The meeting with Sean was racing forward from the horizon, but Bard had wanted to avoid a protracted waiting period. He didn't want Dr. Kline to waste away completely.

Moving forward with his own agenda, Bard added, "I'm meeting a friend in a few days. Actually—a friend's boyfriend. She asked me to help her break-up with him. She's worried he won't take it all that well."

This was partly true, Bard conceded. Sean Kline was a pathetic, rotting excuse for a man. Dr. Kline had practically asked Bard aloud for his help. And after his nocturnal visits, Bard knew that Sean hadn't been warned away from Dr. Kline by his e-mails. What was Bard going to do when he told Sean Kline to pack up and leave for good and the pervert said "No"? Bard had hoped that

Sean would be so spineless that he would leave without a fuss, but with the meeting imminent, Bard worried the situation would prove more complicated.

He heard his sister sucking in her breath through the gap in her front teeth, her side of the telephone emitting a high-pitched whistle. Bard hated that habit of hers.

"What if she's right?" Bard asked.

He remembered the incident where one of Rosie's rejected lovers had tried to break through the barred front door of their home, resulting in police cars and a restraining order. He knew his question would bring Rosie back to that turn in her life, and although he didn't want to cause her pain, he also needed her encouragement, however unintentionally offered.

The line remained quiet for several heavy seconds as Bard waited. The incessant page turns he'd been hearing their entire conversation had stopped. Finally, his sister responded.

"Bard," Rosalind's voice was low and resonant, the way it sounded when she used to read the Gospel verse at church for the entire congregation before their family stopped going. "Listen to me, Bard. Bad men *cling* to good women. They're like parasites. He'll suck the life out of her if you don't stop it." Rosalind paused a second to breathe. Her response had come out in one big rush. "And you know what happens then."

Bard was quiet. He saw Rosalind's face that night so many years ago, when her ex-lover had come to reclaim his seventeen-year-old prize. And he saw the bruises that littered her pale skin from her cheeks to her neck and arms in various stages of healing, which his father and the rest of them had failed to notice. Bard had failed Rosie then, just as he had failed his mother before that. Had failed to save her. It was Rosie herself who had cleaved the rift in that relationship separating herself from the man-boy, and it was the boy's mangled attempt to recapture her that had led to intervention from law enforcement. Bard had done nothing but stand aside and watch, quietly and with judgment. "I won't let him do that, Rosie. Promise." Bard had to choke it out past the shame crowding his throat. And the regret. But still, this was the rush of validation that he needed.

They said their goodbyes and Rosie, back to her previous state of happiness, left for her platonic date with a man whose safety was guaranteed by the confines of a circuit board. Bard felt the weight of the phone in his hand, and his arm dropped to his side as he tried to reconcile his past with his future.

Anna

Wednesday was surreal to Anna. It felt as though her body were moving inside one of those science experiments, where teachers add water to oil to show their aversion to each other. At points, Anna's body stretched slower than time, each movement taking extra seconds and minutes to complete. At other points, she felt like her actions were sped up, racing through the routines of daily life with Sean. And she had no way of knowing when the times of labored breathing and weighted limbs would begin, or when her heartbeat would rush in her chest to the point of almost exploding, like an overfilled balloon.

She put little thought into dinner that evening. As Anna tried to chop onions, she found her racing organs wouldn't allow her the steady hand needed for knife work.

Anna experienced little comfort in the meal preparation, much as she found little comfort in her walk home or her sturdily built house or the imminent arrival of her husband. Words flew into her mind, strung together in her head like cheaply made holiday lights, some flashing and blinking brightly, others extinguishing at random intervals. *Crazy. He wants me gone. He doesn't love me. I'm not crazy. I am crazy. He loves me.* The mental gymnastics required to keep herself from blurting these words out loud were exhausting in their pressure and absorbed significant bodily resources, especially when her activities hurled her into the memories of her marriage. The sight of their wedding portrait, both smiling with such sincerity. The first edition of Faulkner's *As I Lay Dying* on the shelf in the living room, Sean's present for their fifth anniversary. Anna had written down all the details and the website for Sean to purchase it. Now, Anna questioned her wisdom in being so controlling.

Anna went to the downstairs half bath and splashed water on her face. She desperately wanted wine to drown out the voices, the careening sentences in her skull. But she knew that she needed to be sharp if she was going to surmount this. She needed to resist her drive to self-numb. If she buried herself away from these truths, her balance on the razor edge of survival would be preserved. Her courage had failed her once; Anna hoped now that self-preservation, rather than the protection of another, would overrule her natural instinct to shrink away from the decay in her life.

Sitting on the edge of the couch, Anna knew she needed to fill the time gaping between now and when Sean came home. With dinner prepared and heating in the oven, Anna had nothing to keep her mind from traveling back to her worst fears. She could feel her face twitch, and she was annoyed that her childhood affliction continued to make itself known again. Thoughts of her childhood though, brought with them transient yet immediate comfort, like the aroma of fresh-baked bread. She picked up the phone and called her father.

* * *

David picked up on the fifth ring.

"Hi, Dad. What're you doing? I hope I'm not interrupting something."

Anna said the words, even though she knew that her father wouldn't have been occupied with anything too pressing. He always had time for her. She asked more to see if he was doing something he shouldn't have been, like rearranging the furniture in the house for when Lena came home. Anna had noticed he seemed a little out of breath.

"No, no sweetheart. I was just outside in the yard and didn't hear the phone ring at first."

"What were you doing outside? Did it snow?"

Anna knew the weather in her hometown was often different from Winnetka's, even though they were only separated by a few hours. March wasn't a time of year where snow was uncommon, and Anna hoped that was what had brought her father outside.

"No, no snow for us. I was just outside trimming the front bushes."

Anna could swear she had heard her father's voice quicken its pace as he said the last part, as if he were hoping she'd miss it. Her father was a terribly honest man in all details of his life. Except, Anna thought, for the most important one of all.

"Why're you doing that? They've been fine on their own for years."

And they had been, Anna thought. They had been ugly and unkempt, declining into mismatched patches of lush green leaves and gnarled knuckles of branches ever since Lena had moved to the institution. It was as if the bushes had turned to self-mortification to protest the loss of Lena's loving care. Sometimes coming up the walkway on visits to her father, Anna had glimpsed the decrepit bushes and wished for a similar outlet for her grief.

"I wish you'd just get rid of them, Dad." The unspoken but mutually understood part of her response circled the rim of accusation: *They bring up such bad memories. Why are they still there?* Anna felt her face twitch again.

"Oh, honey. They really frame the house so nicely. It wouldn't be the same without them." The hidden meaning was just as clear as Anna's: *Your mother loves those bushes. They need to be here when she comes home.*

Of course her mother had loved the bushes. Anna could easily recall her mother tending to those damn boxwoods in all seasons: in pedal-pushers that matched her gardening clogs in the summer, in a luxurious blanket coat in the winter, in an arrangement of vivid scarves to match the turning leaves in the fall. Her mother had been the sovereign of their family, even when gardening.

With the shrubs in disarray for years, why was her father tending to them again? Up until now, Anna's father had found their withering unremarkable.

As the realization struck her, it was as if an electric jolt surged from her heart to her brain. Anna knew there would be no talk of Sean today. The only aroma she would experience on this phone call would be of something malignant and growing. She had read an article in Ambrose's student newspaper recently about a nursing student who was training a service dog to detect cancer in human patients. Perhaps this was another special talent she possessed, Anna thought, only half-sarcastically.

"What's going on?" Despite her attempts at control, Anna's voice snapped like a rubber band on the last word.

"Well, sweetheart, it's the most extraordinary thing," David began, either ignoring or not noticing Anna's change of tone. It was impossible, though, to ignore the joyful edge to her father's voice. "I went to see your mother yesterday and, well—" here it seemed he paused for effect, as if he anticipated Anna to be surprised by his declaration. "—she's cured, honey. I know you might find it hard to believe, but yesterday we sat together and held hands. We talked about you and Sean, and about so many wonderful times we had together. She was her old self again."

Anna didn't know what to say. A strained "Whaa…" leaked from her lips despite her clenched jaw.

"It's amazing. Yesterday, it was like no time had passed between, well, before, everything and now."

He won't even allow himself to name it, Anna thought. She loved her father so much, but now in this moment when her life was crumbling around her and she needed someone stable and solid, she was angry that her father would let himself slip back into his old weaknesses. Although the fixation on the bushes was new, this was not the first time David had declared Lena cured and ready to come home as soon as they could pack her belongings.

A few years ago, a particularly lucid visit had led David to hire an interior decorator to "brighten up" the house before Lena returned. Anna had discreetly called them the following week to cancel, after David's next visit with Lena had ended abruptly with her accusing David of putting needles in her pillow at night. The suitcases David had brought for Lena had remained in the trunk of his car until Anna discovered them weeks later in the grocery store parking lot. She'd had a full load of groceries in her arms to put in the trunk during a weekend stay with her father. After that, her father no longer insisted that Anna drive his car to run errands during her visits.

Other instances had led to the booking of a second honeymoon in Hawaii, the purchase of a new car (a bright red BMW, Lena's favorite color and make), and invitations to friends and family for a welcome home party. Anna had diligently and quietly handled each of these circumstances with a focus on avoiding as much embarrassment for her father as possible. At least this time, his hope was muted and relatively private. Over the years, the expressions of David's hope had shifted from grand gestures to quiet domestic observances of love. Every time, David's reaction when Lena inevitably returned to a less lucid state was painful for Anna to watch. She wished he would finally learn his lesson. Then, when she really needed his assurance, he would be there for her.

Gathering all of the composure she could muster, Anna fought the urge to scream. Her main goal was to just get off the phone without making the situation worse. After one instance when Anna had tried to convince her father that Lena was not coming home, that she would remain ill indefinitely, and David had actually yelled that Anna didn't know what she was talking about and didn't really love her mother, Anna had learned to weather her father's hopeless hope with care.

This phone call had been a mistake.

"That's great, Dad. Great news. I don't teach on Thursday—how about I come tomorrow for a visit?" And then she added, to help ensure the conversation would end, "We'll have a lot of planning to do."

"That'd be wonderful, sweetheart."

After telling her father she loved him, Anna pressed the button on the phone to end the call. The soft click of the call ending sounded like a door closing.

And then Sean arrived home.

He walked through the door, smiling, crinkles around his eyes. A robot impersonating everything Anna had ever wanted in her husband. "Hi, sweetheart.

How're you feeling? I stopped by and picked up some flowers for the table—thought you might want something to brighten up the day." Smile, touch on the shoulder, light kiss on the cheek. Dead eyes, dark circles underneath.

Anna stood with her throat clenched in a silent scream. Had she driven him to this? Was she the suffocating presence, pressing him into this cubbyhole of existence that he was now so desperate to leave? Was she so accustomed to faulting Sean that she had become blind to her own failings?

Sean moved to the office and put his bag down on his chair.

"Smells delicious. Is it time to eat?" And then, when he spotted Anna's despondent face and rigid body, "Are you okay? You look scared to death." Next, more tentatively and perhaps, Anna thought, with a hint of hope, "Did something else happen today?"

The machinery in Anna's mind and mouth needed to move, to work. She needed to say something. *Stop being a coward. Stop feeling sorry for yourself and stop feeling sorry for him*, a voice screamed inside of her. *Play the game, or you'll lose. Everything.* And finally the filmstrip in Anna's mind stopped on one frame, and then another, and another. Her wall of trophies in her parents' house. Her prom date senior year, Billy Gerholdt, the hottest boy in school. Her English professor reading her essay to the entire class to demonstrate its brilliance. A little girl running up to Anna on the playground to seek out her attention, even as the girl's mother called her to come back. She was special. The most special.

Deep breath. *I am better than you.*

Play the game.

"Not yet. Every time I turn around, though, I feel like there's going to be something awful waiting for me. Who'd do something like that, Sean? They're just song birds. They don't hurt anything that people love."

"I know, I know—but trust me, it's all going to be fine. There has to be some normal explanation for what you saw. You're not going crazy." Sean added the final sentence hastily, all of the words rushing out of his mouth like compressed cardboard: you'renotgoingcrazy.

Anna flinched and looked up at him, her eyes expressing the hurt that she thought he expected from her. "Why would you say that?"

Sean's reaction was smooth and as fluid as mercury. "Because I know you've worried about this for years, with your mom and everything." He grabbed her gently by the shoulders here, turning her towards him, "That won't happen to you. I won't let it."

Had he rehearsed this in front of a mirror before coming home? Anna wondered. And for a moment, a flame of hot white anger surged up Anna's throat. Where had this man, this empathetic and understanding lover, been for all these years? Why was she only the recipient of his perfect love when she knew he no longer wanted her? She clamped her mouth closed to keep the words from vomiting out of her. The resulting expression on her face must have been one of violence, because Sean shifted away from her to avoid the glancing touch of her hip and arm as she moved across the kitchen.

"Let's eat." And Anna, turning after removing the dish from the oven, managed to compose her face and gentle her eyes. *I am special. I am better than you. I am a winner.*

* * *

Dinner passed without incident much to Anna's relief. She had wondered if Sean would attempt another strike during the meal. Something hidden in the food. An effigy hung from the window. A phantom voice, recorded in secret, played through the heating vent. Even though she had prepared the meal herself, fridge to table, Anna found herself sifting through her lettuce leaves and bites of casserole. Sean tried to push Anna to drink the wine, emphasizing that it would help her relax, but Anna refused in as docile a way as possible.

After clearing the plates, both of them still dancing around each other in the kitchen in a parody of marital contentment, Sean excused himself to go take a shower, but only after cocooning Anna on the couch once more. The TV droned, nothing but a gray background of merchandise.

At first, Anna could barely distinguish it. The tapping was muted, like a child's rubber ball against summer-hot pavement, oozing into the asphalt before reversing direction on its return journey. Anna muted the TV. Watching a tan and dimpled face on TV mouthing the words to some trite commercial jingle, Anna's mind inserted the percussive tap-tap for the man's words. Tap-tap, he said, his face all earnest persuasion. Tap-tap.

Where was the sound coming from? Anna moved from the couch, following the noise. She could still hear Sean in the shower, and the noise was not part of the plumbing leaching its water out over his naked body. No, it was coming from the ground level of their house. Walking down the hallway towards the front door, Anna saw the light on the computer tower glowing from the office, the door ajar. Had Sean turned the computer on before heading upstairs? Was this done by design?

She moved her hand towards the door and reticently pushed it open, bracing herself for another vision of horror and death. What lay inside the office waiting for her was not horrible, though, but instead terrible in its beauty. On the windowsill, sheltering from the wind that was kicking up at the end of the March evening, was a cardinal. Healthy and complete. But insistent on getting inside. *There was no way Sean could have done this,* Anna thought. *Right?*

Anna reached over to tap on the window pane, urging the bird to leave for more natural environs. As she leaned over the desk to touch the pane of glass in its frame, her hip bumped the mouse of Sean's computer. He had left the computer on, logged in. His e-mail was up in full screen, shimmering into life as the deadened screen pixilated into existence from Anna's unintentional touch. And there it was, shaded in red: Urgent labeling. DesdeMOANa69. Anna knew instantly that this was her replacement.

* * *

Driving down the interstate again for a very necessary weekday visit, her body hurtling forward at eighty miles an hour (Anna always drove fast, whereas Sean preferred to creep along a few miles an hour below the speed limit) but seemingly static inside the metal cocoon of her car, Anna couldn't bring herself to reminisce about her childhood. Instead, she tried to keep her mind blank, with the expectation that eventually something positive would fill it. Something worthwhile. She was driving to visit her parents in two separate places with the hope of reasserting her own sanity. She wasn't sure how she would get to be alone with her mother, but assumed that at some point during their visit to Pembroke her father would realize his error. When that happened, her father would probably become so upset that he would need to leave the room, and go for a walk outside on the grounds to dissipate his recurring grief. If Anna weren't so desperate to find a foothold in her own shattered life, she would be the dutiful daughter and follow him outside. But she was desperate to know what was happening to her, and no one could help her right now but Lena.

The purpose of her visit was selfish; Anna knew that. She was going to talk to her mother about *Before* (capital B). Discovering Sean's e-mail had almost fully confirmed her worst fears. Everything pointed to Sean (and Desi, as she had resigned herself to think of Sean's accomplice/lover). Except that Anna couldn't conceive of it. The motives for his betrayal slipped from her grasp each time she tried to click the disparate parts together. The dead cardinal. The bushes at the park. The hatred he had for her. His preference for someone else. It didn't fit.

So she was going to see her mother.

* * *

Waiting for her mother in Ward 3, Anna was glad to have left her father at home for this one visit. As she had predicted, his enthusiasm for her mother's recovery had once again been replaced with sorrow. When Anna arrived on Thursday, David managed to convey between full-bodied sobs what had happened when he had visited Lena the previous evening to go over plans for her release and let her know Anna was coming. After Lena had sat down in her chair, David had thought she looked uncomfortable and commented on it, asking if she was cold and perhaps needed a sweater. Lena had responded by telling David that she needed to camouflage her smell.

"That they could smell her through the walls—that's what she said," Anna's father recounted, his face a clay mask of grief.

And then Anna's mother had shit herself, and smiled in relief at her husband.

Her father couldn't even bear to come to the hospital this time, and Anna had the luxury of visiting her mother alone.

Lena appeared, her radiant head of hair tamed in a chic chignon at the nape of her neck. *They must have a new nurse on duty*, Anna thought. Praying that Lena would be relatively lucid, Anna exchanged a discreet nod of acknowledgement with the attending nurse, another large man with a distractingly large tattoo reading 'MOM' in script on his right forearm. Anna and Lena sat in the chairs provided, and Anna paused a second to collect her thoughts. As Anna was considering her opening, Lena spoke first.

"Hi there, sweetheart."

Anna swung her face upwards, surprised and a little elated. She could understand why her father was so easily tempted away from the reality of their situation. A few intelligible comments could be very deceptive. But Anna knew the bald facts from her own training and would not be persuaded that any significant change, given the history of her mother's illness, could ever really occur. Not for the long-term, at least. Anna had accepted long ago that her mother would die at Pembroke Farms, or someplace similar. Indeed, she had begun saving for the time when she would solely be responsible for her mother's care not long after Lena entered treatment.

"Hi, Mom," Anna managed to say with a calmer tone than her face displayed. "How're you feeling today?"

"Oh, just lovely. You see they've set my hair so nicely. And it's such a glorious day out."

In fact, it was gray and overcast, with only a few rays of sunlight peeking through the clouds intermittently. The yard outside looked worn and beaten down, with brown grass and a few charcoal clumps of dirty snow still lingering. But Anna wasn't about to argue.

"Your hair looks gorgeous, Mom. And it *is* a beautiful day."

Anna tread cautiously, trying to move towards her necessary topic without triggering some sort of deterioration in her mother. Using the wrong word, the wrong tone, the wrong gesture could rapidly send Lena back into the shadows of her illness.

"So do you. It's so nice of you to stop by."

Lena smiled, her expression the confident one she had used in all of her school photos years ago. The smile of a woman who knew herself. Anna recognized it now as a mask that so many women wore, herself included. Lena took Anna's hand and they sat there for a few beats, looking out into the garden through the immaculately clean windows. *This place is worth every penny,* Anna thought.

Gathering her courage and bracing for the potential of another form of rejection, Anna asked the question she had come there to ask. She chose her words carefully, in the hopes of masking her pointed inquiry with benign terminology.

"Do you remember what you were working on before you came here?" Anna asked, referencing her mother's delusions as indirectly as possible.

Despite the years Lena had spent institutionalized and in all the visits Anna had made over that time, she had never tried to talk with Lena about *Before*. Before Lena's life became so scheduled and protected, and so sterile. Anna had avoided the questions in part to protect her mother from the potential pain of remembering her life as it devolved into illness, but also to avoid reminding Lena of the richness of her life before Pembroke.

In response to Anna's question, Lena paused for a moment, her brow furrowed. Anna had seen similar expressions on her mother's face before, and began to accept that she had lost her chance for clarity already. After another moment though, Lena's face brightened as if an illuminated thought had just been unlocked from the damp cave of her brain.

"You know, I do. I remember there was this terrible—terrible crisis. Of course, they put me in charge of fixing everything—I was always their little fixer—but I couldn't use my hands." Here Lena nodded her head for emphasis, tapping her right index finger against her temple as she did so. "I could only use my mind."

Anna's mother paused for a second, letting her words settle in to impress her daughter. "Turned out, though, it was a trap. Oh, they didn't want me to succeed! They thought I was weak—some sort of weak and helpless old woman. They wanted it to go on and on and on, hurting the children. But I won, in the end." Lena sat back, an expression of satisfied smugness on her face. "*I* was the special one."

Then, as if a thought had just occurred to her, Lena pursed her lips in distaste. "Listen to me, going on and on about myself. How are you doing, sweetheart? How's Sean?"

But Anna had already decided it was time to leave. Pale and clammy with perspiration, she stood from her chair, kissed her mother on her cheek, and gave only a quick nod to the attending nurse before she was let out of the room; she moved quickly down the hallway, and eventually into the fresh air of the courtyard and car park. She was disappointed in herself for wasting one of the rare visits she could have had with her mother in a state of coherence, but her body literally would not let her stay. Even if her mind had tried to remain seated, she felt as if her legs would have moved her away on their own accord. Turning the key in the ignition to head back to Bristol Ave., Anna knew she had heard enough.

It had to be Sean.

Part V
Friday
March 31

Sean

Friday morning broke cold and bitter. All signs of spring were hidden beneath a jagged frost that came on in the dark night, its icy hands strangling the early spring blooms peppered among the dogwood, cherry, and crabapple trees. He had worked hard, very hard, for days, to play the good, unaware husband. Oh, he had mined the recesses of his memories with Anna, every offense he could remember being accused of, and had met the requirements of his constantly deriding wife to perfection. All of the soft strokes of words, and hands, and mouth had been proffered; he had smiled through the stabbing pains in his stomach, and had nestled her fragile ego into his own now-cavernous and echoing heart, if only for a short time. He had been a good man, and awoke this morning exhausted and empty.

He was thankful for the brief respite Anna's visit to her parents had offered, allowing him time to self-soothe while also calculating his own agenda for their Friday meeting. Wednesday night, after he had put Anna to bed, having crushed a few Tylenol PM into the glass of milk he brought for her, Sean returned to his computer to finish what he had begun earlier that evening before escaping upstairs to his shower.

After no reply had come on Tuesday, he had been certain a message would be waiting for him when he arrived at work on Wednesday, but as he sat down to his coffee and sugary donut (Gary, one of his overly-friendly coworkers insisted on bringing donuts for the office every Wednesday; after the last few days he'd had, Sean figured he deserved a little treat) there was no DesdeMOANa69 flashing at him from the screen. Just mundane work e-mails.

A Flash of Red

Sean plodded through his day, checking his e-mail again every two to three minutes, waiting for her message. He was certain she would send one today. Her performance earlier in the week had been triumphant. Sean had almost been convinced a few times, and he didn't know which was worse, his wife going crazy or his wife pretending to go crazy. He had deleted the previous e-mails from his account, not wanting a trail of this fucked up situation lurking in cyberspace, and had trashed that stupid impulse purchase of IQ pills in a dumpster behind the gas station he passed on his way into work. He'd already had enough trouble with the internet. But he wished he had kept them—the e-mails, that is. He could have reread them now as he waited for the next installment.

And then, like a diamond-encrusted cudgel, her e-mail flew into his inbox, winking at him. *Come here, big boy*, it said. *Let me fuck with you a little more.*

After he read it, he felt a mixture of relief and apprehension. A meeting? What could that mean? Would Anna arrive in the state she was in Monday night, making ludicrous claims and expecting him to comfort her? Or would she be cold and calculating, listing off the ways she would ruin him. Maybe she would send a proxy, some poor asshole she had convinced to stand in her place, to keep the ruse going even further. Sean kept the message to review that evening. He felt there must be clues hidden in the text. He just needed to decode them.

Journey's end in lovers meeting.
5:00 p.m. Friday. Your place.
Repent what's past; avoid what is to cum.

Anna was going to confront him; they were the two lovers. Former lovers, he corrected himself with a sense of loss that surprised him, even now. The time and date left no room for ambiguity, but what did she mean by "your place"? Why hadn't she written "our place"? Was that just a cover for the role Anna was playing in all of this? A breadcrumb to lead him off the trail? Or was

192

it because she considered this place, the meeting place, to be his alone? Knowing Anna's reason for this entire ruse, Sean could only think of one place she would consider both his domain and private enough for a confrontation: the office at home. Of course. Anna would destroy him in the place where she felt he had ruined their marriage. Where he had sought solace from the world, and from her.

And then the final line. She would give Sean a chance. Give it up or accept your fate. So there was a glimmer of hope in this. A chance for him to redeem his marriage, but could Sean really be the husband Anna wanted? Did he want to be? He wasn't sure. *And could Anna love him enough to make his sacrifices worth it?* he wondered, finally.

He wouldn't know until he was there, looking at her. Maybe she would bring sympathy and understanding, or maybe she would show repentance and ask for forgiveness. Sean felt there was still a chance that their meeting would combust all of the terrible horrors from their past, the hurts and judgments and grudges, and they could love each other again. He did love Anna, he could continue to love Anna, but only if she admitted to what she'd done to him. Only if she took credit for her part in this razing of their marriage. If she did that, Sean told himself, and if he took responsibility for his failings, they might salvage something beautiful. But she had to admit it. Anna had to say what she'd done wrong.

Sean slept fitfully and rose early on Friday, not wanting to lose his resolve and not wanting to keep pretending. He dressed carefully and quietly while Anna slept. Stepping out the door to meet the frosty chill of the day, Sean was glad that it was finally coming to an end and that his life would be different after today. Sean buttoned the collar buttons of his coat and braced himself for his walk to work.

On the refrigerator, he had left a note for his wife.

Can't wait to see you.

Bard

Dressing carefully on Friday, Bard chose a cornflower blue sweater and cream-colored corduroy trousers. He felt pure in his purpose, protected in the colors of Mary, the protector of all believers. He'd need her strength today, to stand firm against the sickness in Dr. Kline's life.

Today was his chance to prove his devotion to those worthy of it. She needed protection, and he would be the provider. For her.

Bard had several hours until the confrontation and, although he was thankful that his Friday was full of classes that would provide some much-needed distraction, checking his e-mail after he had dressed changed the tone of his day dramatically. His inbox this morning included a disturbing class-wide note from Dr. Kline stating that class was canceled today because she was feeling unwell. From there, it was only natural that Bard's imagination accelerated in pace and all of the fears that had ticked by until now like a scrolling banner in the background of a television screen grew enormous. Was Sean keeping her there to use as some sort of bargaining chip? Was Bard putting her in danger? Would he fail? Bard's worries bounced inside his skull, never finding a place to land.

Sitting down at his kitchen counter, he tried to weigh the options this new piece of information introduced. He could call off the meeting. But that would leave Anna stuck in her marriage indefinitely. Bring a friend with him—but Bard didn't really have any friends. And, he reminded himself, Dr. Kline had chosen him specifically. He couldn't risk betraying her trust. He could call the police. He could sneak into the house unnoticed and rescue her. Confront Sean at his work. Hack in and send the incriminating evidence to all of Sean's e-mail contacts.

Bard continued like this for several minutes, considering a broad range of scenarios. Each option was quickly eliminated for presenting too much risk to Anna or too little success in actually improving her emotional and physical safety. No, Bard would simply need to stick to the original plan and remain patient until the time came.

He paced his apartment, unsure of how to expend the intense energy his worry created. Finally, after his mind had drifted across all that had happened in the last few weeks, it eventually recounted the initial crisis that had brought him to Dr. Kline's office at the beginning of this journey.

He decided to cook himself breakfast. Bard reached into the refrigerator and pulled out the egg carton, butter, and bread, his hands shaking only slightly.

The ritual of heating the water in the pan brought Bard back to the years of his childhood. His mother was, or had been, a talented cook and Bard had enjoyed watching her in the kitchen throughout his boyhood. Her dark hair was always pulled into a French twist when she was cooking, the stray hairs smoothed with bobby pins. She preferred a chef-style apron in a basic black with white pinstripes. However creative her interior decorating may have been, his mother had always applied an air of assured elegance to her personal style. Even after three children, her figure was enviably cinched at the waist, and looking back Bard felt she dressed to accentuate this without being obvious about her intentions. Knee length skirts in rich wools and tweeds, light linen pantsuits in the opulent colors of cream or white. Never anything too ruffled, too short, or too tight. And she always managed to be the most beautiful woman in the crowd. Or at least that was how Bard remembered her.

A typical Saturday indulgence shared between them was a full breakfast of poached eggs, toast with cherry or peach jam, and bacon. Even in those last few months, his mother would allow herself a nutrient-rich meal on Saturdays in anticipation of the fasting that lay ahead. It had taken Bard years to come to the point where his mother could trust him to cook the eggs on his own, but he eventually mastered the technique. Simmer the water, stir with a large spoon to create a vortex to hold the egg when it was dropped from its shell, a patient five minutes of waiting as the egg took on its proper form under the lid, and then a gentle lift out of heat onto the plate to be devoured, his mother affectionately wiping the drips of yolk from his chin with a napkin. Their last breakfast together had been just before she left.

As he waited for the water to simmer in his small saucepan, he opened his carton of eggs. He preferred to buy brown organic eggs, and these were beautiful specimens he'd purchased earlier in the week from the farmer's market adjacent to campus. He reached out to touch one, his hand now steadied by the familiarity of the routine.

Wrapping his fingers around the smooth brown dome, he pressed in gently, and then more firmly, until a thin crack punctured the rich copper of the shell. *Could he do it, if he had to?* Bard wondered. Were his hands, and his resolve, strong enough? Pushing his fingernail just a little further across the barrier, he was rewarded with a small spurt of the smooth almost-living gel inside. And then, using one hand, Bard cracked the egg in half over the swirling water of the pan, swiveling the top of the shell into the bottom half with practiced ease. The egg gave a susurrant hiss as it hit the water.

Thirty minutes later, Bard was ready to leave his apartment. He might visit St. Anthony's in the hours remaining after his classes. The lingering scent of incense, the dull glow of candles, the powerful memories of his mother triggered by the Catholic infrastructure—much like this morning's breakfast ritual, these would help him focus on the necessary tasks ahead of him.

Then he would walk to their home, Sean and Anna Kline's. And he would knock on the door and enter. And inside, he would do whatever was necessary to ensure her survival.

As he packed his bag for the day, Bard had filled it with his usual notebooks and necessary reading. Just before ducking out the door, Bard decided to include the *Lives of the Saints*, snatching it up from its resting place on his desk. Its heaviness provided a reassuring counterweight on his right shoulder as he left his apartment for the final time.

Anna

Friday rolled in like a thunderstorm for Anna, her head pounding and her body desperately thirsty for water. She lay in bed while her mind and body came together after the separateness that comes with a deep, dissociative sleep. Glancing at the clock, she saw it was after 10:00 a.m. How could she have slept for so long? And where was Sean? Reaching her arm over to his side, her eyes shielded with her other arm from the beams of light arcing through the window, she felt the coolness of the sheets. He'd been gone for hours, if he'd slept there at all.

Last night floated through her mind as she rose to go to the bathroom and begin her day, three hours later than usual. After returning home from visiting her parents and a perfunctory greeting from Sean, Anna had retreated to the couch, her mind whirling with what to do. Soon after, Sean had sought her out, carrying the fresh astringent smells of the shower and a glass of warm milk. "To help you sleep, sweetheart." Anna had drunk it unquestioningly, and now regretted her naiveté. *Wasn't she supposed to stay sharp and focused?* she chastised herself. Stupid, stupid girl. Sinking onto the toilet seat, relieving herself after twelve hours of sleep, Anna marveled at how steadfast the habits of trust were.

In the brightness of the morning, the uncertainty of the last few days dissipated for Anna. After drinking a large glass of ice-cold water and taking two ibuprofen, Anna was decided. This DesdeoMOANa69, this bitch who thought she could fuck Anna's husband with her plastic breasts and rubber thongs (Anna was fairly certain that Desi wasn't the cardigan-wearing type) wasn't going to get away with it. And neither was Sean.

A Flash of Red

The visit to her mother had confirmed it. Her recent episodes were her husband's deception, an attack against her well-being. In her mind, her mother's words were only validation of Lena's illness, and in no way indicated a connection to Anna's own state of mind. At least, that was what Anna had decided to believe. Gazing at her face in the mirror, pale and drained, Anna only wished she had never gone to begin with.

Dressing in jeans and a red turtleneck, Anna pulled her hair back into a ponytail and washed her face. She wasn't going to work today. Her mind was otherwise occupied.

She was going to catch him in the act as he arrived home early for his rendezvous. She'd be here today, at 5:00 p.m. In fact, she'd wait all day in his special place, waiting to sight him through the slats in the blinds, coming home early in anticipation of his tryst. Anna wasn't worried about missing her classes or meetings—she'd cancel them all, giving a made up excuse of illness. For a flash of a moment, she considered the irony of saying it was a mental health issue, but decided against it. Sean probably wouldn't even understand the joke.

Yes, when he arrived home she'd be here waiting for him. And then, she'd make one final effort to salvage her life. Anna no more wanted to be a divorcée—an exposed failure, for the first time in her life—than she wanted someone else to have Sean.

Anna turned to the mirror in their bedroom and caught the glint of her engagement and wedding rings on her left hand. She pulled the rings upwards, but they refused to glide over her joint despite the slimness of her fingers. Anna noticed, in the exposed space where her rings usually sat, that her skin was translucently pale. How long would it take for the patch to blend back in, she wondered? Anna shoved the rings down onto the joint of her knuckle.

She was above this, Anna told herself. There was always a solution, buried somewhere within any quagmire of difficult choices. She'd survived her mother's departure, and she would survive her husband's cruel infidelity, preferably as a married woman. Anna knew herself. She could forgive Sean, as long as he asked for her forgiveness. Yes, she nodded to herself in the mirror, enjoying the sway of her sleek blonde hair tied high on the crown of her head. She could forgive him, and then she would abide his penance as he tried to make it up to her. Anna, she reminded herself, was a winner.

Before moving downstairs, Anna stepped reluctantly into their shared walk-in closet. It felt like an eternity since Sean had emerged from there, so desperate for her. Anna leaned into the row of Sean's shirts hanging on the rod, breathed in deeply, and reminded herself that he was hers.

Sean

Sean meandered through his workday, with only the outward guise of accomplishment, until 3:00 p.m. By then, the aimless shuffling of papers and the torrents of coffee that he had downed were starting to wear on his nerves. He needed a drink.

Heading out, he returned to the same bar he had visited earlier, when this entire disaster had begun. Or had it started even earlier than that? Sean wasn't sure anymore. He was certain, though, that he needed a drink before he met his wife. Creaking open the aluminum door to Marty's once more, Sean sat at the bar and ordered a bourbon. It was time to start acting like a man, Sean thought to himself. Stop being such a pussy and get your house in order.

The barkeep, a round man with a bald spot and scratchy mud-brown stubble on his jawline and chin, poured him a tall shot of brown liquid and returned his gaze to the basketball game playing on the corner television. Not being an expert, Sean wasn't sure, but thought it odd that a game would be broadcast at 3:00 p.m. on a Friday. Maybe he should get into sports? A lot of men found solace in that, it seemed. Sean nursed his drink, sipping the burning liquid slowly and trying not to flinch in a way that was noticeable to the other customers.

His wedding ring clinked on the glass as he picked it up. Sean glanced down at it, recalling with fondness how Anna had painstakingly searched for the perfect ring for him.

"I just want a plain gold band. I'm an ordinary guy—I don't need anything fancy," he had told her when she mentioned that she wanted to pick out his ring as a surprise.

"You're anything but ordinary. You're *my* guy." And she had smiled that crooked smile of hers that showed whenever she was so happy her composure left her.

The liquor burned in his stomach.

The ring she had found was anything but ordinary. It was a hammered rose gold, with a thick line engraved on the top and a thin line engraved on the bottom. Outer wall, inner wall. Just like on the draft sheets he had shown Anna from his senior thesis. Just like he had once felt about Anna—that she was home to him. Sean had loved the ring.

Clink, clink. The glass was empty now. Should he have another? Sean asked himself.

He had had the inscription added before their wedding, showing it off to Anna after their rehearsal dinner and proclaiming it was true and he wanted to remember it every day for the rest of his life. Anna had loved that.

Yes, he would have another drink, and then he would walk home to what lay ahead for them both.

Anna

Anna spotted him through the slats as he turned the corner beyond the trees and carried himself up the path to their front door. She had camped herself in his chair, in front of the glowing blue of the screen, for hours. Her mind had shifted from anticipation of confronting him to dread of the pain that would follow. She wanted it finished, she wanted to know. And yet, she wished somehow she could remain unaware. Coddled for her specialness.

Sean's shoulders were hunched against the wind, and his face was tense and flushed with the effort. He certainly didn't look like a man arriving home for some afternoon delight with his mistress. But looks can be deceiving, Anna had come to believe, and she put the thought away in preparation for when he walked through the door.

She had planned to wait for him in his office, coolly spilled into his chair, and only looking up when he entered the room. She was going to offer him a sideways glance and a terse one-liner: "Expecting someone else?" But when she saw him coming up the drive, she found she couldn't wait for him to emerge through the threshold to that room. She didn't want to wait another second before starting the ending. Or the next beginning.

So Anna rose from her chair and rushed out to the hallway, turning towards the front door just as Sean opened it, catching a glimpse of their wedding portrait hanging on the wall as her body moved from right to left. And then they were together, almost touching each other, in the doorway to their home. So many greetings after a day's work had taken place there that Anna's instinct was to reach up to Sean's neck and kiss him hello. Only Sean's wasted face stopped her. Gone was his smile and attentiveness from the last few days. As his eyes met hers, Anna saw such a raw sorrow in him that she had to stop herself from rushing over to touch him and tend to his wounds, reminding herself that his pain arose from his wish that she wasn't here.

"I thought I'd find you here," Anna finally said, the two of them still standing in the doorway, Sean's feet on the weathered welcome mat, Anna's firmly planted in the doorway, propping the door open. The cold wind whistled through the gap, pushing fiercely into their house.

"So did I." The words came out like his tongue was made of dust, without conviction.

"I know, Sean," Anna said gravely.

She didn't want to be melodramatic, but the situation seemed too rife with clichéd phrases to avoid them. They poured out of her mouth begging for a primetime happy ending.

"I know what you've been doing. It has to stop. I love you and I think you love me. We can still be happy, but it has got to stop." Her voice vibrated just a bit. Anna was proud of herself for not letting her voice break on the word "love."

She watched Sean intently, measuring his reaction with her eyes. Her arm was beginning to go numb from holding the door open in the rushing wind, but she wasn't going to let him into the house now. Not until things were settled. The relief in her came fast and sharp, as she saw her husband's shoulders sink inwards, his chest concave as his breath grew ragged and a few tears streamed down his cheeks. He was confessing without saying a word; he was asking forgiveness, and, oh, she forgave him. She wrapped her arms around his neck, and whispered to him:

"It's okay. I love you, Sean." She could feel him sink into her, like a lost child who has found their parent. And then she added, more for her own satisfaction, "And I forgive you."

It is perhaps a credit to Anna's self-absorption that she didn't at that moment notice Sean's body tense. She continued to stroke his hair, uttering "shh, shh" until he startled her with his sudden rejection of her comfort. In one swift movement, Sean withdrew onto the front porch again and stood at his full height to look her dead in the eye.

"And I forgive you, too." His voice was calm, but thorns were hidden in the sounds, ready to catch and leave a gash.

Anna was surprised. She was the special one, the good wife, and yet she was forgiving him all of his indecencies. She had nothing to apologize for, and she said so.

"But I love you so much, Sean, and I want us to be happy," Anna said. "I'm willing to forgive you. Why don't you just come inside and we can talk about it?"

Anna didn't want a recurrence of that August night years ago at her parent's home. Their raised voices, the confrontation on the porch. It was bound to get the attention of their neighbors and Anna had already had one too many public embarrassments.

And that was when she made her miscalculation. She had never anticipated what came next.

The slap landed hard against her left cheek as she was turning to go inside the house, her hand outstretched to grasp Sean's. Anna fell back into the door, crouching down on the ground with her back against it. She raised her hands up to her face to protect herself, but no further blows came.

"*You* have *nothing* to apologize for! You…have nothing…" Sean's voice was now ragged. His pitch had risen to an unnatural tenor. With his hands clenched at his sides as he spoke, the words shot from him at point blank range into Anna's face, hints of his saliva misting her cheek and lips.

"I've been living under your little thumb for years—years and years. I was never good enough. And you just *loved* pointing out how stupid I was. How embarrassed you were of me. What a *freak* I was." Sean's tears were mixing with his words, garbling his speech. He spit out the next line like it was a rotten seed. "And now, you terrorize me and threaten to ruin my life and *you* have nothing to be sorry for?"

A Flash of Red

Terrorize. Anna couldn't understand what Sean was talking about. Was this just part of the game, part of his strategy again?

Sean brought his hands together and wrung his ring finger until his wedding band came off. Shoving it into Anna's face, he said, "Do you remember what I wrote inside? Do you?"

He appeared to be waiting for a response, so Anna cautiously nodded her head up and down, not daring to speak just yet despite the anger swelling inside of her. "It's a sign of everything that's wrong with us. I hate it. And I hate you." Sean flung the ring into the bushes bordering their yard.

Turning again to Anna, who was still defenselessly propped on her haunches against their open front door, her feet wedged between the door and the hallway, Sean seemed more resolute.

"If only I could get rid of you as easily."

At that moment, her face must have shown the fear that had overtaken the anger in her chest, because Sean's face softened for a moment before he raised his arm. Whether it was to strike her or to help her up, both Sean and Anna would forever remain uncertain. Before Sean could act, a bright flash of red appeared. Caught on a current of wind streaming through the house, a cardinal had flown between Sean and Anna's faces, just inches away, and had landed in their front hall.

It was such a delightful interruption that Sean and Anna both paused to watch the beautiful creature investigate its new surroundings. They turned to each other for a brief moment, forgetting their ordeal and returning to their years of synchronicity, sharing this experience together. Sean remained towered over Anna, his arm poised for action of some kind.

And then Anna saw another flash of red enter her field of vision. Instantly, a heavy black square came down onto the back of Sean's head, once, twice, three times. Caught entirely unawares, Sean fell to his knees after the first blow. When he tried to turn and move his arm to protect his face, the weapon came down again and again. Anna could feel something warm sprinkling her face. She tried to wipe it away, but Sean's blood left streaks on her hand. Disoriented, Anna tried to make sense of what was happening. She scanned her field of vision with her eyes only, trying not to move or attract attention.

In front of her, she saw Sean lying face down on their front porch, his hands stretched out in front of him. The back of his skull was matted and bloody. To her right, the hallway was empty. And to her left, she saw a figure stooping over her, his face splattered with blood and his right hand extended towards her. Clutched to his chest was a heavy book embossed with green: the *Lives of the Saints*. Blood stained the outer edges of the pages. She thought she could place that face, that hair, that figure. When he spoke, she knew. The amber voice flowed over her, with the soft lilt of Kentucky spilling out the sides. "You're safe now, Dr. Kline. He'll never hurt you again."

Only then did Anna start to scream.

Bard

It was a strange experience, Bard reflected. Being processed, that is. He felt like a piece of meat or a bureaucratic memo. Bard couldn't decide which better resembled the rituals involved in his being taken and catalogued by the police. His hands were cuffed behind him and his body prodded and folded into the back of the car, with a tender hand guiding his head below the roof of the cruiser. He felt like a calf being raised into veal, treated gently amid the barbarity of it all.

Bard didn't mind the fingerprinting or the interview room. The coffee he was offered was terrible though. That's one thing he hadn't planned on, Bard observed. It would take him time to get used to the food in prison. He wished he had made himself another cappuccino at home before leaving his apartment.

The questions the two officers asked him tore at the seams of Bard's tolerance for tedium. He felt like he was sitting in a committee meeting to determine the relevance of committees. He was asked the same questions two or three times, with slightly different wording and tone.

"So tell us again," said the officer on Bard's right, "why you went to Dr. Kline's home this afternoon."

The officer, a Det. Bridely, Bard remembered him saying for the benefit of the videotape at the beginning of the interview, looked fatigued. He had dark circles under his eyes and an apparently recently acquired stomach that gapped the fourth and fifth buttons of his wrinkly salmon-colored button-down. Bard noticed a pale circle of skin on his left ring finger, as if it had not seen the sun until very recently after years of protection.

A Flash of Red

Bard recounted his actions that afternoon. Walking against the breeze with his coat open to the elements, his satchel listing to the side with the heaviness of his books. His plan to rendezvous with Sean. The importance of their meeting in order to ensure the safety of Dr. Kline.

"Safety?" the other officer had asked. Det. Malinski was tall with a short brown bob and a slim build. She wore an expensive watch and cheap shoes. Her outfit was sterile, as was her gaze. Bard found her less than interesting.

"Like I told you before, her husband is a repeat emotional and sexual abuser and Dr. Kline asked me to help her." Bard kept his voice steady, although he had explained this twice before.

"When did Dr. Kline tell you to speak with her husband?" Det. Malinski asked before taking a sip from her water bottle. No caffeine for her. *God, the woman was boring,* Bard thought again.

"She never actually asked me, not with words at least. It's a hard thing for her to talk about. Look, she and I have a special—connection. I understood what she wanted and I helped her."

Bridely and Malinski exchanged a look and Bridely wrote something on his bright yellow legal pad. A complete cliché indeed, Bard thought.

It was Bridely who took up the thread now, clearing his throat to ask, "When you arrived at the Klines' home, what happened then?"

Bard described the scene again. He emerged from the trees that were shielding him onto the front path. He saw Sean's raised hand, ready to strike at Dr. Kline, and Dr. Kline was crouched on the ground in the threshold of the door, her face turned away in fear. Then, as Bard instinctively ran towards her, he felt the weight of the bag on his shoulder and quickly retrieved the heaviest item in it, the *Lives of the Saints.* Sean became distracted by something inside the house and Bard saw Dr. Kline smile as he drew closer to the scene, her protector finally arriving.

With Sean's head turned, Bard seized the opportunity and struck him on the back of the head with the spine of the book. The first blow leveled the abuser to the ground, and Bard struck twice more to ensure that he would not get up again to hurt Dr. Kline.

"After that," Bard said, "the police arrived."

"One thing I don't quite get," Malinski continued. "If you could just clarify for us. You said Dr. Kline wanted you to help save her from her husband. But both you and she agree that, after you attacked Sean Kline, Dr. Kline screamed. Why'd she do that, if she'd just been saved by you?"

Bard sighed with annoyance. "I've told you already."

"Just tell us once more. For our records," Malinski said.

"Dr. Kline feels the pain of others so intensely—it's really a great burden for her. That's why she needed me to help her. She needed *me* to end her marriage—to be the one who caused Sean pain. Then she could be totally free to live the life she deserves." Bard folded his arms across his chest. "And that's exactly what I did."

Malinski and Bridely exchanged another look, leaving Bard to wonder for a second if they were going to tell him where Dr. Kline was. He hadn't heard from her since he was taken away in the police car. The last glimpse he had had of Dr. Kline was of her being wrapped in a blanket by an EMT before she climbed into the waiting ambulance alongside Sean's listless body. Bard marveled at her goodness. Could nothing dim this woman's grace?

They did not tell him. Instead, the detectives excused themselves, and Bard was left alone in the interrogation room with only his reflection in the two-way mirrors and his paper coffee cup to contemplate.

Bard was certain that she would arrive soon. He calculated the hours she would need to spend at the hospital, waiting to ensure that Sean was stable and would recover. Then, and only then, would she come to thank him. And after that, she would be free.

All Bard had to do was wait for Dr. Kline. She would be here soon, he told himself. He was certain of it.

Epilogue
Monday
April 3

Anna

Anna was looking out of the one window in the room when Sean awoke. It was almost four o'clock in the afternoon, and Sean had spent most of his stay in the hospital so far in and out of consciousness as he recovered from the procedure to remove the blood clot. The doctors assured Anna they had caught the injury early, that no real damage to the brain had occurred as confirmed by a repeated series of CT scans, and that a full recovery was likely. Still, Anna remained cautious. She did not know what her husband might remember about the events that had led to his hospitalization, and hoped he had not forgotten what he'd done to her.

She was seated in one of the hard chairs hospitals provide as general issue: cheap faux leather the color of chlorinated pool water, as if somehow the hue of relaxation could bring forth healing of its own accord. Anna's chair had a huge crack down the middle, and its innards spilled out obscenely between her legs.

"Anna?" Sean spoke her name as a question.

She squeezed his hand, which she had held intermittently throughout her stay. She had spent the last several nights on the loveseat in the corner of the room, sleeping little. Nurses regularly passed by the open doorway, and Anna felt it only proper to remain, noticeable, at her husband's side. After all, they were now the beleaguered victims of a savage attack. They would undoubtedly need to give interviews, attend hearings, go to trial. During all of those, Anna and Sean would be combined together as one entity—the couple who survived. The couple who loved each other so much that someone was jealous enough to try and rob them of it. Yes, Anna thought, she could make do with that.

A Flash of Red

"Anna?" Sean said her name again, trying to sit up this time, and his wife finally replied.

"Shh, shh," Anna said, placing her left hand on her husband's chest and gently pushing him back down onto his pillows. "I'm right here. I've been right here the entire time."

This was only partially true. Anna had stepped out to buy coffee at the vending machine down the hallway, twice to chat with her father on the phone and assure him traveling all the way to the hospital was not necessary yet, and several other times to pause in front of the bathroom mirror and apply concealer to the bruise that was blooming over her left cheek. Anna had assured the police officer who'd interviewed her that the bruise had come from trying to pull Bard off of Sean. She'd also traveled home to gather a bag of clothes, and had showered in the bathroom attached to Sean's room.

Their eyes connected for three heartbeats—Anna counted, knowing the importance of not breaking her gaze first—until Sean's chin fell towards his chest, tears streaming down his cheeks. To Anna's great comfort, everything she had hoped for prior to their encounter three days ago at the threshold to their home now poured out of her frail and healing husband. Anna fought the impulse to record the conciliatory monologue on her phone as evidence for later use should Sean change his mind, although she was fairly certain he wouldn't. Anna might want Sean, but she knew Sean needed her. Still, if he did change his mind, it would be so easy for Anna to modify her story with the police. She was the ultimate victim, after all. And she had the face to prove it.

"I'm so sorry." Sean's words poured over Anna like honey, sticky and sweet. "How can you ever forgive me? I can't believe it. I can't forgive myself. How could I have hit—"

Anna interrupted him, not wanting any of the hospital staff to overhear. It was one thing for her husband to incriminate himself in front of her, and another entirely to do it in front of others.

"It's not your fault. That student of mine—I had no idea he was so obsessed with me." Anna couldn't help it—the corner of her mouth turned up on the word "obsessed." She continued, "The police said he admitted to everything. He was the one sending the messages." She leaned forward for emphasis here, keeping her voice forceful but kind. "He was DesdeMOANa69."

When the police officer, a slightly unkempt man who introduced himself as Det. Bridely, had come by that morning to update Anna and Sean, he had found Sean sleeping and so delivered all of the details to Anna instead. Det. Bridely stated his opinion that Bard was a danger to both Sean and Anna and that legal action was necessary. The boy was clearly unstable and suffering from some sort of obsession with Anna, he'd said. Not willing to divulge much of the specific evidence, the detective told Anna they had discovered pictures on Bard's phone and messages on his computer that indicated an unhealthy fixation on both Anna and Sean.

It took Anna only a brief moment after Det. Bridely's disclosure to process the information. Sean was not having an affair. Sean was not trying to rid himself of her. It had all been Bard—the messages, the violence to the dead birds. She was not sure how he'd done it all—especially planting the feathers in Sean's pants—but she felt a great relief in knowing that she had no competition for Sean's affection, and in knowing that Sean had hit her anyway.

Eventually, Anna agreed to consider prosecution, acquiescing only after adamantly requesting assurance that Sean's recovery would remain first priority. Det. Bridely gladly obliged, even offering Anna a swift smile as he handed her a large paper bag containing the few items collected from their home and now released as non-evidence. Anna had been asking for Sean's wallet and keys, buried somewhere in the messenger bag he'd carried that day, since his arrival at the hospital.

Now, Anna saw her revelation drop into Sean's brain in a similar fashion, though perhaps taking him a few moments longer to register its full meaning. Sean burst into tears again.

"Oh my God, I'm so sorry." His shoulders convulsed up and down with his sobs. "How can you ever forgive me?"

This was what Anna had been waiting for.

A Flash of Red

"How could I *not* forgive you? I love you so much." She wrapped her arms around his shaking body, being careful to avoid the tubes of his IV. The oxygen had been removed from his nostrils the previous evening, and so now Anna could easily lean in and kiss him fully on the lips, tasting the salty tears he'd shed over his regret of not appreciating her.

A thumping came from the window of Sean's room, and Anna saw a red blur through the industrial glass, clean on the inside but blurry with dirt on the outside.

"I love you, too," Sean said, and Anna was impressed at his ability to ignore the distracting sound in order to attend entirely to her. In fact, Anna was having difficulty focusing and found herself shifting her eyes away from her husband and towards the window as they embraced again. "I love you so much," Sean repeated, his words muffled against Anna's shoulder.

"We can make a fresh start of it," Anna said next, after Sean's crying had subsided a bit. She'd thought about the perfect phrasing, and felt this was the most effective suggestion. While Sean slept in his bed, she'd rejected options involving "You" or "I." And then she added the final knot in the rope tethering her and Sean together.

"I don't want a baby. I just want you." There. She'd said it, perhaps with slightly less conviction given the insistent background noise coming from outside the window, but the reaction from Sean was still as she'd anticipated.

His smile spread broadly across his pale face. "You would do that for me?"

Anna nodded. "For us."

When Anna had asked the doctors earlier that day about Sean's recuperation plan, they'd politely hinted that their sexual life would need to be put on hold for at least a month while her husband recovered. Anna figured that was more than enough time to research the adoption process and get the paperwork moving. She had never wanted to adopt before, but if recent events had taught her anything, it was to be flexible. If she just could find the perfect young mother, healthy, intelligent, and humble, Anna was certain she'd be able to raise the adopted baby properly.

Sean would agree—he couldn't ever say no to her again now. But for the time being, she needed to look as though she were conceding something. She couldn't risk Sean becoming more a victim than he already was.

And besides, she told herself, they would make great parents.

Sean reached up with his hand and stroked her cheek where he'd slapped her three days before. His thumb brushed some of the make-up off her cheek and Anna saw it streak against the white sheets of her husband's hospital bed when he laid his arm back down.

"We belong together," Anna reminded him. The knocking at the window had quieted down finally.

"Things will be different," Sean said next. "I promise. *I'll* be different."

"*We'll* be different," Anna assured him, although she felt his assessment of the situation far more accurate.

They sat there in companionable silence for a few minutes, holding hands and Anna measuring Sean's breathing. She desperately wanted to go investigate the window sill and see what was happening. An atavistic fear gripped her each time she looked over to the window in the corner of the room, as if something terrible lurked there waiting to disrupt the pieces of her reassembled life.

Anna put her hands into the pockets of her jeans and surveyed the room as her husband sank into a deeper sleep. Already there were flowers sent by their neighbor who had called 911 (Anna made a mental note to write a thank-you note to Mrs. Solomon), cards and bouquets from Sean's work, from Sean's father, from Anna's father (who had signed it "David and Lena," making Anna pause when she read it). Anna had spoken to Joyce that morning, and knew that a little stuffed teddy bear was in transit.

Sean's chest was rising predictably up and down by then, and his chin had turned to the side in his typical style of sleep. Once she saw his eyes racing side to side below his eyelids, she knew it was safe to investigate.

Moving slowly over to the window, the red smear began to take on a distinct and familiar shape for Anna. She gently opened the window with her left hand and found herself face-to-face with a male cardinal. After the tumultuous emotions of the last few days, Anna's body was suddenly flooded with a delight more potent than she'd felt even when Sean had asked for her forgiveness. Even more than when he had cried over how much he loved her. There was nothing to be afraid of and Anna chided herself for letting fear back into her mind so quickly again after receiving such wonderful, comforting news about her marriage. Her new life was waiting for her, just outside these hospital doors.

Anna reached her right hand out from her pocket and found the cardinal surprisingly docile and curious. Something in its beak flashed in the sunlight; then, in a burst of color and soft sounds, the bird flew away, leaving its gift on the smooth pebbles filling the industrial trough of the window sill. Picking it up, Anna felt the weight of the object before she saw it, her hand obscuring it with her grip. To Anna's astonishment, she was holding Sean's wedding ring. A short length of white string was tied around it in order to connect a small tag with a series of signatures and the word "Evidence" running across the front. It had been lost since that night, when he had thrown it into the bushes, before everything else that had happened. And now, it was returned to them.

Closing the window and moving back to her seat by Sean, Anna examined the ring. Thick line, thin line. Running in an infinite loop of love. And the engraving on the inside: "You make me a better man."

Anna took Sean's hand in hers again and, removing the tag, placed the ring back on his finger. It glinted in the waning sunlight that filtered through the curtains. Sean moved in his sleep, an ambiguous look on his face. Whether it was one of pleasure or pain, Anna would never be sure.

The End

Acknowledgements

I would like to thank my wonderful team at Pandamoon publishing, including my talented editors, Jessica Reino, Kathy Davidson, and Rachel Schoenbauer, my publicist, Elgon Williams, and the entire Kramer family. Thank you also to my fellow Pandamoon authors, who continue to lend support and encouragement to our writing community every day.

Thank you to my family for supporting me through my journey of becoming an author. To my children—Ethan, Katherine, and Elisa. Thank you for inspiring me with your enthusiasm for life and your fabulous senses of humor. Whenever I felt stuck, I knew I could count on any one of you to make me laugh.

Thank you to all my teachers who have encouraged me in my studies and my love for writing, whether creative or scientific in its scope. I'm fortunate to have encountered a lengthy list of incredible teachers—unfortunately too many to name here individually—but a few I can note include: Mrs. Lippiatt, Ms. Huberty, Mr. Hoopes, Ms. Canal, Dr. Stephen Flora, Dr. Sharon Stringer, Dr. Jeff Coldren, Dr. Keith Crnic, and the late Dr. Peter Beckett. Thank you for committing your lives to emboldening students, like myself, to work hard and work well.

Thank you to Nicole Tone of Tone Editorial, Sue Conrad, and Dr. Jennifer Crissman-Ishler for comments and feedback on earlier versions of this book.

Reading Elyn Saks's excellent memoir, *The Center Cannot Hold*, and Ian McEwan's novel, *Enduring Love*, became, in their own unique ways, starting points for this book.

Finally, thank you to my husband, Joshua. I couldn't imagine any of this without you to share it with.

About the Author

Sarah K. Stephens earned her doctorate in Developmental Psychology and teaches a variety of human development courses as a lecturer at Penn State University. Her courses examine a variety of topics, including the processes of risk and resilience in childhood, the influence of online media on social and behavioral development, and evidence-based interventions for individuals on the autism spectrum. Although Fall and Spring find her in the classroom, she remains a writer year-round. Her short stories have appeared in *Five on the Fifth*, *The Voices Project*, *The Indianola Review*, *(parenthetical)*, *eFiction*, and the Manawaker Studio's Flash Fiction Podcast. *A Flash of Red* is her debut novel.

Thank you for purchasing this copy of *A Flash of Red* by Sarah K. Stephens. If you enjoyed this book by Sarah, please let her know by posting a review.

pandamoon
publishing

Growing good ideas into great reads...one book at a time.

Visit www.pandamoonpublishing.com to learn more about other works by our talented authors.

Made in the USA
Charleston, SC
03 January 2017